Captain Hornigold
AND THE
Pirate Republic

MARTIN A. FREY

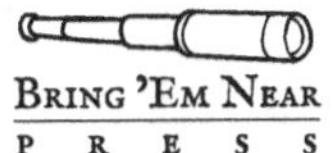

BRING 'EM NEAR
PRESS

ISBN (print) 979-8-9860551-0-7

ISBN (ebook) 979-8-9860551-1-4

Bring 'Em Near Press
Tulsa, OK

Contents

To

Parker, Rose, and Mya
and those of all ages who seek adventure

*May the wind in your sails
be limited only by your imagination*

Preface

SEVERAL YEARS AGO, I was texting one of my former research assistants and we were discussing her precocious ten-year-old daughter, whom she was homeschooling. Her daughter was interested in becoming a writer so I offered to read what she was writing. I loved her dialogue and suggested that for fun, we could write together. We would choose a topic and I would write the introduction and she would write the first chapter and I would write the second, and so on. Because her father was a professor at Clemson University, I wanted a topic close to her home. Blackbeard (Edward Thache) was the obvious choice, but he had been written about extensively so I kept looking. I stumbled upon Captain Benjamin Hornigold, who had sailed in consort with Blackbeard on several occasions. Hornigold intrigued me because he was often mentioned as associating with the other pirates of his day, but I could not find a Hollywood movie or a book devoted exclusively to him. I thought he was historically more important than Blackbeard because he was the non-Jacobite (Protestant) leader of the pirate republic located in Nassau, one of the last safe havens after the Queen Anne's War.

We wrote a little back and forth, and what had started as fun became more serious as did the demands of her home-schooling and outside activities. She drifted away but I was bitten by the "pyrate" bug. I doggedly continued.

Benjamin Hornigold was active as a pirate from 1713 to 1718, so I thought I would have little trouble creating a timeline of his activities during this six-year period. I read a number of "pirate" books looking specifically for Benjamin Hornigold. Little by little my timeline grew as to where he was, what he was doing, and with whom he was doing it. The information I gathered was often vague and sometimes contradictory. I used my best engineering, lawyering, and fraud investigative skills to develop a coherent series of events. The depositions in Baylus C. Brooks' *Dictionary of Pirate Biography: 1713–1720* (2020) supported the events on my timeline and added interesting tidbits of information. What better primary authority than statements made by pirates before they were hanged and by captains who had their vessels seized by Hornigold's pirates? To test whether Captain Hornigold and others could sail from point A to point B in the time that appeared on the timeline, I computed the minimum number of sailing days required, taking an arbitrary 100 nautical miles a day (four knots an hour times 24 hours). Finally, I added a character whose voice could propel the story along.

The events along the timeline are historically accurate. At various times, Hornigold sailed in consort with Blackbeard (and Major Stede Bonnet), Black Sam Bellamy and Paulsgrave Williams, Captain Napping (who seemed to have no first name), and Olivier LeVasseur. Hornigold's archenemies were Henry Jennings and Charles Vane, Jacobite sympathizers, and Thomas Walker, former vice admiral judge of the Bahamas, and Hornigold developed a working relationship with Woodes Rogers, the new governor of the Bahamas.

When there was a lull, I took the liberty to add the hidden cavern, the storm, and a visit to Tortuga, a former pirate safe haven. The taverns were included as locations where pirates could exchange information about the activities of other pirates.

Willie Sutton, a famous American bank robber, when asked why he robbed banks responded, "because that's where the money is." Pirates in the Caribbean in the early 1700s felt the same about Spanish ships carrying silver from the mines of Bolivia, Peru, and Mexico to the king's treasury in Spain. These ships sailed from Cartagena, Porto Bello, and Vera Cruz. Their routes required sailing through one of three narrows: the Florida Straits, the Windward Passage, or the Mona Passage. Spanish ships sailing these trade routes were easy prey. Pirates found no need to scour the Caribbean.

Hornigold's timeline parallels the political-religious conflict in Great Britain. Earlier, King James II and VII, a Catholic, had abdicated his three thrones—England, Scotland and Ireland—and was replaced by co-sovereigns, William III and Mary II, both Protestants. James made an unsuccessful attempt to reclaim his thrones (the Jacobite uprising of 1689). When he died in 1701, James Francis Edward Stuart claimed his father's thrones. As our story unfolds, Queen Anne had died and the Jacobites were staging a second attempt (the Jacobite uprising of 1715).

If being a pirate captain, satisfying his men with plunder ("no prey, no pay"), avoiding being hanged, and attempting to create a pirate republic in Nassau were not difficult enough, Captain Hornigold found himself navigating the political-religious factions within his pirate community.

By researching and writing about Benjamin Hornigold and the other pirates of his day, I came away with a better understanding of this early period of American history and its relevance to current events.

Sailing in the Caribbean in the Early 1700s

SAILING IMPROVED DURING the Age of Discovery (sixteenth century) with the introduction of the Portuguese caravel, which could sail faster and farther than the existing cargo vessel. Fitted with a lateen sail, a triangular sail affixed to a long yard or crossbar, mounted at its middle to a mast and angled down nearly to the deck, the bow of the vessel would be pointed toward the wind so it could blow from one side of the sail to the other, allowing the vessel to sail in the direction of the oncoming wind. The caravel could sail "into the wind," making it largely independent of the prevailing winds.

Vessels, Boats, and Ships

In the Age of Sail (mid-sixteenth to the mid-nineteenth centuries), a vessel was a craft that traveled on water. At one end of the spectrum were the crafts primarily powered by oars such as the rowboats, shallops, longboats, and periaguas (sailing canoes). At the other end of the spectrum were the ships with their three square-rigged masts and a full bowsprit. They were the galleys and the galleons. They sailed the oceans and were employed in commerce and passenger travel. Vessels that were more than boats and less than ships were the fore-and-aft single-masted sloops and the double-masted brigantines with their combination of square rigging and fore-and-aft rigging.

Distances and Speed

DISTANCE	
One foot	.3048 meters
One meter	3 feet, 3.37 inches
One statute (land) mile	5,280 feet, 1,609.34 meters
One nautical mile	6,080 feet; 1,852 meters; or 1.151 statute miles

SPEED	
One knot	1.15078 statute miles per hour
One knot	One nautical mile per hours

A nautical mile is one-sixtieth of a degree of latitude and varies from 6,046 feet at the equator to 6,092 feet at a latitude of 60 degrees. This variation is due to the fact that Earth is not a perfect sphere but is flatter at the poles.

Winds and Currents

In the North Atlantic, the trade winds blow from east to west at about 30 degrees latitude above the equator. They flow from the Canary Islands to the Caribbean. From there, the trade winds push the Gulf Stream north along what was the Spanish Main and up the east coast of America until they veer northeast across the North Atlantic toward Western Europe. Between the trade winds and the Gulf Stream, sailing vessels could follow these clockwise winds and currents as they sailed from Western Europe, down Western Africa, across the Atlantic to America and back to Western Europe.

In the South Atlantic, the trade winds also blow from east to west about 30 degrees latitude below the equator. They flow from western Africa across the South Atlantic to Brazil, down the coast of South America, and then veer east back across the South Atlantic to western Africa.

If a sailing vessel in the 1700s could maintain an average speed of four knots per hour over twenty-four hours, she could sail one hundred nautical miles in a day. Sailing, however, was not in a straight line from point A to point B but needed to take into consideration obstructing land masses, seasons, currents, and wind patterns.

Three examples illustrate the speed of travel. First, when Captain Vincent Pearce sailed the *Phoenix* from her home port in New York to Nassau, a distance of about 1,127 nautical miles, he left New York on January 21, 1718, and arrived in Nassau Harbor on February 23, 1718, thirty-four days later. The *Phoenix* averaged thirty-three nautical miles a day or 1.4 knots.

Second, when the new governor of the Bahamas, Woodes Rogers, and his fleet sailed from London to Nassau, New Providence Island, in the Bahamas, he first sailed south to the Canary Islands, then west across the Atlantic to Barbados, and finally worked his way north to Nassau Harbor, which is on the northern coast of New Providence Island, a distance of over 5,500 nautical miles. If he averaged four knots, he should have arrived in about fifty-six days. But that would have been a perfect voyage. Governor Rogers left London April 22, 1718, and arrived in Nassau Harbor on July 24, 1718, ninety-three days later. His vessels averaged 2.5 knots.

Third, Captain Charles Vane sailed from Nassau Harbor on May 22, 1718, and arrived at Crooked Island a day later in time to capture the *Richard & John*, about two hundred thirty-four nautical miles. He would have been sailing at about ten knots over a twenty-four-hour period.

Distances and Sailing Days

NASSAU TO	APPROXIMATE NAUTICAL MILES	DIRECTION	AT APPROXIMATELY 100 KNOTS PER DAY †
Barbados	1582	ENE	16
Bermuda	1053	ENE	11
Boston	1426	NNE	15
Cartagena, Columbia	1183	SSE	12
Charles Town, SC	631	NNW	7
Curaçao	904	SE	9
Delaware Capes	883	NNE	9
Harbour Island	55	NE	1

Havana, Cuba	407	WSW	4
London	5503	ENE	55
Mona Passage (*between Hispaniola and Puerto Rico*)	641	ESE	7
New York	1127	NNE	12
Port-au-Prince, Hispaniola	746	ESE	8
Porto Bello, Panama	1458	SSW	15
Port Royal, Jamaica	670	S	7
San Sebastian Inlet, Florida (*Vero Beach, Spanish plate fleet wreck*)	226	WSW	2
St. Augustine, Florida	511	WNW	5
Vera Cruz, Mexico	783	WSW	8
Virginia Capes	826	NNE	9
Windward Passage (*between Cuba and Hispaniola*)	400	SSE	4

† Average speed of four knots an hour over 24 hours

British Royal Succession

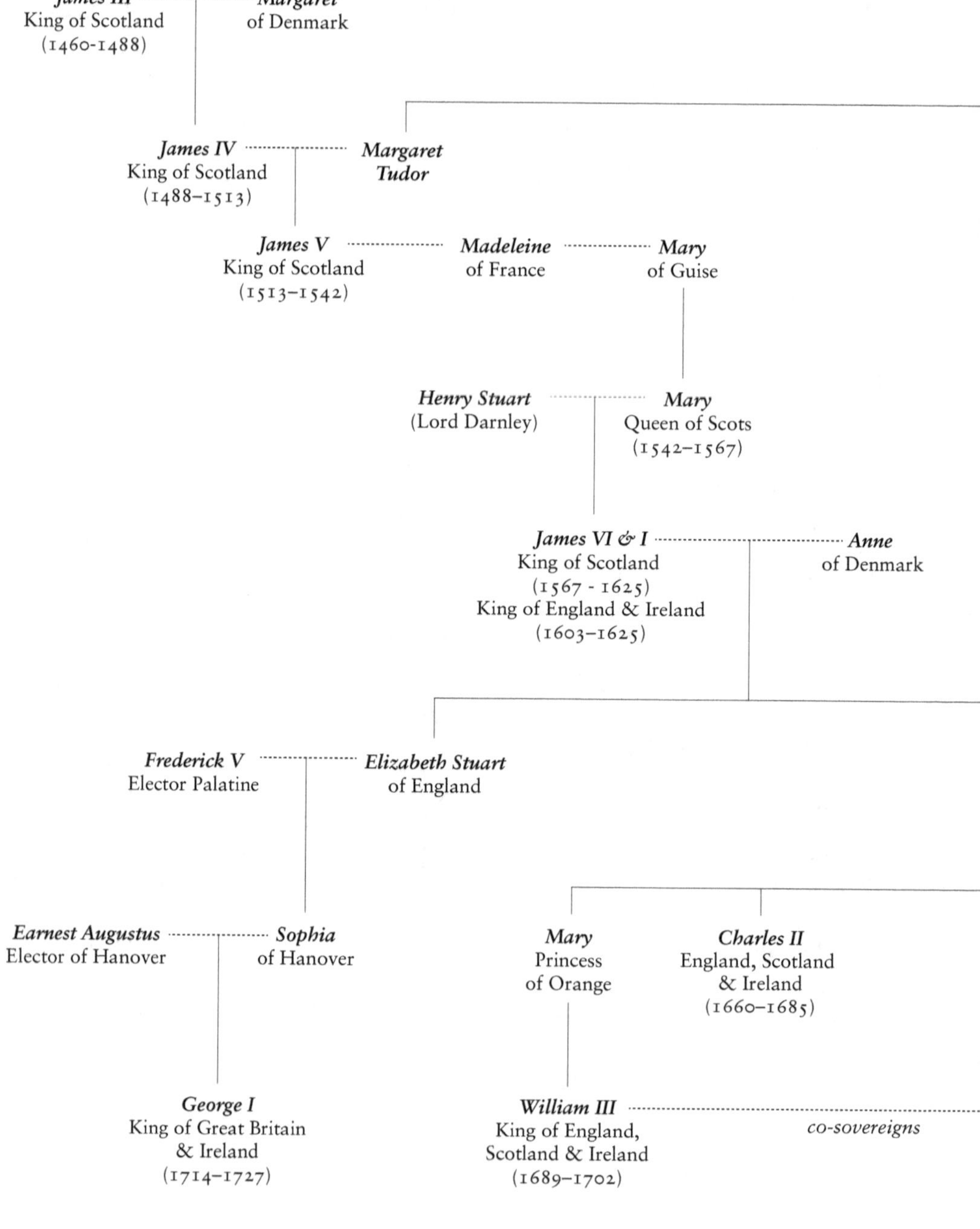

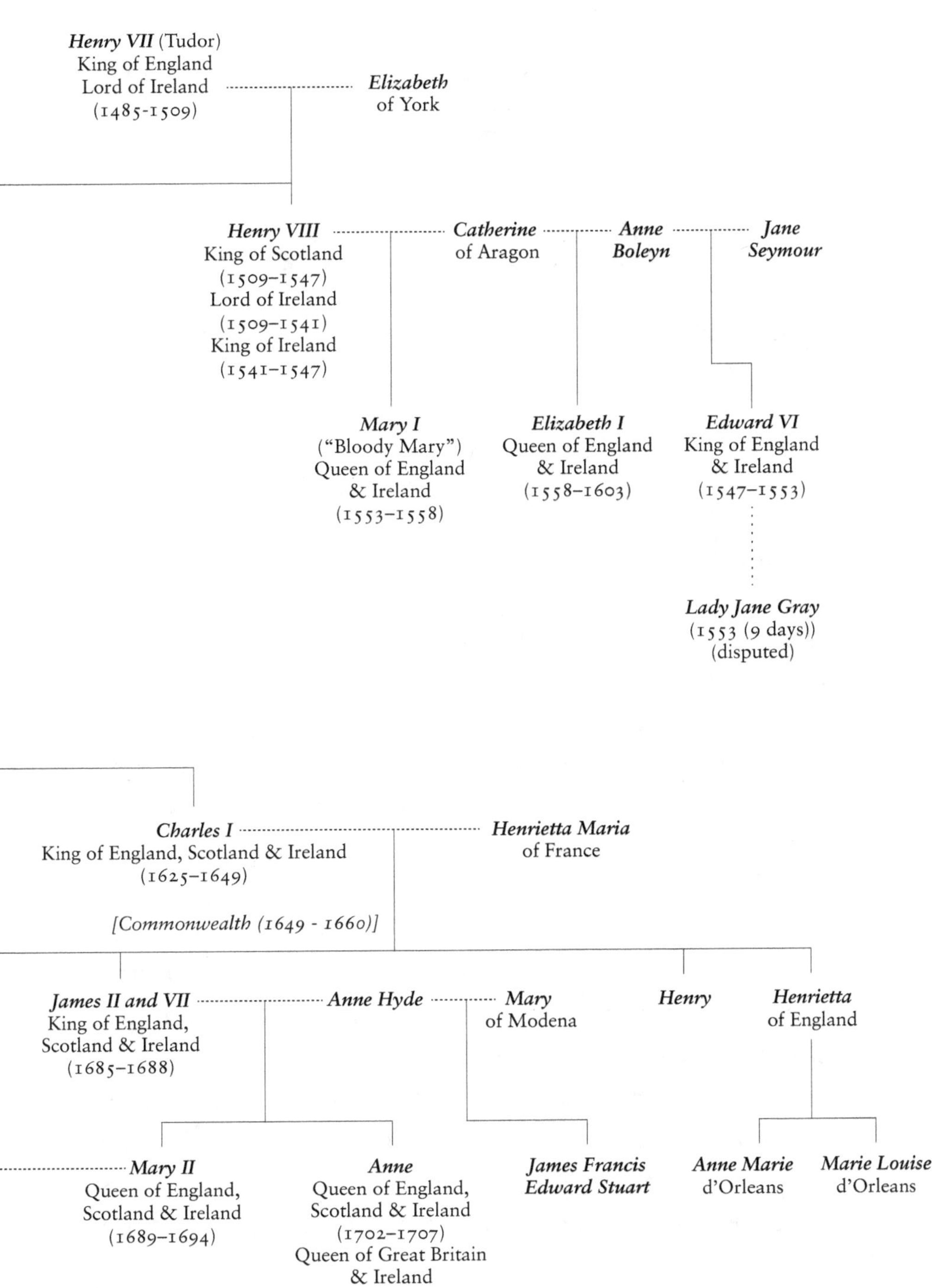

Henry VII (Tudor)
King of England
Lord of Ireland
(1485-1509)

Elizabeth
of York

Henry VIII
King of Scotland
(1509-1547)
Lord of Ireland
(1509-1541)
King of Ireland
(1541-1547)

Catherine
of Aragon

Anne
Boleyn

Jane
Seymour

Mary I
("Bloody Mary")
Queen of England
& Ireland
(1553-1558)

Elizabeth I
Queen of England
& Ireland
(1558-1603)

Edward VI
King of England
& Ireland
(1547-1553)

Lady Jane Gray
(1553 (9 days))
(disputed)

Charles I
King of England, Scotland & Ireland
(1625-1649)

Henrietta Maria
of France

[Commonwealth (1649 - 1660)]

James II and VII
King of England,
Scotland & Ireland
(1685-1688)

Anne Hyde

Mary
of Modena

Henry

Henrietta
of England

Mary II
Queen of England,
Scotland & Ireland
(1689-1694)

Anne
Queen of England,
Scotland & Ireland
(1702-1707)
Queen of Great Britain
& Ireland
(1707-1714)

James Francis
Edward Stuart

Anne Marie
d'Orleans

Marie Louise
d'Orleans

Introduction

Spices To Sugar To Silver To Pirates

THE STORY OF *Captain Hornigold and the Pirate Republic* begins in ancient times when the Eastern and the Western worlds were isolated. Those in the East were harvesting, trading, and enjoying exotic spices such as cardamom, cassia, cinnamon, clove, ginger, nutmeg, pepper, star anise, and turmeric. Many had medicinal as well as culinary uses. At the same time, those in the West had no knowledge of the East or their spices.

In the second century BCE, the Han dynasty in China opened its borders to trade and a network of routes began to radiate westward. The Silk Road, as it became known, started as a series of land paths and evolved into land and sea routes covering the East and extending westward to the Mediterranean. It was long, four thousand miles, the paths ill-maintained, the terrain arduous, crossing deserts and mountains, and personally dangerous. Traders did not travel its length but rather passed their goods to others as trading centers emerged.

The Silk Road offered an opportunity to exchange more than spices. Merchants from the East carried silk, jade, porcelain, and tea westward, and traders from the West brought horses, glassware, textiles, and manufactured goods eastward.

The Silk Road contributed to the dissemination of religions (Buddhism, Islam, Judaism, and Christianity), philosophies, scientific discoveries, and technologies (such as paper and black powder). Diseases, especially the bubonic plague and smallpox, were passed along as well.

Spices generated immense wealth for those who controlled their trade. As spices traveled the Silk Road into the Middle East and toward the Mediterranean, spice merchants created a monopoly that drove up the demand and the price for these "luxury" items.

The control over the Middle East changed from one empire to the next and so did the control of the monopoly. When the Byzantine Empire fell to the Ottoman Empire in the mid-fifteenth century, trade with the West was closed.

The fifteenth century, however, was when Western Europe transitioned into the Renaissance and the Age of Exploration (Age of Discovery). In Portugal, Prince Henry the Navigator organized a navigation school that led to the improvement of navigation tools and vessels, and he arranged for a number of ocean voyages where new lands were found.

In 1415, the Portuguese captured Ceuta, the Moorish port on the North African coast across the Straits of Gibraltar. The Mediterranean was now open to the Atlantic Ocean.

After Ceuta, the Portuguese sailed to Madeira and the Azores and then began exploring the coast of West Africa.

Portuguese navigators picked up the clockwise trade winds that took them south down the West African coast. As the Portuguese ships crossed the equator, the trade winds changed direction, now blowing counterclockwise. By sailing away for the African coast, they avoided being blown back toward the equator and Portugal.

In 1488, Bartolomeu Dias sailed around the southern tip of Africa, thereby demonstrating that the East could be reached by sea by sailing south.

While the Portuguese were seeking a route to the East by exploring south down the West African coast, Christopher Columbus was proposing to the king of Portugal to sail west across the Atlantic Ocean to the "East Indies." The king, preoccupied with sailing south, rejected Columbus' proposal.

Columbus then approached Queen Isabella of Castile and King Ferdinand of Aragon. The king was focused on the Mediterranean, but the queen was interested in the Atlantic and funded Columbus' expedition.

Columbus followed the trade winds south to the Canary Islands and then west, landing on Guanahani in the Bahamas, an island he renamed San Salvador. The "East Indies" was rather the "West Indies." Columbus was impressed with the gold jewelry worn by natives, but try as he might, he was unable to discover the location of their mines. They simply did not exist on the islands. On his next voyage, he brought sugar cane plants and found the climate ideal for their cultivation. Shortly after Columbus returned from his second of four voyages, Spain and Portugal divided the New World. In the Treaty of Tordesillas (1494), a line was drawn from pole to pole down through the Atlantic Ocean. Land east of the line would belong to Portugal and land west of the line would belong to Spain. As a result, Portugal received Africa and Brazil while Spain received the Americas with the exception of Brazil. England, France, and the Dutch Republic were not signatories so they ignored the treaty.

Spain claimed the larger islands surrounding the Caribbean Sea—Cuba, Hispaniola, Puerto Rico, and Jamaica—and began to enslave the native population. They were put to work on the sugar plantations. As the plantations flourished, so did the demand for labor. The natives died from European diseases, brutal working conditions, and armed conflict. Spain turned to the African slave trade for a renewed work force. The Treaty of Tordesillas, however, had placed West Africa off-limits to Spain.

Spain created the "asiento de negros," a monopoly contract, whereby the Spanish crown would award a foreign entity the right to provide African slaves to Spanish America markets for a set period of years. African slave traders would round up Africans from the interior of Africa and bring them to the coast, where they were kept until a ship with the asiento contract could transport them to a Spanish port on the Caribbean. Those enslaved who survived the voyage were auctioned for work on the sugar plantations.

The importation of slaves created a triangular trading system. On the first leg, a ship would sail from her home port in Europe to a port in West Africa carrying a cargo of copper, cloth, guns, and ammunition that would be sold or bartered for slaves. On the second leg, "the Middle

Passage," the ship sailed across the Atlantic to a port in the Caribbean where the slaves would be auctioned. The ship then returned to her home port with a cargo of sugar, rum, molasses, or other New World goods.

In 1497, Vasco da Gama sailed around the Cape of Good Hope and across the Indian Ocean to India, thereby opening a direct trade route around Africa to Asia. Portugal now had access to the riches, including the spices, of the East.

As the Portuguese sailed down the West African coast and across the Indian Ocean, they established permanent trading forts. They were interested in developing trading partners in Africa and the East rather than in colonizing.

At the time the Spanish were developing the sugar plantations on their Caribbean islands, the Portuguese were taking advantage of the Treaty of Tordesillas by harvesting the brazilwood trees located in the coastal forests of Brazil. The dense, orange-red heartwood of these trees produce a marketable red dye. The forests, once cleared, were replaced by sugar plantations. After decimating the indigenous population, the Portuguese imported enslaved people from West Africa. Because they had access to the slave trading ports of West Africa under the Treaty of Tordesillas, they had a direct route from West Africa to Brazil.

Vasco Nunez de Balboa, a Spanish explorer, crossed the Isthmus of Panama to reach the Pacific Ocean. Across the Pacific was the eastern world and all of its riches, including spices.

As the Spanish and Portuguese were developing their sugar plantations, the Caribbean Islands were becoming the staging grounds for Spain's conquest of Central and South America. Cortez sailed from Cuba and landed in the

Yucatan where he established a port at Vera Cruz in what is now Mexico. After conquering the Aztec empire, an alliance of three city-states that ruled in and around the Valley of Mexico, he sent a force south to conquer what remained of the Mayan empire. Neither the Aztecs nor the Mayans had mines. Their gold came from panning riverbeds or from trade with distant sources.

Ferdinand Magellan approached the king of Portugal with a proposal to sail west around the world by traveling around the tip of South America. The king refused to finance Magellan's voyage, so Magellan received funding from the king of Spain. After sailing around the tip of South America and west across the Pacific Ocean, Magellan reached the Philippine Islands and claimed them for Spain.

Francisco Pizarro, on behalf of Spain, began the conquest of the Inca empire that covered a large portion of western South America, centered in the Andean mountains. As Pizarro learned, the Incas also had no mines. Their silver and gold came entirely from surface sources found as nuggets or panned from riverbeds. The year after Pizarro began his conquest, Spain established Cartagena as a port on the northern coast of Columbia on the Caribbean.

In 1545, the Spanish discovered silver mines at Potosi in modern Bolivia. This region, high in the Andes, was rich in mineral ore. Cartagena became a main port for exporting silver and importing enslaved people under the asiento system.

The next year, silver was found in Zacatecas, Mexico. Over the next few years, other sources of silver were found in Mexico. At the same time, sources of gold were being discovered, although in lesser quantities. Vera Cruz became a main port for shipping Mexican silver and gold.

Around 1560, the Spanish discovered silver mines in Peru.

In 1565, the Spanish inaugurated the Manila galleon trade route. One or two Spanish galleons a year would bring spices, porcelain, ivory, lacquerware, and processed silk cloth from the East through the Philippines to Acapulco, Mexico, and return with silver from the Mexican and the Potosi mines. When a ship arrived in Acapulco, her cargo was transported across Mexico by mule train to Vera Cruz where it would be loaded onto ships bound for Spain.

In 1597, Porto Bello on the Isthmus of Panama (now Colon) was founded to serve, along with Vera Cruz, as a port to ship silver from Bolivian and Peruvian mines to Havana and Spain.

These huge shipments of silver from Cartagena, Porto Bello, and Vera Cruz drew pirates to the Caribbean. Spanish vessels would sail from Spain on the trade winds south to the Canary Islands and then west across the Atlantic and around some of the islands of the Lesser Antilles and into the Caribbean Sea and the Gulf of Mexico. To return to Spain from Cartagena or Porto Bello, these vessels would follow the trade winds north through the Yucatan Channel between the Yucatan Peninsula and the western tip of Cuba, and then around the Florida Peninsula through the Florida Straits and north before turning east across the Atlantic. To return to Spain from Vera Cruz, the fleet would still need to pass through the Florida Straits.

These trade routes and their narrow channels and straits provided pirates with the opportunity for easy plunder. They had no need to scour the Caribbean Sea for prey. To combat this danger, the Spanish adopted a convoy system. Instead of sending individual ships laden with silver across the Atlantic, a fleet would sail annually from Spain carrying European manufactured goods, passengers, and troops and return with a year's worth of silver. Pirates would not attack a well-armed convoy but would wait for stragglers and then attack. When a fleet was not sailing, pirates would seize coastal traders or other vessels that needed to navigate the Florida Straits between Florida and Cuba, the Windward Passage between Cuba and Hispaniola, or the Mona Passage between Hispaniola and Puerto Rico.

In the Pacific, the trade route between the Philippines and Mexico also presented an opportunity for pirates to capture goods from the East or silver from Mexico.

As Spain's military power in Europe weakened, so did its dominance in the Caribbean. England and France became powers on the rise.

In the early 1600s, England started settling Bermuda, a group of islands in the western North Atlantic Ocean, roughly eight hundred miles north-northeast of the West Indies and less than sixteen hundred miles from England.

England, France, and the Dutch Republic began to settle the smaller Caribbean islands. England and France partitioned Saint Kitts into English and French sectors. England established a colony on Barbados in the Lesser Antilles. This island, the most easterly in the West Indies, became England's sugar capital in the Caribbean. The English on Saint Kitts settled the nearby island of Nevis and then the islands of Antigua, Montserrat, Anguilla, and Tortola.

From Saint Kitts, the French settled Martinique, the Guadeloupe archipelago, and Saint Barthelemy (St. Barts).

French Huguenots claimed the island of Tortuga off the northwest coast of Hispaniola. They also established the settlement of Petit-Goave on Hispaniola. Tortuga became a pirate and privateer haven and was used by smugglers of all nations.

By the mid-1600s, the Dutch Republic had become Europe's economic powerhouse. The Dutch Republic settled Curaçao, an island off the northern coast of Venezuela. Curaçao would become a major maritime crossroads.

In 1655, England captured Jamaica, the third-largest island of the Caribbean, from Spain. Jamaica is strategically located, ninety miles south of Cuba and one hundred twenty miles west of Hispaniola. Jamaica became a leading sugar exporter and the center for English activity in the Caribbean.

Port Royal, on Jamaica's southeastern coast, became an English trading center and openly welcomed privateers and pirates from around the world. Port Royal, until it was partially destroyed by an earthquake and tsunami in 1692, was known for its wealth and loose morals. Although some activity remained in Port Royal after the major destruction, it was ultimately replaced by neighboring Kingston as the center for trade in Jamaica.

In 1700, King Charles II of Spain died without heirs. His closest heirs were members of the competing Austrian Habsburg and French Bourbon families. The next year the War of the Spanish Succession began between Bourbon Spain and France, whose candidate was Phillip, the grandson of King Louis XIV of France, and the Grand Alliance (Habsburg Spain, England, the Dutch Republic, and the Holy Roman Empire), whose candidate was Archduke Charles, the younger son of Leopold I, the Holy Roman

Emperor. If Phillip became king of Spain, he could ultimately become the king of both Spain and France. The balance of power in Europe was at stake.

In North America, another war, the Queen Anne's War, also known as the Second French and Indian War, broke out. This was a territorial war fought on three fronts: Newfoundland, New England, and the Spanish Florida/Eastern Province of Carolina. Although the West Indies was not within one of these three fronts, the silver being shipped from the Caribbean ports did finance the Spanish war effort both in Europe and America. The presence of the Royal Navy in the Caribbean was very limited, so the involvement of privateers to harass Spanish and French shipping was welcome and effective.

As both wars were winding down in 1713, the letters of marque (the commissions) that legitimized the privateers, were expiring. The Royal Navy was reducing its fleet and dismissing its sailors. The West Indies, especially Jamaica, was being overrun with out-of-work sailors. Some privateers continued to attack Spanish and French shipping but without legal authority. Privateers were becoming pirates.

In 1713, Benjamin Hornigold, John Cockram, and John West, former privateers and now out-of-work sailors, found themselves in Jamaica. They left to investigate what Nassau had to offer. There they acquired three periaguas (sailing canoes) and began pirating. Two years later, in 1715, Benjamin Hornigold, now Captain Benjamin Hornigold, found himself sailing a small sloop around the northeastern coast of Cuba looking for prey.

Then for a moment, all the activity aboard Hornigold's sloop paused upon hearing the lookout cry, "Sail ho!"

1

A Voyage Rudely Interrupted
September–November 1715

"ABIGAIL MARGARET MARY Pennyworth!"
When Mother calls me by my full name, I know I'm in trouble.

"Hurry! Finish packing your chest. Your brothers are downstairs. The innkeeper won't serve breakfast forever! Our ship sails in three hours. The captain won't wait, not even for you. Hurry!"

I dawdle; I know. I'm twelve and all my friends are here in England. I have no friends in America. We're having so much fun. Who am I going to have fun with? I don't want to go!

Here I am in this town called Bristol getting ready to sail for maybe three months on a merchant ship bound for Jamaica and then on to Charles Town.

I don't want to be here! I don't want to go!

"Must Father go on that ship?"

"When your Father was asked by the church to be a missionary, he couldn't refuse."

"Where's Father?"

"He went ahead to prepare our cabins. He'll be back for us within the hour."

"Can't he go without us?"

"Pack!"

"I'll be bored."

"If you make up your mind to be bored, you'll be bored. It's up to you. Enough of this. Just pack!"

"There . . . . I'm packed!"

Mother is pleased as we join the boys. "You know, this will be the last good breakfast you'll have for months."

I shudder. Three months confined to a little merchant ship with all those sailors and none of my friends. I've been told we might be joined by several families, I hope there'll be girls my age. Boys! Who wants to be stuck on a ship for three months with just boys?

I wake up in a panic. My thoughts have taken me back. I'm by the rail with my family watching England fade into the distance, then we're surrounded by water, water, and more water. Mother's trying to assure me all will be fine.

I was on that merchant ship for days on end but where am I now? How did I come to be here? I look around, searching for clues. Nothing's familiar.

I'm not in my cabin. I'm in a hammock on an open deck. Where're Mother and Father? Where're my brothers?

Then it all comes back to me. We'd been sailing for ten weeks. The captain said we would soon pass through the Windward Passage between Cuba and Hispaniola and in a few more days, we'd drop anchor in Jamaica.

My brothers and I decided to camp out on the open deck that night. Maybe we'd see land as we passed through the Windward Passage. If we didn't see land, at least we'd watch the sunrise.

"Look!" my older brother shouted. "Look there!" A vessel appeared from over the horizon. "Maybe she's another merchant ship bound for Jamaica." We watched— she bore down on us—then we saw her black flag. She drew nearer. Fire from one of her cannons interrupted the tranquility of the sea—an explosion, a cloud of smoke, rolling thunder, an object sped across our ship's path and splashed down nearby. Waves—our ship rocked and all was quiet again.

Our captain barked at his crew. "Strike our flag."

Our helmsman swung our ship into the wind. She drifted to a stop.

Terrified, terrified we huddled on deck not knowing what would happen next.

Their deck, crowded with men ready to attack, sent me into a panic. Our crew, merchant sailors, were ill-prepared to fight and would quickly be overwhelmed.

Within minutes, our attackers were among us. They were dirty, smelly, and nasty, and they ran through our ship yelling and screaming in a language I recognized as Spanish, a language I didn't understand. Fifty, at least fifty, all brandishing awful weapons, weapons of death. I was petrified!

I clung to Mother, she clung to me. Father tried to protect us, but he was knocked to the deck. My brothers were nowhere in sight. Hopefully they had found a safe hiding place.

Hands ripped me from Mother's grasp. I was thrown over his shoulder and carried to another vessel. I screamed, they laughed. I was carried down a ladder to the deck below. Oh, the smell, the smell of black powder was overpowering. I was pushed into a room, a tiny, dark, damp room and I heard the bolt securing the door. *Alone . . . . I was alone. . . . And I was cold and frozen with fear.*

The vessel's sails caught the wind and she began to sway. A beam of light through a small knothole pierced the darkness. I saw my family's ship disappear over the horizon. *Will I ever see them again?* I fought back tears and sleep. Fatigue overcame me. I drifted off.

My sleep was fitful. I awoke and peered out my knothole. The darkness was broken by the moon's reflection on the sea. I couldn't stay awake. I drifted back to sleep.

I woke up again. Shouting and running boots, where? The deck above. This vessel was being boarded. I recognized fragments of their language, English.

Voices were not far away. I had to attract their attention. They were English, at least.

I was saved, I was saved!—Someone English was unbolting my door.

I heard him say, "There's an English girl! What should I do with 'er?"

"Take her to the Captain."

The Captain was not in a good mood. "What do you want? Bad time to interrupt. I'm meeting with my officers! I've that sloop's papers here and she's English, from Jamaica. Better sloop than ours. We're trading. We're busy!"

"Sorry sir, found this English girl locked in a cabin below deck, sir."

Someone muttered, "Can't be bothered with her now! Anyways, she's a girl. Give her to the sharks!"

"Could be useful," another replied. "Charlie washed overboard, need a new cabin boy. What you think, Captain?"

"Aye, take her to Charlie's trunk, find her something decent to wear, see what he left behind. She'll work for her keep. Move his hammock and things to our new vessel, and chop off that hair, and don't bother us again!"

I was taken to a little alcove next to the captain's quarters where the previous cabin boy had his hammock and trunk. The pirate who found me crudely chopped off my long blond tresses. "Stop crying," he muttered as he motioned for me to pick among Charlie's things.

There was not much to choose from. I did find boots, pants, a belt, a shirt, and a vest. A crumpled hat would keep me shaded from the hot sun. A knife I stuck in my belt. A ribbon, I tied back what was left of my long, beautiful hair.

Through my tears, fear, and confusion, I caught myself thinking an absurd thought: *I look like a pirate and therefore I am a pirate.*

"Hurry! Trading vessels. Stay with me or be left behind with the Spaniards."

And so began my adventures as the cabin boy to Captain Benjamin Hornigold, one of the most notorious pirates of the West Indies.

2

Pirate Life
November–December 1715

THIS MUST BE a bad dream.

I drift back into a hazy sleep and lie there. Afraid to get up to face what the day has in store for me, I rub my eyes to erase away the memories. I count the days on my fingers, five, seven, ten? The days are a blur—a week, yes, a week. I've been Captain Hornigold's cabin boy for a whole week.

I remember being yelled at a lot. Cabin boy, where's my dinner? Cabin boy, you're so slow. What's the matter with you? Cabin boy, don't you know nothing? You aren't a patch on Charlie. As hard as I tried, I felt I couldn't do anything right.

I catch myself daydreaming and quickly leave my hammock, get into my clothes and scurry off to do my rounds. A moment later, three members of the crew corner me. "Which's starboard and which's port, boy?" Before I can answer, another growls, "Where is the bow and where is the stern?" The third yells, "Who runs this vessel, the captain or the quartermaster?"

An officer I know only as Mr. Howard sees me trapped and comes to my rescue. "Leave the cabin boy alone. Get on with your work or I'll issue punishment."

"Thank you, sir," I whisper.

"Don't thank me, get to your work, boy!" I soon discover Mr. Howard is William Howard, the quartermaster. He controls the day-to-day operations of this vessel.

Quickly, I learn what is expected of me. If I can't do the job of a cabin boy, I'm useless to them. I don't want to be discarded and thrown overboard. Tho' my tasks are mundane, including running messages for the officers and fetching whatever they want, I'm determined to make the best of my situation. Each day passes and I'm criticized less and less; slowly I'm becoming accepted as Charlie's replacement.

This vessel, the *Mary* of Jamaica, is a sloop. She looks to me like a very big sailboat with her single mast and triangular sails. She's substantially smaller than the merchant ship my family sailed off on. That ship, with her three masts, rectangular sails, multiple decks and two dozen crew, seemed spacious when compared to this vessel. Everything is happening on a crowded deck and where all eighty of the crew work, eat, and sleep. Even the four cannons and four pattarareas (mounted swivel guns) are on this deck. Below's the hold where the provisions, black powder, and captured goods are stored. Under the hold is what the crew calls the bilge, the lowest innermost part of the vessel where the ballast keeps the vessel upright and foul water collects.

I find myself running back and forth between the officers and the galley where the cooks, Cooky and Stewy, prepare the meals. They're the nicest of the crew and they make me feel at home. They also provide me with a place to hide away from the ever-watchful eyes of the captain, the quartermaster, and the other officers.

After seven long days, I've had my fill of dirty, smelly sailors who curse like, well, sailors. Just being on the *Mary* is exhausting, the rocking from side to side and the twisting and lurching. Hearing the bell every half an hour and the incessant shrill call of the boatswain's brass whistle every time he wants to bark an order are getting on my nerves. The food is bad beyond description and not seeing land—and not even knowing our destination makes me weary. When I ask a member of the crew where we're going, he points to the empty horizon and always says the same: "thar," and obviously that's no answer. Eventually, I overheard several of the crew talk about heading back to the island of New Providence in the Bahamas.

I seek out Cooky, who, by now, will answer some of my many questions. "Why New Providence?"

"The pirate colony? Safe haven for pirates, boy."

"Why?"

"You'll see," and he turns away shaking his head at my ignorance.

I don't dare inquire further. I'll bide my time. Once we reach New Providence, I'll see for myself.

The sun rises again as I lie in my hammock trying to get my thoughts together for another day. Boots, the sound of boots, coming towards me. Do I dare open my eyes?

I peek and there's William Howard, the quartermaster.

"CABIN BOY!" He takes a step forward. "SHOW A LEG!"

Tho' I've only been on the *Mary* for a week, I've learned not to question the quartermaster. He's the next in command after the captain and tho' the captain decides when to give chase and leads the crew in battle, it's the quartermaster who manages the vessel and the crew. He keeps custody of the plunder, distributes rations and black powder, schedules work, settles quarrels, administers punishment and leads the boarding parties. No way I'll question him.

I mumble something, fiddling with the gold chain around my neck—the chain with my grandmother's locket—my only physical reminder of home. I slip into Charlie's ill-fitting boots, tuck my knife in my belt, and wrap my cloak over my dirty, torn pants and shirt. That's the best he left behind.

Mr. Howard is about to berate me for my "slowness" when the Captain's voice booms, "SAM!" He chooses to call me "Sam," a name I despise. He knows my name is Abby, but he calls me Sam for spite.

"Sorry, sir. The Captain's calling me." I escape from Mr. Howard and I find the Captain examining the empty horizon.

"Sam, where've you be? We're about to make Nassau. Much to do. Take these maps to Smithy, the helmsman. Stay with him, he may need you."

I tuck the maps under my arm and head to the wheel hoping to find Smithy. Yes, he's there on his watch.

"Good! Glad you brought the maps. Nassau's an hour or two out. Shifting currents, reefs, and sandbars makes this harbor's narrow entrance especially treacherous. Open the maps, find Nassau Harbor."

My hands carefully unroll the maps and I search for Nassau Harbor. "Nassau, but no Nassau Harbor, sir."

"Look just north of Nassau. What do you see?"

"An island, a long island."

"What direction?"

"Stretches east to west."

"Name?"

"Hog Island."

"Harbor's not necessarily a bay or a cove. A sheltered spot along the coast will do. Hog Island, a natural barrier between Nassau and the ocean. Provides shelter for vessels dropping anchor at Nassau, a good place to hide from the British."

I look at the map again. "Hmm! Hog Island follows the Nassau shoreline. Harbor has two entrances."

Smithy points to one entrance and then the other. "Aye, harbor's main entrance here to the west, kind of a backdoor entrance here to the east."

"What's these written notes on the map?"

"Current's constantly changing the entrances. Captains who sail here note what they find. Very helpful. No one wants to run aground on a sandbar or to scrape his vessel's bottom on a reef. We've been out for two months and our hold's full. The *Mary* sails low in the water, need to be extra careful."

Smithy takes a quick look at the notes on the maps and then glances at the sandglass near the wheel.

"Can you read?"

"Yes, sir."

"Read me the notes on the map."

I begin but he interrupts. "Sand's about to run out, when it does, turn the sandglass over and strike *Mary*'s bell three times, first two, pause, then the third."

"Why three times?"

"Day's divide into six four-hour watches, except for the fifth watch, the sixteenth to twentieth hour watch. That's dog watch—divides into halves—each two hours, so those on watch can eat an evening meal."

"Why pause after two bells and before the third?"

"The pause makes it easier for the men to count the time. How'd they know six bells from eight?

"Now's the third watch, forenoon watch. Began at the eighth hour with the sandglass full. Sand ran out in thirty minutes. Sandglass was turned over and the bell struck once, everyone knew it was eight-thirty. Sand ran out, turned again and the bell was struck twice, began the ninth hour.

"Now, turn the sandglass and strike the bell three times: two strikes, a pause, and a third strike, nine-thirty, see?"

I turn the sandglass and strike the bell once and then again. Smithy nods and I pause. He nods again and I strike the bell again. Wow! Its beautiful tone is clear and commanding.

In a few minutes, Hog Island and the coast of New Providence Island comes into view. Smithy brings the *Mary* to the western entrance of the harbor. From the map, that entrance appears larger than the eastern entrance and from the notes, deeper. Smithy shouts commands to the quartermaster, who relays them to the boatswain, who blows his whistle, relaying the commands to the crew. They constantly adjust the sails as the *Mary* carefully picks her way into the harbor.

One of the crew shouts numbers to Smithy.

"What's he doing?"

"Sounding, he's sounding."

"What?

Sounding. There's a weight on the end of his line and he's measuring the depth of the water as we make our way into the harbor. He can tell when the water is getting dangerously shallow."

I listen and hear the numbers change back and forth.

One by one, the sails are furled, stern sails first. The *Mary* drifts to rest. The boatswain whistles, splash, splash, the anchors drop, one by one.

"Why two anchors?"

"Holds the *Mary* steady. Otherwise, she'll swing around the anchor as the tide changes."

It's now late November. I look around the harbor from the *Mary* expecting to see a bustling seaport, something more like Bristol but on a newer, smaller scale.

"Smithy, what happened?"

"Nassau was sacked and burned four times by the French and Spanish during the war. The fort over there, on the knoll, destroyed. The people, the few who were left, fled. The island's abandoned with no government and no security. We needed to leave Jamaica, no work, so we moved here. Now it's not just New Providence—it's 'The Republic of Pirates.' Well, you got work to do, boy. Stop staring and get moving!"

The *Mary* is heavily laden with cargo captured during her months at sea. She's anchored a little distance from the wharfs. I watch the longboats ferry her cargo to shore.

I'm told the cargo will be sold by Hornigold's agents, who will sell to the local merchants, who in turn will sell to the townsfolk and sailors at prices below what they can usually find. Merchant ship captains also buy to sell at other ports. European fabrics, especially scarce in the colonies, sell well here.

The cargo is being offloaded when a smaller sloop drops anchor nearby. Smithy's pleased to see her. "Our Spanish prize. She'll bring a nice price."

"What do you mean?"

"Well, after we captured the *Mary*, we seized this Spanish sloop, a small merchant vessel. She was a coastal trader traveling between ports. Nice cargo. Her hold was filled with barreled sugar and dry goods."

Once the cargo from both sloops is offloaded and sold to the Captain's agent, Mr. Howard distributes the proceeds to the crew. One by one they receive their share and they pile into longboats heading for shore to spend their time and their riches at the tavern or on the women who flock to Nassau.

"Sam! Where've you be!" My daydream is interrupted by Mr. Howard.

"Find the boatswain, tour the *Mary* with him. Report back how long he thinks repairs will take."

Peters, the boatswain, is waiting for me near the bow. He keeps the vessel fit for travel and battle. We walk and he checks the vessel's wood, sails, lines, and cables. He stops to chat with the cooper, who maintains the food barrels, and with the carpenter, the sailmaker, the cooks, and the master gunner. All have needs.

"Tell Mr. Howard I'll take a longboat and three men to buy supplies and find material for repair. I'll need three, maybe five days."

After I finish with the boatswain and report to Mr. Howard, I return to the rail to watch the men board boats for shore. *Will I ever get the opportunity to go with them?*

I absentmindedly find myself holding my grandmother's locket and thinking about my family. *Although it's less than two weeks since I was snatched from Mother's arms, it seems like an eternity.*

The day passes and the longboats begin returning with lumber, barrel staves and hoops, and canvas. Each long-boat quickly unloads and returns to shore for more. The men who stay on the *Mary* begin the repairs so she'll be seaworthy again. On the last day, barrels of food and fresh water are taken aboard and stored in the hold.

Four days after the *Mary* dropped anchor, she sets sail, leaving the small Spanish sloop behind for Hornigold's agents to sell.

That evening, when I'm in the galley having supper, I ask Cooky where the *Mary*'s heading.

"The shipping lanes between Cuba and the Florida coast, called the Florida Straits."

"Why there?"

"Silver and gold mines. The ore's smelted near the mines and the bars and coins carried overland to the coast and loaded on ships heading for Havana. From Havana, fleets of ships take the silver and gold through the Florida Straits and catch the currents and the prevailing winds as they sail to Spain. When vessels come up the shipping lanes through the narrows of the Florida Straits, we'll be waiting for them."

At sea, one day melts into another. The *Mary* approaches the shipping lanes near the Florida coast and meets several other pirate vessels. Captain Hornigold sails with them. I'm told that it's called sailing in concert. By sailing five to ten miles apart, the *Mary*'s lookout can still see the next vessel. With several vessels sailing in consort, they can almost stretch from Cuba to Florida. Soon we begin seeing Spanish merchant ships making their way from Vera Cruz, Porto Bello, and Cartagena to Havana or Spain. Captain Hornigold spots one lagging behind the others and nods to Mr. Howard and Smithy that this will be the *Mary*'s prize.

Word spreads. A level of excitement and urgency makes its way throughout the *Mary,* and the men prepare for the chase.

I seek out Smithy. "How does one vessel communicate with another when they're so far apart? They're too far away from each other to call out by speaking trumpet or by whistle."

"Watch Scotty at the bow. He has flags. Watch."

Smithy and I watch Scotty work his flags.

The Spanish vessel is a substantial distance in front of the *Mary* but she can still be seen. Slowly, very slowly, the distance closes. Smithy positions the *Mary* so when she's very near, she'll be on the windward side of her prey.

"Why do you want to be on the windward side?"

"Ahh, when we get near and if she tries to escape, we'll cut off her wind and she'll find herself helpless."

When the *Mary*'s close, Mr. Howard calls out, "Hoist our flag." Peters blows his brass whistle and the black flag is raised.

Mr. Howard passes the order to the master gunner, "Run a shot across her bow!"

"This is a warning," Smithy says. "Tells the captain to strike her flag, head into the wind, and come to rest. He knows she'll soon be boarded."

The *Mary* draws near and Mr. Howard prepares a longboat and his boarding party—about ten men, including himself. I've been on a ship that was captured and boarded, but I've never seen one captured and boarded. Eagerly, I stand at the rail alongside Smithy.

I sense Smithy is rather nervous. "Seems too easy. Never know whether she's waiting for us to get close enough to pounce. Sometimes a Spanish warship's disguised as a merchant ship, only to spring at the last moment."

We lean over the rail to watch Mr. Howard and his boarding party climb down into their longboat. They push off. We each draw a deep breath. We watch.

What's happening? Flashbacks. All I see are flashbacks of when those despicable Spanish pirates ripped me from Mother's arms. What's happening?

My world's going dark!

3

The Captain's Secret
December 1715

*W*HY AM I *lying on the deck of the Mary with eighty pairs of eyes staring down at me?*

"What's happening?" I moan.

Smithy is first to answer. "You leaned too far over the rail and fell overboard. Fortunately, Mr. Howard and his longboat weren't far away and they fished you out. You'll recover in a few minutes."

With that, the crowd disappears and Smithy helps me to my feet. "Off with you and get dry clothes."

A short time later, Mr. Howard and his boarding party return with rum, a little sugar, black powder, shot, and a little silver and gold. He says the *Mary* didn't need much because she just left Nassau.

"You never know what awaits when you board another vessel," is all Smithy says.

After a few more vessels are seized, Captain Hornigold spots a sloop sailing low in the water. The capture takes place with ease and Mr. Howard signals his boarding party to prepare the longboat. They bring back the captain and a few of his crew. Captain Hornigold reviews the sloop's papers and concludes she's indeed Spanish, and because he's never accepted the treaty that ended the Queen Anne's War, she's the enemy and a legitimate "prize of war." The Captain's prize crew, a dozen men, go aboard to escort her to New Providence.

The *Mary* stays in Nassau Harbor just long enough to offload her cargo. The longboats return and those who went ashore bring back the gossip. I notice a level of excitement I haven't seen before.

"What's happening?" I ask Smithy, who is becoming more receptive to my questions.

Smithy laughs, "Didn't you hear about the hurricane and the Spanish plate fleet before you left England?"

"I heard something but I didn't pay any attention."

"Well, Nassau's abuzz with news of the Spanish plate fleet that sailed from Havana the end of July. Those ships were loaded with silver from the mines in the Andes and Mexico. They'd been waiting for the war's end before they sailed to Spain. A hurricane took its toll. All eleven Spanish ships either broke up on the Florida reefs or capsized. Only the French frigate *La Griffon*, that sailed ahead of the Spanish fleet as the escort, survived."

"So why all the excitement?"

How would I know my question would cause Smithy to roar with laughter.

"Never seen a wreck before, I guess. When we're close to shore and the water's clear, you see silver, gold, and all the cargo just shimmering in the sand. All you need to do is pick it up. Instant riches! Those who know say the value of this treasure in the sand's unimaginable."

"Are the Spanish in Havana planning to do anything?"

"Well, they've sent salvage vessels and divers from Havana. They're 'fishin' for the silver, gold, and any items of value that lay on the ocean floor. I'm told they've a salvage camp at San Sebastian Inlet with two storehouses filled with treasures just waiting for vessels from Havana. Some coins, ingots, and jewels have already been brought back.

"But here's the rub," and Smithy starts speaking in a hushed voice, "the rumor's that Henry Jennings and his friends, John Wills and Edward James, had their vessels refitted at Port Royal. Captain James changed his mind about sailing and invested as a third owner in the *Eagle*, Captain Wills' vessel. Jennings and Wills will be heading along the east coast of Florida to the wreck site. Rumor also has it that they've acquired commissions—letters of marque—from the British governor of Jamaica, Lord Archibald Hamilton, authorizing them to strike against Spanish and French pirate vessels. Hah! Everyone knows that despite the rights granted by these letters, Jennings and Wills won't be hunting Spanish or French pirate vessels but rather they'll be attacking the storehouses and fishing the wrecks. Knowing Lord Hamilton, won't be surprised if he receives a share of the silver and gold."

Later in the day, I happen to see Captain Hornigold. I can tell the news that Jennings is heading for the wreck site does not sit well with him. His deep dislike for Jennings is obvious, even to me. Smithy tells me the Captain desperately wants to fish for silver and gold alongside the others, but he knows his vessels need to be careened so they'll be seaworthy.

Once the cargo is ferried ashore, the Captain orders the *Mary* and his Spanish prize to sail for what he calls Eleuthera, a sparsely populated island to the northeast of New Providence.

Smithy says Eleuthera is only a day away and has a number of secluded coves. He says the Captain will select a cove on the Caribbean side of the island. "Eleuthera's a strange island, over a hundred miles long, sometimes no more than a mile or two wide, eastern coastline faces the Atlantic."

Captain Hornigold finds a cove and sends Scotty, the lookout, to the crest of the island to watch for approaching vessels.

The *Mary* and the Spanish prize anchor side by side. The men begin transferring everything from the *Mary*, including her guns and ballast, to the Spanish prize. What they can't store on the prize, they take by longboat to the beach.

Smithy and I row over to the Spanish prize. Those remaining with the *Mary* tow her towards shore and leave to make camp on the beach. Unlike the *Mary*, the prize's anchored a significant distance from shore. Why? But I know better than to ask.

The tide's receding and the *Mary*'s coming to rest on a sandbar. "Heave down," I hear Mr. Howard order as the *Mary* rolls on her side. While some of the men tie her down, others begin scraping the seaweed and barnacles from her hull. They scrape and bring tar and oakum from a boiling tar pot on the beach to make her watertight again.

With the underside of the *Mary* out of the water, I notice small holes bored into her planks. "What are those?"

"Sea worms—sea worms have been at work. Love the warm waters of the Caribbean. Their holes'll be sealed. *Mary* won't leak, not for a while."

I'm almost overwhelmed by the dense smell of boiling tar coming from the beach.

A few days later, the men began careening the Spanish prize. They move all her cargo to the *Mary* and we follow.

I notice the Captain, Mr. Howard, and two of the crew preparing to launch a rowboat. The Captain sees me watching.

"Sam, I trust you and the cooks to watch over my vessels while we search the island. Don't leave. Do you understand me? Don't leave!"

I nod a quick reply and watch as they finish lowering their boat, climb down the ladder, and row towards shore.

They reach the beach and pull their boat out of the water. Each carries a burlap bag. From the way they struggle, the bags are heavy.

They disappear into the brush. I watch for a moment but my curiosity gets the best of me. Where're they going? A few minutes pass and I carefully lower a small rowboat into the water. Over the rail and down the ladder I go. Silently, I drop into the boat and take the oars.

The water's amazing! Beautiful aqua against the pink sand—and so clear. I row and pass over schools of fish wearing the most gorgeous colors: bright reds, oranges, yellows, and blues. I can't help but be mesmerized.

Before long I'm on the shore and beach my rowboat near the Captain's. They don't have much of a head start. With care, I can catch up without being seen or heard.

I look around. I'm in awe. I've never seen such beauty. Exquisite, the water's clear and shimmering, the sky's a rich blue, and the dazzling sand's a light pink against the rich green foliage, dotted by an array of tropical blooms. Self-satisfied, I continue up the beach to where the sand meets the brush and trees. What a magnificent place! I fight the urge to linger, they'll soon be back and I'll be discovered.

Now, where did they go?

My question is answered when the Captain whispers to Mr. Howard, "Not far now." A chill goes down my spine, they don't sound far away.

I creep in the direction of the voices, I see the Captain pointing and saying, "Across the pond—behind them rocks."

Hmm. There must be a passage!

I wait. Seems like an eternity. Now—should I go? I'll be careful not to splash. Slowly, I begin to cross the water. Sure enough, behind the rocks is a small opening. It's above the waterline for now but won't be when the tide is high.

I squeeze into the darkness. So dark, my eyes aren't adjusting. I'm surrounded by this vast darkness, I can't see. Can I move up the passage? I think I can but it's narrowing. The ceiling's forcing me to crouch. I'll feel my way along this damp wall. Careful, I need to be careful not to splash—water's still under my feet. Must keep moving. Ever so slowly, my eyes begin to make sense of the darkness. Hmm, the path's rising slightly, no more water, no more mud. What's scampering up my arm? I shudder. What just crashed into my face? Wings are brushing the back of my neck. *I want to scream!*

Hmm. The passageway is now opening, just a bit. Can I stand up? Yes, but as I do, I'm forced to duck back down. Bats—hundreds of bats—they're flying at me. And they're singing, their singing's getting louder. I'm shuddering again. Should I take another step? More bats. The Captain's lantern must be rousing them from their peaceful slumber. I'm sliding. Oh, the floor's slippery from their droppings.

I know I made a grave mistake following the Captain. How can I turn back now? Must move forward, yes, must move forward. Careful. Forward's my only option.

I'm close, ever so close.

Echoes of the Captain and Mr. Howard talking and laughing begin to greet me.

I creep on, carefully, feeling along the wall. Where's the wall? I search for the wall. Oh, it veers to my right. I take another step. The soft flickering glow from the Captain's lantern breaks the darkness and casts dim shadows. I can take a few more steps. The passage turns sharply again—I step from darkness into a breathtaking, pristine cavern.

The soft glow from the Captain's lantern becomes beams of light bouncing off the stalactites and stalagmites. Gasping in sheer amazement, I realize I've stepped too far. Now, I can be seen as well as heard. I must formulate a plan to sneak out. Can't get my mind working. I'm still disoriented from the unexpected light.

What's that I tripped over? I'm afraid to raise my head, can't look up—oh no, boots, all I see are boots, large boots, boots of a very angry Captain, and his face, crimson. And who's behind him? Mr. Howard. I'm doomed. Can't escape now. *Escape is impossible!*

"YOU! YOU!" The Captain stammers. "I'll deal with you when we get back to the *Mary*. Not a word to no one. CURSED! Not a word, you hear? CURSED!"

A meek "yes, sir," is all I can muster to say.

When we arrive back at the *Mary*, the Captain discovers I'm the least of his concerns. Scotty's spotted the three masts of a British frigate picking her way south along the eastern side of the island. Her crew's looking for signs of life.

For the moment, the gravity of this news surpasses any punishment I'll receive. With the Spanish prize still being careened, only the *Mary*'s seaworthy. If the warship spots any of the Captain's men, she'll be upon them before they can sail into a position where they can fully defend themselves. *We all know the consequences of being discovered and they're not good.*

"Sam! Go find Scotty and report to me. Need to know what that frigate does when she clears the end of this island."

With that, I climb to the island's crest and join Scotty.

When I look back at the cove, the *Mary* is closer to shore and her starboard guns face the open sea. Those careening the prize have taken refuge among the trees. The British warship must keep her distance. She's much larger and heavier than the *Mary* and has a deeper draft. She'll run aground on a sandbar or scrape her bottom on a reef if she gets too close. The tide's a concern. The *Mary* will be beached when the tide goes out. She'll roll and her cannons will be useless.

I remember where the frigate was first spotted. She was lurking in the distance. Now she's coming closer and closer. I count ten cannons pointing directly at me. *She'll pin Captain Hornigold's sloops in the cove. The odds are not in his favor. My heart's pounding.*

4

The Jacobite Threat
December 1715

WE WATCH AND wait, watch and wait. Our waiting seems interminable. Slowly, ever so slowly, the warship reaches the tip of the island.

"She's stopping. Why's she stopping?" I whisper to Scotty.

"Don't know, maybe she saw something. Keep your head down, don't move. Spooking the birds will cause her to come back. She seems undecided whether to check our side of the island."

After hesitating for a few minutes, the frigate resumes her southerly course.

"Run down to the beach. Tell the Captain the immediate threat has passed, the reprieve may be only temporary."

With this news, the men show a new urgency to finish careening the Spanish prize. When the work's done and the tide's high, the two vessels anchor side by side and their crews return.

I'm surprised when Captain Hornigold announces that they'll sail back to New Providence so his men can spend Christmas and New Year's Day in Nassau.

Once the *Mary* sets sail, I hear him bellow, "Sam!" My worst fear is about to happen. My time to face the Captain has come. I build up my courage and make my way to his quarters. He growls as I approach. Just seeing me makes him angry again. His eyes flash and his face turns beet red. Sweat starts streaming down his face. He's even more disturbed than when we're in the cavern. He's very, very angry at me!

"YOU!" he shrieks. "I told you to stay on the *Mary* with Cooky and Stewy! Was that too difficult to understand? What did you do but disobey me! I had half a mind to leave you there. USELESS! JUST USELESS!"

I wince at his anger.

"I'm sorry, Captain, but I was—."

"SELFISH, UNTHINKING, YOU PAID NO MIND TO MY ORDERS!"

His quarters become silent, absolutely silent. The air is still, nothing is moving. I can't say I am relieved by the sudden change because he's still fuming. Even his pacing stops, adding to the awkward silence.

Smithy enters and the Captain returns to his pacing. I go back to cowering in the corner. At any moment he'll lash out at me again.

"Sir," Smithy says politely, "if I may—."

"YOU MAY NOT! Not till I've deal with this ungrateful—." He glares at me as his voice trails off.

"What did I do that was so wrong?" *I should have held my tongue. I know better than to whine. I may have gotten away with this with Mother, but not with the Captain.*

"You violated my orders, that's what you did!" He's quieter now, a sign of his true rage.

Never thought that leaving the *Mary* would make him so mad. But he hates being disrespected, and I know I was extremely disrespectful.

"I'm sorry, Captain. That will never happen again—am I dismissed?" I beg politely, trying to make him less angry.

"I WARN YOU! SAY NO WORD ABOUT THE CAVERN TO NO ONE! No one! That cavern's cursed, I tell you, and you'll die a most unpleasant death! You'll die a most unpleasant death. Do you hear?"

"I hear, sir. I'll say nothing," I reply timidly.

"Dismissed!"

I back away from the Captain but I don't go far. I strain to listen.

"Smithy, what do you want?" the Captain asks, still upset.

I'm thinking about what has happened and forget to listen for Smithy's boots leaving. I lose my balance and fall forward but steady myself quickly and disappear around the corner. I know Smithy saw me eavesdropping but I can only hope that the Captain hasn't.

I need time to catch my breath and so I head to the galley seeking out Cooky and Stewy. After my encounter with the Captain, I'll find comfort in seeing their smiling faces. I can't tell them what happened, I'll make an excuse for visiting. The first thing that comes to mind is "Where're we heading?"

"You're impatient. Wait and see, boy, wait and see," is all Cooky says.

I feel a little foolish because I know where we're going.

I avoid the Captain while we're at sea, but after we drop anchor in Nassau Harbor, I hear him call, "Sam!" He's at the rail gazing across the harbor at the town.

"Here, Captain!"

He seems to have forgotten our previous encounter. He greets me warmly. "Going ashore. Want to go? Never been before, have you? Take the next longboat."

"Oh yes, absolutely, thank you, sir!"

But with the next breath he cautions, "You need to remember, don't go ashore alone. Not safe for you alone! You disobey and go alone, you won't come back. Do you hear? Only go ashore with me or Smithy!"

I follow the Captain into the longboat and take my place behind him. The trip from the *Mary* to shore is no more than a few minutes, but with my excitement of being on shore after three months at sea, not counting my brief visit to the cavern, the trip seems like an eternity. Our longboat docks at the wharf and I quickly follow him ashore. I take a few steps. *I'm dizzy, disoriented. Why are my legs beginning to wobble?*

I find myself sitting on the wharf and everyone around is laughing.

Captain Hornigold grabs my arm and yanks me up. Slowly I find my land legs. He's tall and I can't match his strides. Not wanting to ask him to walk more slowly, I find myself running just to keep up. After what he's told me about going alone, I don't want to be left behind.

We walk and approach two taverns. We pass the first, The Killiecrankie Tavern, and enter the second, The Lion and the Unicorn.

The Captain is well received. He makes his rounds, moving from table to table greeting each sailor by name. Some have a story or two to tell. Others can't resist having a little fun with him. "Didn't know your kid tags along? Teaching him to be a pirate?"

"Me? A kid? Hah! Found Sam on a Spanish pirate ship. Either throw him in the sea or take him with me. Couldn't leave an English kid with *Spanish* pirates!"

The room erupts in laughter, followed by the clinking of bottles and mugs.

"Made him into my cabin boy," the Captain adds as he points to a table in the corner. I push my way through the crowd. He soon joins me with two tankards. "Drink up, boy. Show what you're made of."

I act casual and take a big gulp, and choke. Embarrassed, I clear my throat. The taste is awful, strong and bitter! I didn't realize that what I've been drinking on the *Mary* was watered down. I manage my best and the Captain seems pleased I don't make a complete spectacle of myself.

With Christmas approaching, everyone at the tavern is in a festive mood and drinks flow freely. The fiddlers play and the sailors sing, dance, and tell stories on one another. The afternoon passes quickly.

On our way back to the wharf, we pass The Killiecrankie Tavern and the shrill wailing calls of the bagpipes comes to meet us. They sharply contrast with the bright, lively tunes of the fiddles at The Lion and the Unicorn.

The Captain stops walking and turns to me. He sees I'm curious about Nassau. "Nassau, hmm, once a thriving little harbor. Great location in the Bahamas. North of the Caribbean. Easy two to three days to the Florida coast; four to Havana; seven to Hispaniola; seven to Jamaica; and five to Charles Town. Nassau was burned to the ground and the fort destroyed by the French and the Spanish during the early days of the Queen Anne's War. Once the war began, the town had no governor and no government. With the war over, we're no longer privateers. We came here and squatted before Nassau could be rebuilt. Declared ourselves to be the government, a republic. Scared off most of the locals who remained. Spent freely, merchants, arms dealers, smugglers, and women flocked to Nassau to get rich quickly. Nassau's a great place but needs work, lots of work."

At that point, the Captain becomes absorbed again in his thoughts about Nassau. We quietly make our way to the wharf where his longboat is waiting. Spending the afternoon with him and his friends gives me a lot to think about.

Not being at sea is a welcome change. Neither the rocking and lurching of the *Mary* nor the groaning and creaking of her hull bothers me. I've become accustomed to all that. What I hate is the food! After a few weeks at sea, all the fresh food runs out. Everything left is old, stale, salted, pickled, dried, and out of a barrel. And the water, what little there is, is foul. When the *Mary* is in the harbor, the food is real, fresh food. I can enjoy eating at the tavern if either the

Captain or Smithy will take me, or I can eat in the *Mary*'s galley with Cooky and Stewy. Everything's fresh: fresh fish and seafood, fresh meat, fresh fruits, and fresh vegetables. Best of all, I have fresh water and uncut rum and wine.

The next morning at breakfast, I have a chance to talk to Cooky about my visit to the tavern. "I noticed we passed The Killiecrankie Tavern on our way to The Lion and the Unicorn. Why did the Captain choose The Lion and the Unicorn?"

Cooky pauses for a moment and then answers my question with a question. "Did you notice how many men spoke to the Captain when you entered?"

I conjure up the image. "Yes, I think everyone made a point to speak to him. Yes, that's right, everyone!"

"Well, Captain Hornigold isn't any old captain," joins Stewy. "Captain's their leader."

"Know anything about English history?" Cooky asks.

"Mother taught me some, and I heard Mother and Father talk about the queen when we're eating supper."

"Well," says Cooky, "about thirty years ago, England, Ireland, and Scotland were separate kingdoms with separate parliaments but with one king, James. He ruled over all three kingdoms. For England and Ireland, he was called James II. For Scotland, he was James VII. So for short, he was King James II and VII.

"Ireland's predominantly Roman Catholic. Scotland's Church of Scotland's called the Kirk Presbyteran. Pockets of Catholicism are present, including in the Scottish Highlands. As you know, England has a checkered past between the Roman Catholic and the Anglican Church. Although England's predominantly Anglican, when James, a Catholic, came to the English throne, he was acceptable because he was married for eleven years and had no male heirs. When he died, the throne would pass to his eldest daughter, Mary, a Protestant. Mary's his daughter by his first wife, Anne Hyde, a Protestant."

"But James had a son, didn't he?"

"Aye. Well, as faith would have it, Anne died and James married Mary of Modena, a Catholic. In a few years, a male heir, James Francis Edward Stuart, was born. James Francis was raised Catholic. Under English law of male preference, the throne passes to the male heir, James Francis, and not to his older half-sister, Mary. England would have a Catholic dynasty again.

"Well, James II and VII, as a Catholic, attempted to create religious liberty for Catholics in England and Scotland by having their parliaments repeal of the anti-Catholic Test Acts. Those laws prohibit Catholics from serving in public office. When the English and Scottish Parliaments refused to repeal those acts, James suspended the parliaments. Not good! Very unacceptable to the Anglicans!

"The final straw was when seven Anglican bishops were prosecuted. Anti-Catholic riots broke out across England and Scotland. James' political authority was destroyed. The Anglican nobles were furious with him."

"How was peace restored?"

"James' authority collapsed and that created the opportunity to restore the original plan: Mary, James' Protestant daughter and his eldest child, could ascend to the throne."

"But how did they do that?"

"Well, with all the chaos, William of Orange of the Dutch Republic was invited to land an army on English soil."

"But why go to the Dutch Republic?"

"As you know, many of the royal houses in Europe have intermarried for political reasons. The Dutch Republic and England are no exceptions. Let me take you back to Charles I.

"Remember King Charles I? He's the son of James VI and I, the king of Scotland, England, and Ireland. Charles was beheaded and England had no monarchy for about a dozen years. Oliver Cromwell was lord protector. After Cromwell's death, his son Richard became lord protector and a short time later renounced power. The monarchy was restored and Charles' son, Charles II, became king. When Charles II died without heirs, his brother James became king and was known as James II and VII.

"The brothers, Charles II and James II and VII, had a sister, Mary Stuart. She married William II, the Prince of Orange, and she became the Princess of Orange. She's the mother of William of Orange."

"Oh, so William of Orange's James' nephew."

"Aye, when William of Orange's army invaded, most of his Uncle James' troops deserted. James disbanded the army that remained and fled to France. No one's surprised when James and his court were welcomed by his Catholic cousin, King Louis XIV. All related, you see.

"By fleeing England, James abdicated his English and Irish thrones, and William of Orange, a Protestant, and his wife Mary, an Anglican, became joint monarchs of England and Ireland. Scotland soon followed. Was called 'The Glorious Revolution.'"

"Is this the same Mary who's the daughter of James II and VII?"

"Aye, she's his daughter," Cooky responds.

Stewy adds, "And her husband, William of Orange, was James II's son-in-law as well as his nephew. Hah! All family, you see!"

"But when did Mary marry William of Orange, and weren't they cousins?"

"Mary's uncle, Charles II, arranged the marriage when she's fifteen, a marriage arranged for political reasons. William and Mary were first cousins. They had the same grandfather, Charles I. He's the grandson of Mary, Queen of Scots."

"Wow! Mary Queen of Scots was their great, great grandmother."

"But Mary's father, James II and VII, became a Catholic. Why was Mary not a Catholic as well?"

"Well, tho' Mary's from the House of Stuart, as was her father, she and her younger sister, Anne, had a Protestant mother and were raised Protestant at the insistence of their uncle, Charles II. He's king at the time and a Protestant until his death. Some say he became a Catholic on his deathbed, but that is a story for another day."

"So what happened to James II? Did he attempt to regain the thrones?"

"Oh, aye. The next year, he and his followers landed in Ireland but were defeated. James spent his last days in France."

"When did he die and who succeeded him?"

"James died in 1701, and his son, James Francis Edward Stuart, claimed the thrones as James III and VIII. He still lives in France and his supporters are still trying to take back the thrones. Matter of fact, they're trying right now.

It's called the second Jacobite uprising. Does that answer your questions?" Cooky asks.

"I think so. Let me think about it."

"Good." Cooky seems pleased with himself.

"But why are James' followers called Jacobites?"

"*Jacobus* is Latin for James, so they're called Jacobites," Cooky answers.

"So why's the first tavern named Killiecrankie?

"You sure are full of questions, boy. But I'll tell you. Aye, the first tavern's the Jacobite tavern, Killiecrankie, the name of a famous battle during the first Jacobite uprising, twenty-five years ago. The Jacobites were outnumbered but still won that battle."

"And what about the purple thistle on the sign outside The Killiecrankie Tavern?"

"Oh, that thistle. The purple thistle's the Scottish thistle and dates back over four hundred years. Many Jacobites are Scottish Highlanders and to them, this thistle stands for bravery, courage, and loyalty in the face of treachery. Goes along with the name of the tavern, Killiecrankie."

"Oh, I see."

"Aye, and the crest of King William and Queen Mary, The Lion and the Unicorn, it's the name of our tavern."

"Let's bring this up to date," Cooky adds. "William and Mary ruled together as co-sovereigns. When Mary died, William ruled by himself. When he died leaving no heirs, he was succeeded by Anne, Mary's younger sister, who was also a Protestant.

"A year ago when Queen Anne died leaving no heirs, James Francis Edward Stuart, a Catholic, thought he could claim the throne. When he refused to renounce Catholicism,

Parliament turned to Queen Anne's closest living Protestant relative, her second cousin, George Ludwig, the Elector of the German state of Hanover.

"George is not any old German. His grandmother, Elizabeth Stuart, was the sister of King Charles I. George's great-grandfather was King James I and his great-great-grandmother was Mary, Queen of Scots.

"Enough royal British blood? Not too shabby."

"Enough mussing. Back to Nassau," comments Stewy. "And as you now know, Nassau divides into two camps, Jacobites and everyone else. Captain Henry Jennings leads the Jacobites, those who want James Francis Edward Stuart and the Catholic Stuarts returned to the throne. Everyone else, those who support King George, falls in behind Captain Hornigold. King George's followers won't be seen in The Killiecrankie Tavern."

"Oh, so that's why the Captain and Captain Jennings dislike each other."

"Aye!" Cooky adds. "Another reason, the Captain's a working man, a privateer who left Jamaica because of no work. Came to New Providence and Nassau to sail again.

"Jennings' a landowner in Jamaica and Bermuda and thinks he's a gentleman pirate. Hah! Calls Captain Hornigold a common pirate. How humiliating!"

"Oh, this is all becoming clear now. So what will happen to Captain Hornigold and all of you if the Jacobites succeed and James Francis gains the throne?"

"Won't happen! Won't happen!" Cooky seems adamant.

I leave the galley thinking, *I'm not so sure.*

5

Christmas
December 1715

HE NEXT MORNING, I'm in the galley for breakfast as usual. Stewy greets me. "What you think of
Nassau, boy?"

His demeanor and question take me aback for a moment.
"Let me think. Well, this was my first opportunity to see
what a pirate colony's really like. From the *Mary*, Nassau
had no buildings except for a few taverns, a carpenter's
shop, a sailmaker, and a few trading companies near the
wharf. When I walked with the Captain, I got a better view.
The old governor's mansion, the fort, and the church were
badly damaged. Found it hard to believe that Nassau had
been reduced to a tent city with a few one-room huts scattered around. We'd some trouble walking down the streets—
everywhere's overgrown—our way's often blocked by trash
and waste. Never seen so much trash. Everywhere! And

the stench and the animals—chickens, dogs, cats, goats, pigs, cattle, horses—they all roamed at will. The rats. Oh, the rats! Except for their tails, they'd pass for Millie, the *Mary's* cat."

My description gives both Cooky and Stewy a good laugh.

The days roll by, I look at palm trees but daydream about snow—this my first winter away from England. Thoughts of my family follow me everywhere. *Will I ever see them again?*

When Christmas Day arrives, I wake in tears. All I can think about is Mother and Father. This is my first Christmas without them and without all my friends in England. I even miss my brothers.

Everything happens to me and I have no control. It's bad enough we were sailing to the Carolinas, a place I don't want to go, but then Spanish pirates, English pirates, and now—who knows? I'm a prisoner, overwhelmed, yet this is Christmas and that makes being away from my family and my friends all that much worse.

I stay by myself for most of the day. Except for the Captain, Cooky, and Stewy, everyone's ashore. Jack, the ratter dog, and Mollie, the cat, keep me company. Where are they going? Guess even they're growing tired of me. Must be wondering off to root out a mouse or a rat.

Cooky and Stewy invite me to join them in the galley for Christmas dinner. At first, I'm reluctant but as they keep insisting, I relent.

Much to my surprise, they've decorated the galley and have a small package for me. I'm embarrassed, I never thought to have something for each of them. I open their gift and find a beautiful pair of boots.

"We noticed you're often barefooted. Thought Charlie's boots hurt your feet," Cooky comments as he puts dinner on the table.

The dinner is exceptionally good. We finish, clear, and clean the galley. Stewy pours us each a beer and we talk, mainly about my family. I tell them all about Father and Mother and my brothers, the church, Father's ministry work in the Carolinas, and my friends. I feel uncomfortable probing into their lives, so I think I'll not ask and they can tell me when they feel comfortable doing so.

At one point Stewy leaves the table and Cooky takes this opportunity to whisper, "Christmas is a sad time for Stewy. See, Stewy was married and they were expecting a baby. She's born around Christmas but Stewy's wife died giving birth."

"Where's the baby now and how old is she?"

"Oh, she's about five. Being raised by Stewy's sister and her husband—live in Charles Town—he's a blacksmith. Stewy visits when he can, holidays make him very sad. Don't say a word."

Stewy returns and we chat a while longer. The conversation turns to the Captain. "How long have you sailed with Captain Hornigold?"

Cooky is the first to answer. "Well, me and Stewy was friends in Charles Town. The war was winding down and we found ourselves in Jamaica with no work. All the letters of marque, you know, the governor's commissions to capture Spanish and French vessels, expired with the end of the war. Privateering was no longer legal. Jamaica's getting crowded with out-of-work sailors. Captain Hornigold, John Cockram, and John West decided to see what Nassau on New Providence Island was like. They heard there's no government but a good harbor. Could be a nice place to be for a while.

"They talked up New Providence and Stewy, and me, and a bunch of others decided to join them. What's to lose? At least we would get out of Port Royal and do something.

"You know New Providence's an island in the Bahamas, north of the Caribbean. The old king, Charles II, gave a charter to a group called the Carolina Lords Proprietors. They was to govern north of Spain's claim to Florida and south of the Virginia colony, all the islands of the Bahamas, included in the charter, with the capital being Nassau. The Lords Proprietors didn't give a fig about the Bahamas. No money to be made here. So they provided no protection. For us to claim Nassau as the pirate republic was of no interest to them."

Stewy then speaks up. "Me and Cooky sailed with the Captain to New Providence. Captain Hornigold, Cockram, and West each bought a periagua. You know, one of them sailing canoes made out of a hollowed-out tree trunk, fore-and-aft rigged sail, and oars for twenty to thirty men.

"Hornigold, Cockram, and West sailed using Nassau Harbor as a safe haven. No one comes to these islands to look for us. Plenty of places to hide.

"We attacked small Spanish trading vessels and isolated sugar plantations from the Straits of Florida to the shores of Cuba. With a periagua and twenty or so well-armed men, no small trading vessel and no isolated sugar plantation could escape us.

"Had some profitable cruises. One day, Captain Cockram came back with Asian silks costing the Spanish merchants around thirty-two thousand pieces of eight. On another day, he came back with copper, rum, sugar, and silver coins worth two thousand pieces of eight. Captain West raided a Cuban plantation and came away with fourteen slaves valued at twenty-one hundred pieces of eight. Captain Hornigold came back with bales of expensive linens from Silesia and Prussia worth fourteen thousand pieces of eight."

"What did you do with all those slaves and goods? They're not money and can't be spent?"

Stewy pauses and Cooky answers, "Richard Thompson lives on Harbour Island, a very small island with a great harbor, about fifty miles northeast of Nassau, off the northeast tip of a long, narrow island called Eleuthera. You know Eleuthera. We careened the *Mary* and our Spanish prize there when you first joined us. Thompson fences pirated goods. He has his own vessel and sails to Nassau and Charles Town. Sometimes he even sails almost nine hundred miles down to the Dutch spice island of Curaçao. He makes money for himself and for us and for everyone in Nassau, Harbour Island, and Eleuthera. The money's made to be spent.

"Me and Stewy sailed with Hornigold for about six months, but shortly after Christmas, they decided to divide their plunder and split up. West quit pirating, took his share, and moved on. Never knew where. Cockram left to marry one of Thompson's daughters and moved to Eleuthera Island. A rumor was spreading that the Spanish were preparing to raid New Providence Island, so Captain Hornigold followed Cockram to Eleuthera. Me and Stewy sailed with him. Only a few farmers lived on Eleuthera and they welcomed us as protectors."

Stewy adds, "Captain Hornigold befriended Jonathan Darvell. The Darvell family were early settlers of Eleuthera. Darvell owned a small sloop, the *Happy Return*. Darvell was getting too old to sail but his seventeen-year-old son, Zacheus, wasn't. So in the summer of fourteen, me and Cooky joined Hornigold, Zacheus, Daniel Stillwell, who is Darvell's son-in-law, James Bourne, and Ralph Blanken-ship, and we sailed the *Happy Return*, a nice little vessel, probably around fifteen tons. Although the cruise was short, was real, real successful. Raided the shores of Florida and Cuba and returned with forty-six thousand pieces of eight."

"What's a piece of eight?"

"Well," laughs Stewy, "a piece of eight's a Spanish peso. Spanish money's used around here. Silver from the mines of Peru, Bolivia, and Mexico. The ore's mined here, smelted here, and made into pieces of eight here. Very little British money around. You'll just see pieces of eight and a few gold Spanish coins."

"Why's it called a piece of eight?

"A piece of eight's an ounce of almost pure silver. A piece of eight's eight reales and can be broken into eight reales. That's seldom done but can be. A piece of eight's stamped with the number eight. Does that answer your question?" Stewy asks.

"Yes, thanks, so how many pieces of eight would I get for a pound sterling?"

"You sure is full of questions, boy," Stewy smiles. "Well, let me see. Pieces of eight's not exchanged for English pounds. The value of a piece of eight depends on what it can buy, often barter. Same for the pound, people haggle. A seller might get one English pound for something, or four pieces of eight, maybe less, maybe more. Depends. Does that help?"

"Four pieces of eight might be one pound sterling. Hmm, two hundred forty pence in a pound, twelve pence in a shilling, twenty shillings in a pound. One piece of eight might buy the same as sixty pence, or five shillings. OK, I think I understand.

"Might forty-six thousand pieces of eight buy the same as about eleven or twelve thousand pounds?"

"Aye, but back to my story. Something happened between Captain Hornigold and old Darvell because the Captain never sailed the *Happy Return* again. Maybe Darvell took more than his share of the plunder as the *Happy Return's* owner, leaving what was left to split among us who risked getting caught and hanged."

Stewy pauses, seeming to dream about their cruise on the *Happy Return*. That gives Cooky the opportunity to pick up the story. "In late fall, Captain Hornigold, Thomas Terrill, and another of the Captain's friends bought an open boat, a shallop, from an Eleutheran settler."

"What's a shallop?"

Cooky chuckles. "Think of a shallop as an overgrown rowboat. Instead of one set of oars, there's several oars on each side. A single mast and a fore-and-aft rigged sail, sometimes more than a single sail."

"In early December, me and Stewy joined Hornigold and a few others, and we sailed in his shallop to Cuba."

"Aye," Stewy laughs, "turned out to be some adventure. We captured a small vessel and a periagua belonging to a

Cuban noble—Señor Barrrihone was his name—from Port-au-Prince, I believe. His vessels were overflowing with goods and money. Think about striking it rich!"

Cooky can't restrain himself. "Word spread and Captain Hornigold became the most respected pirate in the Caribbean!"

"I can't imagine all those pieces of eight. I've never seen a piece of eight—not one—not a boat full."

"So, as I was saying, by the time we sailed back to Eleuthera and finished dividing our treasure, the threat of the Spanish attack had passed. Was a good time to move back to New Providence and Nassau.

"That brings me to Daniel Stillwell. Remember, Stillwell sailed with me and Stewy on the *Happy Return*. Well, shortly after we returned from Cuba with all the thousands of pieces of eight, Stillwell sailed the *Happy Return* for Darvell. He wanted to try his hand as a captain, so he sailed the *Happy Return* and was joined by Matthew Lowe, John Cary, Benjamin Linn, and Zacheus Darvell.

"They sailed from Eleuthera along the coast of Cuba and seized a vessel with eleven hundred pieces of eight and tanned hides and other goods valued at another three hundred pieces of eight. This was not near the forty-six thousand pieces of eight Captain Hornigold seized. Stillwell was disappointed, real disappointed.

"Meanwhile, Señor Barrihone was extremely angry. He complained to the governor of Cuba, who complained to the governor of Jamaica, Lord Archibold Hamilton, and threatened to invade the Bahamas if Lord Hamilton didn't do something about the 'pirates nest,' as he called it. Governor Hamilton's a Jacobite sympathizer and you'll hear about him from time to time. Anyways, Hamilton wrote to Thomas Walker in New Providence saying Walker needed to do something.

"That brings me to Thomas Walker. I don't think I've spoke of him before. The Walker family homestead's about three miles out of Nassau. Walker was a judge of the vice admiralty court of the Bahamas before the war and when New Providence had a government. He thinks he's still the acting deputy governor. Huh! He can think all he wants.

"Walker sailed from Nassau to Harbour Island and captured Stillwell, Zacheus Darvell, and Matthew Low. Both Darvell and Low were willing to sign documents blaming Stillwell if Walker would turn them loose. They didn't want to be hanged for so little.

"Walker seized the *Happy Return* and sailed her back to Nassau with Stillwell. He had the gall to arrange to send Stillwell to Jamaica for trial. The vessel with Stillwell sailed from Nassau right after New Year's Day. Captain Hornigold got wind of what's happening, and he and his sloop slipped out of Nassau Harbor not long afterwards. Somehow the Captain rescued Stillwell, so Stillwell was never delivered to Governor Hamilton in Jamaica. Standing up to Walker and rescuing Stillwell certainly caught the attention of the pirates in Nassau. If Captain Hornigold wasn't the leader of the pirates in Nassau before then, that made him their leader, and when he says New Providence's the pirate republic, that makes Nassau the pirate republic. Captain Hornigold says everyone in Nassau's under his protection and he gave Walker a warning that if Walker interferes again, he'd personally burn Walker's house down."

"Was that the end of it?"

"No, far from it," Stewy responds. "Reports spread in Nassau that the Spanish in Cuba were preparing a massive assault on the Bahamas, retaliation for the acts of Captain Hornigold and Daniel Stillwell.

"Walker still had the *Happy Return* and sailed her to Havana hoping to talk the Cuban governor out of invading Nassau. He spent most of February in Havana due to a big hurricane. Strange, hurricane season won't start till June."

"I assume Mr. Walker succeeded in stopping the attack."

"The Spanish never invaded, so I guess you can say he succeeded. But when Walker returned, Nassau's abuzz with what's happening in Havana and along the Spanish Main. Want to hear about that?"

"Don't tease the boy," Cooky warns.

"Here's what happened. Anyone for another mug of beer before I begin?"

"Aye, but don't take too long, Stewy."

"Well," begins Stewy, "need to go back in time a bit. The king of Spain financially supported the War of the Spanish Succession and Spain's involvement in the Queen Anne's War with silver from the mines of Peru, Bolivia, and Mexico. That silver ore was mined there, smelt into bars there, struck into coins there, and packed across the mountains from Peru and Bolivia to Cartagena on the Colombian coast and Porto Bello on the Isthmus of Panama, and from the mines in Mexico to Vera Cruz on the Gulf Coast. From there the silver was shipped to Havana and then on to Spain. Sailing to Spain required the ships to sail north through the Florida Straits and then across the Atlantic. These fully rigged, square-sail ships needed the currents and the prevailing trade winds.

"Spain sailed twice a year in large fleets that were well protected. Towards the end of the war, even sailing in fleets became unsafe. No fleet attempted to sail for two years and the king was getting mighty desperate. All that silver and gold's piling up at the New World ports and in Spain his treasury's empty.

"When Walker came back from Havana, his crew talked about all the ships in the harbor there. General Echeverz's fleet of seven ships was waiting for General Ubilla's fleet of eight ships from Vera Cruz. Ubilla was in Vera Cruz for two years just waiting for the war to end before he sailed to Havana to join Echeverz's fleet. They were sailing together for safety. The official cargo was valued at fourteen million pesos, that's fourteen million pieces of eight. That's not counting the passengers' unofficial cargo. I'm told those sailing back to Spain had much of their personal wealth aboard.

"Captain Hornigold knew General Ubilla's fleet was coming up from Vera Cruz, and with General Echeverz's fleet waiting in Havana Harbor, the *guarda costas*, the Cuban coast guard, was on high alert. Captain thought it wise to avoid Cuba west of Havana, especially when sailing alone.

"In March, word came back to Nassau that the February hurricane wrecked four of Ubilla's ships and his flagship was damaged and needed repair. General Ubilla figured that would add another month before what's left of his fleet could sail from Vera Cruz to Havana.

"In late March, Captain Hornigold began fishing the wrecks far from western Cuba, more around the Windward Passage and Hispaniola. Sometimes he would fish, sometimes he would capture a small vessel. In and out of Nassau, a week here, two weeks there.

"Come the end of July and another deadly hurricane came across New Providence and Nassau heading for the Florida coast. We're lucky to be in Nassau Harbor and were able to ride out the storm.

"Sometime in September, we heard that the Spanish plate fleet—the eleven Spanish ships and a French frigate—had sailed from Havana on the twenty-fourth of July. Seven days later, the thirty-first, they're caught in the hurricane. All but the French frigate were wrecked. The rumor's that the wreckage was up and down the Florida coast, on either side of San Sebastian Inlet. Soon, the Spanish from Havana were on site with vessels and divers to salvage what they could.

"With all that silver and gold in the water near shore waiting to be picked up, many English flocked to the Florida coast to try their luck at fishing the wrecks."

"One last adventure," Cooky adds, "the *Mary* of Jamaica. You tell that one, Stewy."

Stewy begins, "In early November, we're coming back from a longer cruise, sailing off the northern coast of Cuba near the Windward Passage, when we came upon a sloop that looked English but was flying a Spanish flag. Captain's curious, real curious, so he ordered an attack. That was when you're discovered locked in a cabin below deck. That vessel's a sloop, the *Mary*, and she originally sailed from Jamaica.

"So, Captain Hornigold traded his sloop for the *Mary*.

"We went on to capture a small Spanish sloop off the coast of Florida. She'd a nice cargo of sugar and dry goods.

Mr. Howard sent our prize crew over and told them to bring her and her cargo back to Nassau.

"The *Mary* then sailed back to Nassau. Once anchored in the harbor, the plunder from the *Mary* and her Spanish prize were taken ashore and delivered to the Captain's agent to fence."

With that, I see that Cooky and Stewy are tired and so am I. We sit in silence. A few minutes pass. They're remembering their past and I'm overwhelmed by their adventures.

Cooky breaks the silence. "Need to prepare a Christmas plate for the Captain. You'll take it to him."

"I will, Captain Hornigold seems to stay by himself."

"Aye," said Cooky, "except when he goes to the tavern. Never tells no one about his past. He isn't much of a talker. Takes good care of his men, tho'. Never killed nobody that Stewy and I know about."

"Won't attack British or Dutch vessels," Stewy adds. "Says he doesn't accept the peace treaty. Never was consulted, he says. Must be something else, but don't know what.

"He's English for sure, and the rumor's he might be from Ipswich, a port town nor'east of London. Hornigolds live there and a few now live around Massachusetts Bay in a town also named Ipswich—good Puritans."

Stewy goes on, "He's older than most around here. He might have served in the Royal Navy and then as a privateer before the war ended. Some think he was married and when his wife died, he hooked up with Corkram and West, and that's when me and Cooky threw in with him. But he never talks about the past."

I bent over to give Jack and Mollie their final holiday treats. Cooky, meanwhile, waits with the Captain's plate.

"Here, boy, wish him a Merry Christmas from me and Stewy."

I enter the Captain's quarters. He's lost in thought.

"Sorry to interrupt, sir, but I've your Christmas plate. Cooky and Stewy want me to wish you a Merry Christmas."

The Captain smiles and points to where I should leave his plate.

"Merry Christmas, sir."

I begin to leave when he's calls me back. "Merry Christmas" and thrusts out a little package. "Thought you might like this."

Inside, I find a notebook marked *DIARY* in big letters and a stick of graphite.

"Thank you very much, sir, and Merry Christmas."

I hear him whisper, "Merry Christmas, Abby."

6

No Risk, No Reward
Late December 1715–March 1716

THE DAY AFTER Christmas, the men of the *Mary* are preparing for their next cruise. Captain Hornigold's restless and decides to sail within a day or two.

The *Mary* is stocked with only those provisions needed for a few weeks at sea. Smithy says we're heading to the Florida coast. He's not sure whether we'll fish the wrecks or capture vessels. So the *Mary* sails from Nassau Harbor for the Florida Straits, the sea passage between Florida and Cuba.

A few days pass. The sea is calm and the prevailing wind gently guide the *Mary* towards her destination. That gives me time to check on the livestock we always carry onboard.

When the cow or goats produce extra milk or the chickens lay extra eggs, Cooky and Stewy save me a special breakfast treat.

I have time to mingle with the men. I pause to listen to Matthews, Sanders, and Johnson. They huddle together telling stories about their lives before they joined the Captain.

"I lived somewhere in England," Matthews sighs. "Been sailing with the Royal Navy when the war ended. With no war, sailors like me were no longer needed, so we're discharged, unemployed. That's what I was, all the good years serving the queen, discharged, unemployed! That's two years ago. I signed onto a merchant ship heading for Jamaica. That's where I found myself, Jamaica, unemployed! I heard Nassau's the place for unemployed sailors like me, so I made my way there. Captain Hornigold sailed into the harbor looking for a few men because his sloop had lost some to sickness. I joined and haven't been back to England since."

Sanders nods thoughtfully. "Me and my family was wanderers. Sometimes here, sometimes there. Moving around kept me on my toes. I's sailing on a merchant ship when we was attacked by pirates, and 'cause I wasn't married, I was forced to join. Sailed with them for a while and when we're in Nassau, I was able to join Captain Hornigold's crew. I liked sailing for the Captain and grew to like pirating, so stayed on. Do wonder what me mum and dad's doing and how they're getting along without me."

Johnson looks a little uncomfortable, but sensing it's his turn, he begins. "My past? Not sure what to make of it. Lived by myself somewhere. Joined so long ago, can't remember. Was eighteen, maybe twenty, and ready for adventure. Joined up with the Captain back when he's a privateer during the war, been with him ever since."

Sanders chuckles briefly. "Yeah, you get used to this life. Is that the cabin boy over there?"

Their eyes follow Sanders' gaze and fall upon me. I linger, do they want me to leave? I slowly back away, shooting Sanders a half-apologetic look. Sanders replies with a crooked smile.

I hunt around till I find a place near the rail where I make myself comfortable. I've been carrying my prized possessions the Captain gave me, the diary and the stick of graphite. I would like to understand the history of William and Mary, so I pay no attention to all those eyes that look at me. Have they never seen anyone write before? They're curious, and I hear them whisper but no one comes to see what I'm doing.

I make an effort to look at my notes. My mind drifts back to the tangled families of William and Mary. First, I trace William of Orange. Hmm, Mary, Queen of Scots; her son, James VI and I; his son, Charles I; his daughter, Mary Stuart. She married William II, the Prince of Orange, and became the Princess of Orange. Her son's William of Orange who became William III, king of England, Scotland, and Ireland. Good, I think that family line's right.

Now for William's co-sovereign, Mary, Mary II. I'll begin with Mary, Queen of Scots, again. Her son, James VI and I; his son, Charles I, king of England, Scotland, and Ireland. He's the one who's beheaded and the royal line interrupted by Oliver Cromwell. After the restoration, Charles' son, Charles II, became king of England, Scotland, and Ireland, and he died without heirs. Charles II's succeeded to the throne by his brother, James II and VII. James was a Catholic when he abdicated and fled to France. James was followed by his daughter, Mary, who became Queen Mary II of England, Scotland, and Ireland. She's the wife of William of Orange and they ruled as co-sovereigns. William and Mary were first cousins. Yes, I'm quite pleased with myself.

When I finish, one of the men approaches me.

"Sir, I don't mean to interrupt, but could you read this letter I have here?"

"Yes, I will." I wait as he digs around in his pocket and pulls out a crumpled letter. He takes great care in unfolding and smoothing it out.

"Here," as he sheepishly thrusts it out at me.

He squats beside me and I read quietly because I know the letter must be private. The letter was written with great care and in a nice hand.

Dear Homer,

These months without you have been very difficult for me and the little ones. We miss you dreadfully and wish you were home. Please be safe and come home quickly. Your loving wife, Jessie.

I fold Homer's letter and hand it back to him. He seems very pleased, and I see a tear run down his cheek. A little embarrassed, he rises, bows, and shuffles off. He makes me think of Mother and Father. *I wonder where they are? I know they miss me as much as I miss them.* Without thinking, I find myself holding my grandmother's locket.

The men on the *Mary* seize a few vessels in the Florida Straits and with mid-January approaching, Captain Hornigold decides it's time to sail for home, Nassau Harbor. On our way, we capture a Spanish vessel that's heavy with cargo. Mr. Howard leads the boarding party. The men are given an option: sail with us or be marooned naked on a nearby island. I have discovered after wearing Charlie's hand-me-downs day after day, that clothing is scarce and among a pirate's most prized possessions. The thought of being stranded naked is enough for some to join our crew. Our boarding party discovers that the Spanish prize is carrying commodities that can readily be sold by Hornigold's agents in Nassau. Captain Hornigold takes the vessel and her cargo back to Nassau.

While the *Mary* and our Spanish prize are offloaded, Captain Hornigold and I go to The Lion and the Unicorn. We enter and one of the Captain's friends motions for us to join him at his table. He's anxious to update the Captain on the local news. "While you're sailing the Florida Straits, I'm in Jamaica. Well, Henry Jennings and John Wills accepted commissions from their friend, Lord Archibald Hamilton, the governor, to seize French and Spanish pirate vessels. They sailed to the wreckage of the Spanish plate fleet off the Florida coast."

"That isn't all," another adds. "From what I hear, they've one hundred fifty men. Right after Christmas they marched

in formation to drums and all that to two salvage storehouses at San Sebastian Inlet and chased away about sixty
Spanish guards."

"Oh?" the Captain says.

"Aye, and reportedly, they stole much of the silver and
gold the Spanish had fished from the wrecks, 350,000 pieces
of eight. That treasure was stored, waiting for salvage vessels
to arrive and take it back to Havana."

"How do you know this?" the Captain asks.

"Well, Jennings and his lot came back to Nassau, bragging. Jennings said he was leaving for Port Royal to give
Lord Hamilton his share and to fish the wrecks again before
his commission expires."

With that, everyone at the table becomes silent till one
of the Captain's friends speaks up. "What do you think,
Captain?"

"Hmm, raises a lot of questions.

"Whose idea was the commission, the letter of marque?

"Did Jennings and Wills ask the governor for their letters,
or did the governor ask them whether they each would like
one?

"Were Jennings and Wills the only ones? Did the governor give letters to others?

"Where did the one hundred fifty men come from?
Pirates? Can't see one hundred fifty pirates marching in
formation to a drummer, can you?" And everyone laughs.

"Did they come from the militia barracks in Jamaica, and
why were they sailing with Jennings and Wills to begin with?

"All interesting questions, wouldn't you say?

"Who owned the vessels? Did Jennings own the *Barsheba* with her eight guns and eighty men? No, don't think
so. I'm told Jasper Ashworth and his partner Daniel Axtell,

two merchants of Port Royal, own the *Barsheba* and loaned her to Jennings, or maybe she was owned by John Cavalier and William Hayman.

"Did John Wills own the *Eagle* with her twelve guns and one hundred men or was she owned by John Beswick and William Hayman?

"Who would have gotten a share of any plunder as owner of the vessel and how much?

"Why did the vessels return so quickly to Jamaica? Did Jennings and Wills plan this would be a short voyage with a particular purpose, to raid the storehouses?

"And what happened to the 350,000 pieces of eight? Was it divided, and how? Did Jennings and Wills get shares? Did King George get a share? Did Governor Hamilton get a share? Did Jasper Ashworth and Daniel Axtell or John Cavalier, John Beswick, and William Hayman get shares? Or was it all sent to the Earl of Mar in Scotland to support the Jacobite uprising?"

The group's quiet in thought. Finally, the Captain breaks the silence. "Hamilton's clever, but he'll get his just deserts one of these days. Mark my words."

There's a lot of shaking of heads and then some mumbling. Finally, each in turn gets up, nods to the Captain, and leaves the tavern.

On our walk back to the wharf, the Captain stops by his agent's shop. "Want to check on that small Spanish sloop I left with you December last. Were you able to get the court to declare her a forfeiture so she could be auctioned?"

The Captain's agent pauses for a moment. "Sorry to tell you, but Captain Jennings came by a couple of weeks ago, just after he raided the Spanish storage camps in Florida, and claimed that vessel. Showed me his commission from Governor Hamilton and I had no choice but to release her to him."

"I understand. That vessel's probably more trouble than she's worth. What about the cargo—the sugar and dry goods?"

"All sold. Did quite well for you."

"Good! I'll send William Howard to collect."

And with that, we continue to make our way to the wharf and our waiting longboat.

The *Mary*, now resupplied, is ready to depart again for the Florida Straits. After sailing for a couple of days, Scotty, who's on his watch at the bow, calls out, "Sail ho!" Captain Hornigold scans the horizon. He spots a large merchant vessel he thinks looks familiar except she's flying the Spanish flag. We follow for an hour or two and then begin our approach. She has a deep draft, so there's a good possibility of a hold full of cargo. By now, our men can see the vessel and all are anxious to seize her.

She's a large sloop. As I admire her, Captain Hornigold gives Mr. Howard word to prepare a cannon. Mr. Howard relays the command to the boatswain, who blows his whistle to alert the main gunner.

When the bow of the *Mary* is even with the stern of the merchant vessel, Captain Hornigold nods to Mr. Howard, who calls out, "Hoist our colors!" Our black flag, the flag of a pirate vessel, is raised as Mr. Howard barks, "Run a shot across her bow!"

The rhythmic whipping of the wind in our sails and the waves lapping our vessel are interrupted by the thunderous clap of our cannons making our intentions known.

In response, the merchant vessel dutifully strikes her flag, turns into the wind, and drifts to a stop. Mr. Howard and our boarding party lower a boat, row over, and soon return with the captain along with his vessel's papers. She's a Jamaican sloop that was captured by Spanish pirates, renamed, and sold.

Because she was captured by Spanish pirates, Captain Hornigold's not going to just plunder her. Mr. Howard selects several of her men to join the *Mary*. Some join willingly, most do not. He orders those not selected to be transported to a deserted island nearby. We set sail with our freshly captured Spanish vessel following us to New Providence Island.

It's late January when we drop anchor in Nassau Harbor. Captain Hornigold sends Mr. Howard to discover the owner of the *Mary*. He soon returns with the news that she's owned by Augustine Golding, of Vero Parish, Jamaica. Now that we've a seaworthy vessel, the Spanish sloop we just seized, the Captain orders Mr. Howard to gather a small crew and return the *Mary* to Golding.

During the month of February, the seized Spanish vessel, now renamed the *Benjamin*, is refitted as a pirate vessel. Structures on the deck are removed, and cannons and swivel guns added. The *Benjamin*, although a sloop, is larger than the *Mary* of Jamaica and can accommodate two hundred men. The *Mary* can accommodate only one hundred forty. Even at one hundred forty, the *Mary* is much larger than the ordinary pirate sloop that can accommodate around eighty.

The Captain and I continue visiting The Lion and the Unicorn. On one occasion, a couple of the Captain's friends pull chairs up to our table. "I heard rumors the Jacobites are preparing another attempt to retake the throne."

"That's what I hear too," comments the Captain. "My sources tell me that last March, James had the audacity to write Pope Clement seeking his support for another Jacobite uprising. James thought the timing was good with the death of Queen Anne and the coronation of King George. From what I heard, the pope never answered. He's too smart to get into another failed conflict. His support of France during the War of the Spanish Succession created enough problems for him within his church. He'll stay out.

"I also heard that late in August last, the Earl of Mar sailed from London to Scotland and held the first council of war, and the next month he raised the standard of James. My sources tell me that a month later, Mar had twenty thousand men and controlled Scotland above the Firth of Forth. I also heard Mar wanted James to appoint him commander of the Jacobite army. Serious business, aye, serious business!"

In early March, the *Benjamin* is ready to sail. I know we're sailing south but I don't know our destination. So I visit Smithy, who is on his watch at the helm.

"Where're we heading?"

"Florida coast to do a little fishing," is Smithy's chipper reply. He's happy to sail again, and especially anxious to try out our new vessel, the *Benjamin*.

We sail south to Cuba—about three days—then west following the Cuban coast till we come to the Florida Straits, and then north another couple of days, up the Florida coast till we come to the wrecks of the Spanish plate fleet. Six of the wrecks were marked by the Spanish with buoys. I'm surprised to see the debris from those and previous wrecks stretching along the coast for miles. They'd been scattered by storms on the reefs and sandbars. We drop anchor near a sloop that has come up from Port Royal. Smithy said Captain Hornigold knows the captain, Edward Thache, from their privateering days. Smithy says Thache's family owns a plantation in the vicinity of Spanish Town, Jamaica, but Thache likes the sea better than tending the land.

A number of our men are excellent divers, and they take to the water to prove the stories of the great sunken treasure are true. Early on, they decide to follow our usual practice and share equally regardless of the finder.

We drop anchor and our longboats are lowered into the water. Once near a wreck, the men dive in pairs to retrieve the silver and gold coins, ingots, and various other objects that are spread across the ocean floor. With the tide out, everything's not far from shore. The shallow draft of our longboats keeps them bobbing safely just above the sharp teeth of the reefs.

Periodically, a longboat comes back to the *Benjamin* to unload her treasures. We gather around and marvel at what's found: coins and ingots of silver and gold, jewelry, weapons, utensils, personal items, and even a cannon.

We stay at anchor for a week, almost two. By then, our men are exhausted from diving even tho' the lure of the treasure just waiting to be picked up keeps them returning for more. From the description of the size of the wrecked ship and our review of what's being retrieved, Captain Hornigold concludes we're at the *San Roman*, one of the largest ships in the Spanish plate fleet.

Towards the end of one day, a diver comes back to his longboat in a panic. "I'm diving with Jonathan near the stern of the hull that's still intact. Went to the bottom to retrieve some coins and when I looked around, Jonathan's gone. At first, thought he swam inside the wreckage to see what's still there. Told me he might do that. If he did, he'd run out of air."

Smithy and I watch as Mr. Howard sends fresh teams down to look for Jonathan. They keep returning to the longboat saying there's no sight of him.

"Jonathan must have entered the wreckage, been pinned by the shifting beams, run out of air struggling to get free, and drowned."

Mr. Howard and the Captain confer and decide that with the sun setting, sending another team inside the hull is too risky. That effort can start in the morning.

Even with all the riches spread on the deck of the *Benjamin*, gloom settles over our vessel.

7

Silver, Gold, and the Marianne *of St. Domingue*
March–April 1716

THE NEXT MORNING as the sun's breaking the horizon, all's exceptionally quiet except for the calls of the gulls feeding and the gentle waves lapping the *Benjamin*. The sea breeze is light and billowy white clouds begin to fill the sky.

On my way to the galley for breakfast, I stop to visit with Smithy, who's standing by the rail looking pensively at the fractured hull of the *San Roman*. I start to greet him when he motions for me to wait and listen. At first, I hear nothing but the gulls and the waves. I listen more carefully and my ears become attuned, I begin to hear a faint tapping.

"Get the Captain and Mr. Howard," Smithy whispers.

When they arrive, they too hear the tapping. Mr. Howard is quick to call his divers to join him in a longboat.

They row to the *San Roman* and several pairs of divers enter the water and carefully swim towards the wreckage. Two by two, they disappear under the water. Periodically, they bob up and disappear again. Time passes slowly.

Then the cry. "He's here! Jonathan's here! Trapped but here."

Another calls out. "One more longboat, winch, cable, plenty of cable. Hurry!"

An hour later, we gather around Jonathan, who sits on one of the chests he discovered. "I entered an airspace in the wreckage and discovered a chest and then another. I tried to move them but as I pushed, a timber fell, trapping my leg. I knew the sun's setting and my rescue would be delayed until the next day. I did my best to be patient."

Mr. Howard opens the chests—in the first, silver and gold coins, and in the smaller chest, silver jewelry inlaid with precious stones.

With that, the Captain calls a halt to the diving, and the *Benjamin* prepares to return to Nassau with her enormous find.

Upon our return, Captain Hornigold and I proceed to The Lion and the Unicorn. An old friend of his approaches our table. "While you're away, I heard that Jennings sent out word he's making another cruise to the Spanish wrecks. The six months of his commission has not expired. Leigh

Ashworth and his sloop, *Mary*, and James Carnegie and his sloop, *Discovery*, will join him. That isn't surprising. Everyone knows Hamilton's commission's just a ruse to sail around the Florida coast. I'll bet Jennings and company really plan to fish the Spanish wrecks."

When we return to the *Benjamin*, the Captain gives orders to sail in two days.

Once underway, I listen carefully for information about Jennings and Ashworth. One of our men's saying, "Heard Jennings and Ashworth sailed from Bluefields Bay, that secluded bay on the southwestern coast of Jamaica. Sailed on the morning of the ninth of March. Snuck out of the bay real early. Sailed to the Isle of Pines. Met Samuel Liddell and his sloop, *Cocoa Nut*. The three, Jennings, Ashworth, and Liddell, then sailed on to Cuba."

"And I hear," adds another, "they sailed to Cape Corrientes and then to nearby Cape Antonio, the far western tip of Cuba. Met up with James Carnegie and his sloop, *Discovery*. Planned to stay there for a while to fish the wrecks."

I go to Captain Hornigold's quarters and find him meeting with Mr. Howard and Smithy. Mr. Howard's saying, "I guess after Jennings, Ashworth, and Liddell met Carnegie, they fished the wrecks around Cape Antonio and then sailed east along the northern coast of Cuba towards Havana. At Bahia Honda, they're probably planning to veer north for the Spanish wrecks off the Florida coast."

They all nod.

"We'll sail south to Cuba," Smithy comments, "and then west till we come to the western tip of Cuba. We'll catch the currents till we reach the wrecks."

We sail south for two or three days, and once we reach Cuba, west. On the seventh of April, as we sail west, we come upon the entrance to Mariel Bay.

Smithy is at the helm and I daydream by the rail. I'm roused by Smithy who's shouting, "What ho! See there!" I look in the direction he's pointing. "A merchant vessel at Port Mariel, painted blue and yellow, flying French merchant colors!"

"Ahh. A French merchant vessel, a sloop," exclaims Captain Hornigold, who's standing nearby. "We'll see how easy she'll be to take."

We watch at the harbor entrance. There's little, if any, movement on her deck.

"Where's her crew? Ashore?" Smithy wonders.

"Move in cautiously. She's at the southeastern corner of the bay," the Captain orders.

An eerie silence engulfs the harbor as the *Benjamin* approaches the French vessel.

Mr. Howard boldly calls out, *Puis-je monter a bord?*

Oui, responds a voice, *permission accordée.* The French sloop is lightly manned and her captain knows he has no choice but to welcome us aboard.

Mr. Howard and his boarding party lower a boat and row over. In a few minutes, they return with the captain, Ensign Le Guardeu.

Captain Hornigold asks, "Where's your crew?"

The ensign replies, "Sent half to trade with a French frigate about twenty miles to the west, Bahia Honda, I believe."

After a quick glance at the sloop's papers, Captain Hornigold announces the vessel is indeed French, the *Marianne* of Saint Domingue, and because he doesn't recognize the treaty that ended the war, he considers her a prize of war. "Take her back to Nassau. She'll bring a pretty price."

The men of the *Benjamin* set to work preparing the *Marianne* for her voyage to Nassau. "Look," Smithy calls out, "a sloop and two periaguas are entering the harbor. No, they're hesitating. I think they saw us with the *Marianne*. One periagua's breaking away and beginning to row towards us. Can't tell what the sloop and the other periagua are doing. Seem undecided."

Smithy now shouts to Captain Hornigold. "There! Look! That's Carnegie in his sloop, the *Discovery*. I'll be—. He's spying on us."

Aware that Captain Hornigold is watching him just as he's watching the *Benjamin*, Carnegie gives the order for the *Discovery* to turn and leave the harbor. His periagua escort follows.

With Mr. Howard still preparing the *Marianne* to sail with the *Benjamin*, we're not able to pursue. The remaining periagua, however, continues rowing towards us.

"Know these men rowing towards us?" Captain Hornigold asks.

Oui, responds Le Guardeu. "My men. I sent them to Bahia Honda to trade with the French frigate. And I gave them a packet of mail for Havana. Sent them hoping they'd bring back sailing information. I've never sailed these parts before."

The newcomers tie their periagua to the stern of the *Marianne* and join us onboard the *Benjamin*.

The officer in charge of the periagua, already distressed, told Le Guardeu why they were sailing with the sloop and the other periagua. He recounts, "Four pirate vessels captured the *St. Marie* of Rochelle, the frigate you had sent us to trade with. Their leader's a pirate named Jennings and his sloop *Barsheba*. The others, Leigh Ashworth, the captain of the *Mary*, and James Carnegie, the captain of the *Discovery*, that was the sloop that's with us when we entered the harbor. The two periaguas must have joined Jennings before he seized the *St. Marie*. Their captain's a pirate named Sam Bellamy. Has a friend with him, Paulsgrave Williams. One of Bellamy's periaguas was with the *Discovery* when we entered the harbor."

Captain Hornigold asks, "So you think Jennings, Ashworth, Carnegie, Bellamy, and Williams' all involved in seizing the *St. Marie*?"

Oui.

"When Howard gets the *Marianne* ready to sail, we'll take a look. Yes, we'll take a look. You say about twenty miles to the west at Bahia Honda?"

With the *Marianne* now flying the "red ensign" designating her as a British merchant vessel rather than the blue and white ensign flown on French merchant vessels, Captain Hornigold prepares to see what Jennings, Ashworth, and

Carnegie are up to. He's also interested in Bellamy and Williams. He has never heard of them before.

Peters, our boatswain, cuts the periagua loose from the *Marianne* so Le Guardeu and his men can sail back to their home base, Saint Domingue, or on to Havana.

Sure enough, Jennings, Ashworth, and Carnegie are in Bahia Honda with the French merchant frigate, the *St. Marie*. Although the *Benjamin* and the *Marianne* are sailing in consort, Captain Hornigold considers approaching the *St. Marie* and possibly joining the pillaging. He soon thinks better, though, when he sees the *Barsheba* and the *Mary* raise anchor. Not wanting a confrontation, he orders Smithy to change course and sail back to Nassau.

We sail for a couple of hours trying to put some distance between Jennings, Ashworth, and ourselves. Then out of nowhere, the *Benjamin* is hailed by about twenty men in a periagua.

"Ahoy! Permission to board," is the cry from the captain of the periagua.

"Permission's granted," replies Captain Hornigold.

Safely aboard, one of the newcomers gives his name. "Bellamy, Sam Bellamy, and my partner here's Williams, Paulsgrave Williams."

"What're you doing way out here?" Captain Hornigold asks.

"Well," Captain Bellamy answers, "a few days ago, Paulsgrave and me helped Jennings, Ashworth, and Carnegie capture the *St. Marie* in Bahia Honda. Sure you know.

When Jennings and Ashworth went to chase you, we saw an opportunity to take all their silver and gold from the *St. Marie*. After Jennings and Ashworth left the harbor, our men seized the *St. Marie* and loaded all her silver and gold into this periagua and made our escape from the harbor without them seeing us. The rest of our men are following in another periagua—need to keep a watch for them. When Jennings returns to the *St. Marie*, he'll discover me and Paulsgrave are gone with all his silver and gold. He'll be furious, real furious."

The *Benjamin* and the *Marianne* continue on their course for Nassau, but now with Bellamy, Williams, and their periagua crew aboard. Their periagua's tied to the stern of the *Benjamin*.

I know Cooky and Stewy would like to know what is happening, so I slip off to the galley. "The Captain and Mr. Howard knew Jennings and Ashworth saw the *Benjamin* at the harbor entrance and they'd be coming for us because we had the *Marianne*. They'll be determined to catch us and claim the *Marianne* under their commission from Governor Hamilton."

I tell them about our being joined by Bellamy and Williams. "They told us Jennings and Ashworth hadn't seen them leave the harbor so they wouldn't know that their silver and gold's gone. They'll find out when they return to the *St. Marie*. Bellamy and Williams also said there's no reason to doubt that after Jennings and Ashworth discover their silver and gold's been taken, they'll try to recapture it.

"What Jennings and Ashworth don't know is that by pursuing us, they'll be pursuing Bellamy, Williams, and their silver and gold, as well."

I leave Cooky and Stewy thinking about what Jennings and Ashworth will do if, and when, they catch us.

8

Seven Pirates and the St. Marie *of Rochelle*
April 1716

CAPTAIN JENNINGS' GREED works to our advantage. Both Jennings' and Ashworth's vessels are weighed down with plunder. We sail along quickly with our two vessels lighter in the water. Captain Hornigold's *Benjamin* is fresh from Nassau, and much of the cargo of the newly captured *Marianne* has just been sold while at Port Mariel.

We don't see Jennings and Ashworth and hope they've returned to Bahia Honda, at least temporarily. They're no longer an immediate threat.

The next morning, a strong southerly breeze rapidly propels the *Benjamin* and the *Marianne* towards the friendly waters of Nassau Harbor. The seizure of the *Marianne* and the episode concerning the periagua, as well as our encounter with Jennings, Ashworth, and Carnegie, had kept the *Benjamin's* crew on edge all of yesterday. With the sunrise comes a new day along with time to ponder those events. Who are the two pirates Captain Hornigold saved from Jennings and Ashworth? Where do they intend to go once they arrive in Nassau?

Captain Hornigold invites Captain Bellamy and Mr. Williams, Mr. Howard, Smithy, and a few others to join him for breakfast in his quarters. They seat themselves around his great round table. I take my place in the corner.

Within minutes, Cooky and Stewy appear with an exceptional breakfast they set up English style on the sideboard near me. After yesterday's excitement and a good night's sleep, everyone is hungry. Quickly, plates are filled.

The Captain introduces his officers and then turns to the more outspoken of the two strangers.

"Bellamy, Sam Bellamy's my name. Raised in Devonshire, England. Joined the Royal Navy during the Queen Anne's War. After the war, like many, was discharged and looking for something to do, so I signed onto a merchant ship bound for Boston. Found myself in Eastham on Cape Cod where I met a pretty girl, Goody Hallet. Planned to marry her, but her parents thought I wasn't husband material, being only an out-of-work sailor. Needed to go out in the world and make something of myself and show 'em. By luck, met Paulsgrave in a tavern."

Paulsgrave Williams picks up where Sam Bellamy leaves off. "Paulsgrave Williams' my name. Silversmith by trade.

I've money. My father was a wealthy attorney in Rhode Island and at one time the attorney general. Money's not my problem, boredom was. Met up with Sam and he talked about all the wrecks off the Florida coast. Sam knew how to sail and I could raise money, so I invested in a small sloop and signed on some men. Packed my stuff, left my wife and kids, they're already grown, and sailed down the coast to Florida with Sam. We soon learned to sail as a crew and became pretty good at it. Arrived at the Florida coast in early January. Heard about the wreck of the Spanish plate fleet and anchored our sloop alongside seven or eight English vessels near where they thought one of the wrecks went down. No matter what we tried, weren't able to locate the main hull of the ship. Instead, we fished for scattered cargo and coins. After weeks of work, didn't have much to show. Around the twenty-second of January, Captain Escobar arrived from Havana along with Spanish reinforcements and chased all us English away."

Paulsgrave Williams pauses for a drink and Captain Bellamy picks up the story. "Sailed south through the Florida Straits and down to the Gulf of Honduras where we traded our little sloop for a couple of periaguas, nice sailing canoes. Have one tied to your stern. Needed to rest our men and recruit a few more so we'd have about thirty for each canoe. Met several log cutters who wanted to leave that mosquito-infested area around the Bay of Campeche and join our crew. A young Miskito Indian from that region said he's a pilot and knew the area joined us, John Julian's his name.

"While in the Gulf of Honduras, we captured a Dutch ship. Her captain's John Cornelison. You probably know him. Took what provisions we needed. An older Dutchman, Peter Cornelius Hoff, joined us. He'd been sailing for years around Vera Cruz and Porto Bello.

"Then we captured Captain Young's English sloop. Poor Captain Young, a dark day for him."

Paulsgrave Williams interrupts, "Ah, yes, Captain Young's sloop, a real find. Tied our periaguas to the stern of his sloop and ordered him to sail towards Havana. He had no choice.

"Off the northwest coast of Cuba, we spotted four sloops flying British colors bearing down on us. Because we're pirates, we had to avoid capture at all cost. Scared, real scared. They were gaining every minute and we had to do something, so we had our men load our valuables into the periaguas.

"Within an hour, one of the sloops, Jennings' *Barsheba*, came alongside Young's sloop. We jumped into our periaguas, abandoned Young's vessel, and rowed into the wind. Rowed with all our might. The *Barsheba* couldn't catch us before we reached the Cuban shore and hid in a shallow cove."

Williams pauses and then continues. "Watched from our safe haven among the reefs and mangroves as Young's sloop's forced to join Jennings' sloops and sail east along the Cuban coast. Soon our curiosity overcame us. Came out from hiding and followed at a safe distance. Before long, the *Barsheba* and the others anchored at the entrance to a quiet harbor, Bahia Honda, it was. Because they'd captured Young's sloop, we now knew Jennings' a pirate, just like us.

"Time passed and Sam became more curious. 'What's going on? Why didn't Jennings enter the harbor?' Sam decided because we're all pirates, it's safe to make a move.

Around seven that evening when the sun's setting, me and Sam in our periagua rowed past Carnegie and Young's sloops and came alongside Jennings' *Barsheba*. To our surprise, he invited us aboard. Our second periagua waited nearby.

"We discovered he was watching a large armed French merchant frigate, the *St. Marie* of Rochelle, in the harbor. Jennings told us because she's French, he could seize her under his commission from the governor of Jamaica. But because the *St. Marie*'s so heavily armed, fourteen to sixteen guns, he's concerned that a direct attack was very dangerous.

"Well, Jennings had this plan. Had three of his men in a dory row into the harbor and up to the French ship, just to assess the situation. The captain, Jean d'Escoubet, thought they're traders and invited them aboard. Jennings' men discovered that half of the *St. Marie*'s small crew was ashore collecting water and firewood. With this information, Jennings knew me and Williams would be useful in his plan."

Williams pauses and Bellamy picks up the story. "A little before ten that evening, me, Paulsgrave, and some of our men rowed one of our periaguas over to Jennings' *Barsheba* and some of the others rowed our other periagua over to Ashworth's *Mary*. Jennings' men threw my periagua a cable. Ashworth's men did the same for the other periagua. Our two crews rowed across the bay towing the heavily armed *Barsheba* and *Mary*.

"We approached the *St. Marie*, cut our cables, stripped down naked to our deeply tanned skin, and showed our weapons. We whooped and hollered and made such a terrible commotion that Captain d'Escoubet didn't know what to make of us, especially with us being followed by two armed sloops. Confused and without his men to defend his ship, d'Escoubet surrendered without firing a shot. The *Barsheba* and the *Mary* then came alongside the *St. Marie* to complete the seizure.

"The next morning, the fourth of April, I think, a periagua, not ours, sailed into the harbor and made her way to the *St. Marie*. One of her crew, a French merchant officer, asked for Captain d'Escoubet. He said they're from the *Marianne* of St. Domingue and she's anchored at Port Mariel, about twenty miles to the east. They said they came to trade with d'Escoubet. Upon hearing this, Jennings took them captive and offered to release them if they'd take him back to the *Marianne*."

Williams continues, "The next morning, Jennings said that him, me, Ashworth, and Sam would stay with the *St. Marie* and guard our treasure, while Carnegie in the *Discovery* and one of our periaguas would follow the captured periagua to Port Mariel. Carnegie'd come back with information and we'd capture the *Marianne* in a day or two."

Captain Hornigold interrupts. "Oh, that explains why we saw Carnegie's *Discovery* and two periaguas enter the harbor, and the *Discovery* and one periagua turn and leave."

Williams nods. "Aye, that periagua that stayed with Carnegie was ours. She and Carnegie's *Discovery* came back to Bahia Honda the next day and told us you'd captured the *Marianne*.

"Two or three days later, and before we'd developed a plan on how we'd seize the *Marianne*, we saw the *Benjamin* and the *Marianne* stop at the entrance of Bahia Honda. Jennings' upset, real upset. Not only did he lose the *Marianne* but he lost her to you!"

Captain Hornigold chuckles, "Yes, that's us. We're thinking of sailing into the harbor and joining Jennings, Ashworth, and Carnegie as they plundered the *St. Marie*. Before we could enter the harbor, we saw Jennings' *Barsheba* and Ashworth's *Mary* raise their anchors, set their sails, and come after us. Not wanting a confrontation, we resumed our journey to Nassau Harbor with our prize, the sloop *Marianne*."

Williams continues, "You know that Jennings and Ashworth did leave the harbor. Carnegie and his small sloop, *Discovery*, Captain Young's sloop, and our two periaguas were left behind. We watched the *Barsheba* and the *Mary* disappear over the horizon."

Bellamy interrupts. "At that moment, I looked at Paulsgrave and we both had the same idea: *Here's a golden opportunity*. Our men knew what was coming. Sam gave the signal and they rose up, surprising the men Jennings left behind, and seized control of the *St. Marie*. Some of our men held Jennings' men at gunpoint, and the others quickly moved one of our periaguas alongside the *St. Marie*. We threw sacks and chests of coins to our men below.

"Quickly, we boarded the periagua and began rowing out of the harbor and into the open sea. Made sure we wouldn't be on the route Jennings and Ashworth would take when they returned.

"In a few hours, we came upon the *Benjamin* and the *Marianne*. You gentlemen took us aboard."

William Howard looks puzzled and asks, "What happened to Captain Liddell and the *Cocoa Nut*?"

Bellamy laughs. "Poor old Liddell. Samuel Liddell's a merchant who trades between Jamaica and Carolina, never a real pirate. While he's in Jamaica gathering produce, he received orders from his vessel's owners to ignore his produce and search the Spanish wrecks for silver and gold. Just happened to meet up with Jennings and Ashworth and later with Carnegie. The rumor's that the morning after the capture of the *St. Marie*, Liddell and his sloop, *Cocoa Nut*, slipped out of the harbor and haven't been seen since."

Mr. Howard then asks, "What happened to the rest of your men, and Young and his men?"

Williams replies. "Our men were to join us in the other periagua once we cleared the harbor entrance to Bahia Honda. We waited but they never came. Young, his men, and his sloop, never saw them again either."

Captain Hornigold concludes the breakfast by saying, "Of course, you'll stay with the *Benjamin* as members of our crew till Nassau. We'll talk again and you can decide whether you want to continue sailing with us."

Four days later, the *Benjamin* and the *Marianne* drop anchor in Nassau Harbor with Bellamy and Williams aboard, and their periagua still tied to the stern. The Captain is enjoying the fact that Bellamy and Williams have outmaneuvered his nemesis, the arrogant Henry Jennings. But time can't be wasted. He knows that Jennings will claim the *Marianne* under the bogus commission from the governor of Jamaica. The silver and gold from that vessel must be kept out of Jennings' clutches.

A week or so later, Jennings' *Barsheba* and Ashworth's *Mary* drop anchor in Nassau Harbor. Jennings wastes no time hunting down Captain Hornigold who is heading to meet us at The Lion and the Unicorn.

"*Wait up. Wait up, thief!*" Jennings shouts.

9

No Prey, No Pay
April–May 1716

CAPTAIN HORNIGOLD KEEPS walking.

"I'm talking to you, Hornigold, you common pirate!"

The Captain turns and gives Jennings a stare. "Fighting words, Jennings. What do you want?"

"The *Marianne*. She belongs to me. Here, see!" and thrusts out Governor Hamilton's commission for the Captain to read.

"We all know what that says, not worth the paper it's written on. I'm not in the mood to spill your blood over that worm-eaten vessel. Don't need her, she's not worth my time. The *Marianne*'s yours if you know how to sail her." With that, the Captain turns and enters The Lion and the Unicorn.

The Captain finds Mr. Howard, Smithy, and me at a table in the corner. He describes in great detail his encounter with Jennings. "You know, stripped her bare of her silver and gold. He can have what's left. Nothing but a shell and some rags. This round's on me."

"I'll drink to that!" Mr. Howard and Smithy are quick to accept and we all have a good laugh at Jennings' expense.

We know the Captain had no choice but to release the *Marianne*. Jennings has Governor Hamilton's commission, no matter how unsavory a deal he made with the governor to get it.

Although it's mid-April when the *Benjamin* drops anchor in Nassau Harbor, this is the first time I have an opportunity to actually look around the town. I take to heart the Captain's warning and I won't go ashore alone. Smithy, who has the afternoon off, is more than willing to join me explore.

I look up at the old fort, Fort Nassau. It's on a knoll that overlooks the entrance to the harbor. "Smithy, can we explore the fort?"

"Aye, if you like."

We walk along what was the road to the fort, now overgrown and barely passable. Although the fort once guarded the western entrance to the harbor, only ruins remain.

"What a beautiful view," I look at the harbor between my fingers, trying to blot out the town. The harbor's magnificent with its light blue and green water and its white sandy beaches. Hog Island, the northern shore of the harbor, is another story. The bones of fifty vessels litter its beautiful beaches. Some were burned, while others were dismembered and their remains left unattended. They remind me of the carcasses of the sperm whales I once saw, washed ashore, picked clean by birds, and bleached by the sun.

From the *Benjamin*, I notice the harbor's divided by a small island into two basins. "Smithy, I didn't notice that little island before."

"Oh, that's Potter's Cay. Large vessels with deep drafts can't sail in one entrance and out the other. Even smaller vessels find the east entrance quite challenging—twisting channel, hidden reefs, and small islands."

We walk back to the wharf, absorbed in our own thoughts. Finally, I break the silence. "Nassau's a beautiful harbor with a tropical climate. I can understand why pirates claim it as their own."

Smithy adds, "When word spread about Nassau being a safe haven, pirates including Jennings, Burgess, and our own Captain, began coming and going. Most were interested in finding a safe, quiet place to rest and resupply. The Captain had imagined a pirate republic. Jennings even had said that but really, he just wants a safe haven for his Jacobite followers."

Smithy seems to dwell on the fort's condition. "Captain dreams about rebuilding the fort. Can't be done. Just can't be done!"

I thought Smithy's dreaming about what could have been.

Meanwhile, I'm thinking about why some pirates gravitate towards Captain Jennings while others towards my Captain. I now know about the Jacobites, the religious differences, and the class distinctions that separate the pirate population.

The fact Nassau is ungoverned is evident in the town's condition—garbage, decay, and rats everywhere. We walk back to the beach and the sight and smell become almost overwhelming. I'm happy to seek refuge on the *Benjamin*.

Once aboard, I look back at the town, the fort, and the harbor. Unlike the town, the harbor is surprisingly active with a semblance of order. At least ten vessels are making the harbor home. Some belong to pirates while others are merchant vessels. "See that merchant vessel there?" Smithy points. "Her captain's selling her cargo to the captains of other merchant vessels, to the captains of the pirate vessels and to the merchants on shore. Watch what the longboats take from her and what they bring back."

"How can merchants and pirates use the harbor at the same time? Aren't the merchant captains afraid their vessels will be captured?"

Smithy laughs. "Unwritten rule. Merchant vessels are generally safe when they're in the harbor. See, pirates may need to buy what's on a merchant vessel, and the pirate captains want to sell to whomever has an interest in buying. If pirates seize a merchant vessel while she's in the harbor selling, other pirates can't buy. That sows discontent, everyone loses.

"Pirates want a safe, quiet harbor to rest and resupply. That won't happen if they attack merchant vessels and merchant vessels try to defend themselves while in a harbor. The rule is different when a merchant vessel is on the high seas."

I shift my gaze to shore. "How many pirates do you think are ashore on a day like today?"

Smithy thinks for a while. "Hmm, well, hard to say. Five hundred, six hundred, maybe more. Pirates outnumber the locals but pirates just come and go. The sick stay, they have no choice. The disillusioned stay too. Some don't want to risk being caught and hanged. Some have families somewhere and want to just get home."

Captain Hornigold comes by, "Join me at The Lion and the Unicorn."

We enjoy our tankards with a few of his friends and I begin to think about the incident with the *Marianne* and the *St. Marie*. "Wonder what happened to Captain Liddell and his sloop *Cocoa Nut*?" That brings a bit of laughter from those at the table.

"Oh, Liddell never was a pirate. Turns out that the merchant owners of the *Cocoa Nut* who live in Carolina heard about all that treasure on the ocean floor, just there for the picking. Thought they'd get rich by diverting Liddell and the *Cocoa Nut* from Jamaica to the Florida coast. Somehow, Liddell got caught up with Jennings and his crowd and found himself at Bahia Honda, discovered he's over his head, got out fast, real fast."

"And what about Captain Carnegie?"

"Oh, guess we'll see him one of these days."

Sure enough, several days later, Captain Carnegie sails into Nassau Harbor. To our surprise, he's sailing the French merchant frigate *St. Marie*. I ask around and the answer is he traded his sloop *Discovery* for the *St. Marie*. I guess the captain of the *St. Marie* was happy to have any vessel to get his men back home. Anyways, he really had no choice.

A day or two later, Smithy and I are at the rail looking over the harbor. All's not quiet at the *Barsheba* and the *Marianne*. We watch and Mr. Howard comes over with the story.

"Seems like a day or two after Jennings seized the *Marianne*, he went ashore, leaving Allen Bernard, his quartermaster, in charge of both the *Barsheba* and the *Marianne*. Poor Bernard, had no experience as quartermaster and only took the job because Jennings told him he'd have nothing to do. With Jennings ashore, most of the men from the *Barsheba* boarded the *Marianne* and began looting her remaining cargo. It's all being piled up on Hog Island."

We see the cargo being hauled from the *Marianne*'s hold, piled onto longboats, and rowed over to the desolate shore of Hog Island.

"There! Look there!" exclaims Smithy. "Bernard's leaving the *Barsheba*. Guess he's going for Jennings."

We learn later that tho' Bernard found Jennings, Jennings refused to return to the *Barsheba*. Instead Jennings told Bernard, "Too busy! You're the quartermaster, you handle it!"

Bernard came back to the harbor in search of Ashworth and Carnegie. Carnegie refused to go to the *Marianne*; instead, he went back to the *St. Marie* to make sure the chaos on the *Marianne* didn't spread.

Ashworth did go with Bernard to the *Marianne* but by the time they boarded, her hold was picked clean and most of Jennings' crew were on Hog Island, sorting their loot.

Several days later, Jennings reappears. In a day or two, his three-vessel fleet, his *Barsheba*, Ashworth's *Mary*, and Carnegie's *St. Marie*, sail out of Nassau Harbor heading for what we're told are the wrecks on the Florida coast. Jennings' newly acquired *Marianne* is left behind. The rumor around Nassau is what pirated goods Jennings' crew had saved for the vessels' owners were packed aboard another vessel, the *Dolphin*, and sent on to Jamaica. We wonder whether the owners received their third of the plunder. We also wonder who owned Carnegie's original sloop, *Discovery*, and whether they now have an interest in both the *St. Marie* and the *Marianne*.

With the departure of Jennings and his companions, some degree of tranquility returns to the harbor. During a lull, the Captain asks me to go with him to The Lion and the Unicorn.

We are walking to the tavern when a young man approaches from the opposite direction. Captain Hornigold stops and snarls, "Thomas, where's that old rogue, your father?"

The young man grudgingly replies, "At home."

To that the Captain growls, "Tell him he's a troublesome old rogue and when I see him, I'll shoot and kill him!"

"If you have anything to say to my father, tell him yourself. Speak to him face-to-face." With that, the young man shrugs and stalks off.

After that outburst, I don't know what mood the Captain would be in once we arrive at the tavern. Fortunately, he's pleased with himself.

We're enjoying our tankards when suddenly he stands and walks to another table.

"La Buse, you old Frenchman, what're you doing here?"

The man he addresses as La Buse rises. "Why if it isn't my old friend and enemy Benjamin Hornigold. I heard you'd be around here, so I thought I'd camp out till you came by. Knew you wouldn't be caught in The Killiecrankie Tavern." That gives his friends at his table a good laugh.

"Thought you'd got back to France after the war when your King Louie cancelled your commission. Now you can't make an honest living seizing British and Dutch vessels," replies the Captain.

"Nah! Commission, just paper. I enjoy hunting and catching British vessels too much. When the war ended, I thought I'd stay here for a time. Privateer or pirate, what's the difference? Be around for a while. Have a tankard with me tomorrow?

"Oh, by the way, heard the latest about the Jacobite uprising?"

"No," the Captain replies.

"Well, my friends in France tell me the Earl of Mar received a commission from James to raise and command the Jacobite army. T'was not long before Mar's army met

King George's army at Sheriffmuir, near Dunblane in Scotland. Told the Jacobites outnumbered King George's army but the battle was inconclusive. Mar mistakenly believed his army had won, left the field, and marched his troops to Perth. By the time James landed in Scotland and made his way to Perth—around Christmas—Mar's army was down to five thousand. Seeing no hope, Mar led his army out of Perth. A few days later, James sailed back to his haven in France."

"Interesting, very interesting," the Captain comments. "King George now will seek out Jacobites and Jacobite sympathizers and exile them to Jamaica or some other island around here. Queen Anne's done that before. Not a good time to be a Jacobite. Wonder what this means for Archibold Hamilton and Henry Jennings, both sympathizers. Can't exile them back to Jamaica. They're already here," he chuckles.

On our way back to the wharf, I ask about the man he calls La Buse.

"Full name, Olivier LeVasseur, French. Was the enemy during the Queen Anne's War. Had a commission from the king of France to be a privateer and hunt British and Dutch merchant vessels. Very cunning, very cunning indeed. He's called 'La Bouche,' the mouth, and 'La Buse,' the buzzard. He's nicknamed the buzzard because of the speed and ruthlessness with which he attacks his enemies. LeVasseur has no need for the money. His family's rich. Just needs the excitement."

By early May, Captain Hornigold in the *Benjamin* and Captain LeVasseur in his vessel, the *Postillion*, sail in consort and head to the Isle of Pines to careen their vessels and then sail on to Hispaniola to avoid the hurricane season. Sam Bellamy, his friend, Paulsgrave Williams, and their crew of twenty or so from their periagua, continue to sail with us as crew of the *Benjamin*.

I find Smithy at the helm. "Smithy, where's the Isle of Pines?"

"Sail west, round the tip of Cuba, then east along her southern coast. You'll find the Isle of Pines. Very big island. Can't be missed."

It's not long before we're sailing along the northern Cuban coast. "Sail ho," calls Scotty from the bow. "Let's take that ship!" shouts LeVasseur.

"Can't!" replies Captain Hornigold. "Dutch!"

"So?"

"I was a British privateer during the war. Dutch our ally. Won't attack a Dutch vessel."

With that, LeVasseur orders his helmsman to track the Dutch ship.

I hear Captain LeVasseur give the order *Hissons notre drapeau.* His flag takes me by surprise, a white ensign with the image of a black skeleton laying horizontally.

The *Postillion* approaches the Dutch ship and LeVasseur's quartermaster commands his master gunner, *Un coup de semonce!* The Dutch ship strikes her colors and her captain orders her sails furled. In a few minutes, she drifts to a stop and is easily boarded.

A number of hours later, the *Benjamin* and the *Postillion* sail in consort again. The Dutch ship and her cargo of logwood, a cargo she's transporting from Honduras to Holland, are now LeVasseur's. She sails behind the *Postillion*.

That evening, after my chores are done, I find myself by the rail next to Captain Hornigold. He's deep in thought. "You know, LeVasseur's educated and comes from wealth. He's a good sailor and a good leader—for his youth, not yet thirty. A risk-taker, tho'. He likes adventure and challenges. That'll get him into trouble. Yes, that'll get him into trouble."

I pass by the helm where Smithy's on watch. "What's so important about logwood?"

"Well, it's not the lumber but the heartwood, makes wonderful dye. Only comes from the Bay of Campeche, east of Mexico and north of the Gulf of Honduras. The land's swampy and insect infested but the heartwood's sought after. Excellent market in England. The logs are chipped, soaked, and boiled. Brings a very good price."

For the next week or so, Captain LeVasseur is busy selling his logwood. He doesn't notice when a sloop flying the Spanish flag comes over the horizon. Captain Hornigold tells Mr. Howard, "Make her our prize. We'll see what she's carrying."

The sloop is seized and the captain comes aboard the *Benjamin*. Captain Hornigold discovers that the vessel had been English, the *Betty*, and was captured by the Spanish. There's no way that Captain Hornigold will return her to those Spaniards. He selects John Perrin to captain a small prize crew and sail her to Nassau. He's to turn her over to the Captain's agent, who will sell her cargo, have the vessel declared a prize vessel, and then sell her at auction.

Perrin and his crew will wait in Nassau for our return. So off they sail.

Eight to ten days after the capture of the Dutch ship, Captain LeVasseur releases her to her captain, Captain Kingston.

That evening, I meet Smithy, who's at the wheel. Naturally, I'm full of questions. "Why did Captain LeVasseur keep that ship for so long?"

"LeVasseur had no need for the ship. We're not going back to Nassau anytime soon—he can't sell her or her cargo there. The cargo's not like silver or gold, so he can't store it on the *Postillion*. No need to burn her, either. Captain Kingston cooperated. He didn't do anything wrong. La Buse only took one of Kingston's sailors, a Jamaican named John Brown. No need to maroon the others on an island. So La Buse took his time selling the logwood and then released her. La Buse's quartermaster has already distributed the proceeds from the sale."

The celebration on the *Postillion* didn't go unnoticed by Captain Hornigold's men. They're indeed envious. As I did my rounds, I hear them grumble, "*No prey, no pay.*"

10

At the Mercy of the Men
May–August 1716

W E RETRACE OUR steps west along Cuba's northern coast, round the island and begin to sail east.
Scotty spots two Spanish brigantines off Cape Corriente.
"Raise our flag!" is the call and our black flag, flapping in
the salty breeze, declares our intention.

The explosion from our cannons signifies a shot was fired
across the bow of the closer brigantine. Both vessels lower
their flags, turn into the wind, and prepare for the worst.

Captain Hornigold and Captain LeVasseur send boarding parties that make quick work of ransacking the vessels:
hogsheads of rum, barrels of sugar, indigo, money, jewelry,
linens, woolens, bedding, and any other item that can be
removed and easily sold or used. The brigantines' maps are
among the most important items taken. They note sailing
channels and obstacles. Hidden sandbars and reefs can
wreck a vessel.

The main cargo, however, is disappointing, cocoa. When Smithy learns of the cargo, he remarks, "If we were near Nassau or Harbour Island, the cargo could easily make a nice profit, but not here. We're in Spanish waters and heading to careen our sloops. Neither the cargo nor the vessels are of any value to us here."

"What do you want to do?" Captain Hornigold asks, deferring to the younger Captain LeVasseur. "They're cooperating and we've got all they can give us. Let them go?"

"No, can't just let them go. No, can't do that!" Captain LeVasseur adamantly replies. "Need to make a statement. We mean business. Ransom, yes, demand a ransom."

"Fine if they pay, but what if they can't?"

"We'll cross that bridge if we get there." With that, Captain LeVasseur puts the ransom demand to the two captains. After a few days, it becomes apparent that a ransom can't be paid.

"What now?" Captain Hornigold asks.

"We're pirates, are we not? No choice, burn their vessels."

And so it is. The cocoa is dumped into the sea, and those men who don't want to sail with us are marooned on a nearby island.

Smithy can see my surprise and asks, "Thought we'd kill the crew after taking everything and burning their vessels?"

"Sort of," I meekly answer.

"Just because we're pirates don't mean we're barbaric," Smithy replies with a huff.

I nod, honestly glad the seizure doesn't end in bloodshed.

"Treated you pretty good! Huh?"

"So far," I mutter.

We continue on our way, past Cape Corrientes and on to the Isle of Pines. I make my rounds and hear the grumbling grow louder. "No prey, no pay." Burning the brigantines doesn't sit well. A few provisions for our sloop are not silver in their pockets.

Farther along the way, Scotty, from his vantage at the bow, spots a small Spanish sloop. Captain Hornigold calls to Captain LeVasseur that the *Benjamin* will take her. Her capture is uneventful. To my surprise, Captain Hornigold asks Sam Bellamy to be the captain of this Spanish prize and for Paulsgrave Williams to be his quartermaster. Mr. Howard sends Bellamy's men from their periagua days and a few of our crew to sail under Captain Bellamy's command.

Our little fleet, the *Benjamin*, the *Postillion*, and our new Spanish prize, soon arrive at the Isle of Pines, just as Smithy had said—a large island between Cuba to the north and Jamaica to the south. The Isle of Pines is well off the beaten path. Vessels from the Spanish coast sail the prevailing winds and currents through the Florida Straits between Cuba and Florida. Vessels from Jamaica and other islands leave the Caribbean through the Florida Straits or one of the other passages, the Windward Passage between Cuba and Hispaniola or the Mona Passage between Hispaniola and Puerto Rico. Neither of these routes is even close to the Isle of Pines.

Captain Hornigold finds a quiet harbor for our vessels to be careened. To our good fortune, our men discover three or four empty British sloops and they make careening our sloops easier. Everything, including our guns and provisions, can be moved to those sloops rather than transported to the beach and back. In less than a fortnight, the *Benjamin*, the *Postillion*, and our Spanish prize sail east along Cuba's southern coast and then southeast to Hispaniola.

The end of May signals the approach of the hurricane season. Captain Hornigold finds a secluded harbor where our sloops are hidden from the open sea. They anchor in calm waters and our men encamp along the shore.

"Smithy, how long will we stay in Hispaniola?"

"Maybe two, three months, maybe more. Need the worst of the hurricane season to pass. No need to be caught in a hurricane if we can avoid it. Why hurry and risk every-thing?"

Two camps are set up along the shore, one for the *Benjamin*'s English-speaking crew and the other for the *Postillion*'s French-speaking crew. Scotty choses several men and sets up a watch schedule to monitor activity beyond the harbor. If a British, Dutch, French, or Spanish navy vessel prowls, the Captain needs to know. Our sentries also provide information about passing merchant vessels so they are easy prey without disclosing our hiding place.

Mr. Howard has assigned duties. Some men will supply the galley with fish, seafood, turtles, and small game. Others will provide fresh water, a real treat. I'm assigned to help Cooky and Stewy gather fresh fruits, nuts, and vegetables.

On occasion, one of the sailors, John Julian, asks Cooky whether I can fish with him. Except for the powder monkeys, those young boys whose primary role is to ferry black powder from the powder magazine in the hold to the gunners at the cannons on the deck, John is the youngest member of the crew, maybe three or four years my senior. He's tall, lean, and self-assured, with a rich copper skin tone.

John chooses a rowboat and we push off. The sea and sky could not be more beautiful. Rhythmic waves lick our little boat, a light breeze cools us from the hot sun, and the billowing white clouds create interesting patterns against the otherwise blue sky.

"Ever fished?" John asks.

I lower my eyes in embarrassment and sheepishly answer, "No."

He chuckles and in his strange speech says, "I teach you. I'm an expert and my people are good fishermen. I teach you to be a good fisherman, too."

He reaches for a long pole and makes his way to the front of the boat. The pole's about eight to ten feet long with a line attached to one end. "Hold the boat steady. I fish." John stands, his spear poised to attack. He gazes intently at the water and then with determination, hurls his spear towards his prey. A minute or two later, he pulls in the line. A fish struggles to escape from the end of his spear.

John motions for me to pick up a line near where I sit. "I catch, you string."

One by one, I string flapping fish on the line so they can be returned to the water.

After a while, John takes a break and sits down. "I left my family at thirteen to fish with the men of my tribe, the men of the Miskito empire. We live along the shores of this sea you call the Caribbean. After a couple of years, sailing and training to guide vessels in and out of shallow coastal waters, I became more skilled and my elders called me a pilot.

"One day, two periaguas were sailing in the Gulf of Honduras and they captured the small coastal trader I was on. The captain of one of the periaguas, Sam Bellamy, asked if I knew how to sail along the coast. I answered, 'Yes,' and he asked me to join his periagua crew."

John looks up at the sun. "Getting late. Better get back to work. You like to fish?" he asks.

"Sure." Fishing looks easy. All I need to do is raise the spear and when I see a fish, I quickly throw the spear and then pull the line, the spear, and the fish out of the water.

I try over and over, but no fish. John laughs. "Not easy, I show you."

So John patiently gives me instructions. "Water plays tricks. You aim too high. The fish not there," as he raises one hand above the other. "You see fish here," as he wiggles the fingers of his top hand. "Fish not there." He then wiggles the fingers of his lower hand. "Fish here. Aim here."

I do as he says, but the fish dart away before my spear arrives.

"When you move your arm back, the fish sees you moving. Scaring the fish. Hold the spear ready, then hurl. Can't pull back and then hurl. One motion forward, hurl."

After several more tries, I have a fish. John smiles. "See, I good teacher, huh?" We are both pleased with ourselves.

We fish and talk. At first, I had a hard time understanding him. Some of his words are English, some Spanish, and some are just incomprehensible to me. I soon learn that John is from a native tribe who lives along the coast of the Gulf of Honduras and the Bay of Campeche. He calls them the Miskito empire.

"Never heard of the Miskito empire," I say.

John, ignoring my ignorance, responds, "We live along the coast. When the Spanish came to the Caribbean and began bringing slaves to work the plantations, slave ships would wreck and slaves would escape. Some settle along the coast and marry members of my tribe. Their children called creole."

He holds out his arm so I see that he's neither black nor white. I hold my tanned arm next to his. We laugh. He thinks my pinkish-white skin is funny.

John laughs when at times I can't understand him. "Some of my words come from Africa and some from my native Miskito." He then pauses and laughs again, "Sometimes I don't understand you 'cause you talk too fast. Sometimes your words, very strange to me." And we both laugh.

After a few hours at sea, we row back to camp. Cooky and Stewy are pleased that we bring a good number of fish for dinner.

John's a good fisherman and many a day we spend together. Some days we concentrate on fish, while other days we find green sea turtles or an occasional manatee.

When I don't sail with John, I help Cooky and Stewy. That gives me an opportunity to bring up that unpleasant incident between the Captain and the young man we met when the Captain and I were walking to the tavern.

"Oh," laughs Cooky, "probably one of Thomas Walker's sons. Old man Walker and the Captain have been at it from the time we set foot on New Providence Island. We talked about Walker when we're at Christmas dinner, remember?

"Well, Walker, his wife, four kids, and his father were one of the few families remaining on New Providence. They live about three miles out of town. Old man Walker was a judge of the Vice Admiralty Court in the Bahamas till his commission expired when Queen Anne died. Walker still thinks he rules New Providence even tho' his commission was never renewed. He says that his duty's to root out pirates from his island. Captain has a different idea. As I said, Walker went so far as to try to get one of the Captain's friends, Daniel Stillwell, tried in Jamaica as a pirate. Captain put a stop to that. Captain said everyone on the island is under his protection. Funny thing, to this day, Walker still deals in pirated goods. Hah! Don't fret. Captain can take care of himself, and Walker, too, if need be. Will never come to that."

I thank Cooky and tell him he has made me feel much better.

The free time I have is spent among the men chatting. I see one of the older sailors sitting alone by the fire. I approach and he motions me to join him.

"Name's Hoff, Peter Cornelius Hoff. Born in Sweden. You know where Sweden's at? You can see I'm older than most around here, except for Captain Hornigold." He pauses for a moment and then adds, "Guess I'm about thirty-three. Left Sweden when I's about sixteen and been sailing ever since. Sailed mostly with the Dutch off the coast of Porto Bello. Sailing with Captain Cornelison on a Dutch merchant vessel when we's captured by Bellamy and his periaguas in the Gulf of Honduras. Bellamy forced me to sail with him because I's unmarried and knew the seas."

We talk for a while and Peter bends close to me so no one can hear. "Help me escape!"

"What?"

"Help me escape!"

"Why?"

"Don't like pirate life. Want to get back to Sweden with my mom and dad."

I'm taken aback. "Sorry, mate. Can't help you. I'm the Captain's cabin boy and he'd skin me alive if he knew I helped you escape."

One evening as everyone's winding down for the day, I come upon a small group of men sitting by the fire having their last drink before turning in. They're exchanging stories about how they became pirates. The man regaling the others I recognize as John Brown. He sees me listening.

"Cabin boy, remember when La Buse captured my ship from Campeche?"

"Yes, I remember that quite well. Captain LeVasseur captured your ship off the northern coast of Cuba. Captain Hornigold wouldn't join Captain LeVasseur because the Dutch were our ally during the war."

"Yes, I's on that ship, and La Buse forced me to sail with him as a member of his crew. I was hoping to get home to Jamaica but La Buse wouldn't let me go. Born in Jamaica, about twenty-four years ago. La Buse wouldn't let me go because I'm young and unmarried.

"Aye, sailing on a Dutch merchant ship. Just picked up a load of logwood from the Bay of Campeche, sailing to Holland. Captain Kingston's our master. Our ship's captured off Cuba by La Buse. Kept Kingston's vessel and joined up with Captain Hornigold's *Benjamin*. La Buse kept Kingston's vessel for eight maybe ten days and then returned her to Captain Kingston. La Buse kept me and a couple of others and wouldn't let us go back to Kingston's ship. Been with La Buse ever since. Can't do much about my situation so I'm trying to make the best of it. Don't know what's ahead. I'd like to get back to a Dutch or an English vessel. I don't like sailing with the French."

John Brown's friends seem to agree about sailing on a French vessel even tho' the war is over and France is no longer the enemy.

The days pass and I sense the seeds of discontent growing among Captain Hornigold's men. His unwillingness to take British and Dutch vessels doesn't sit well with them. After all, each member of the crew receives a share of the plunder and not a wage. Periodically, Captain LeVasseur and the *Postillion* venture out to pluck another Dutch vessel that sails by from the Dutch islands. Watching the men from the *Postillion* count their plunder doesn't do much to raise the morale of our men. I hear them mumble, "no prey, no pay." And who knows what Bellamy, Williams, and their men are up to? So far, they've contributed nothing.

By the end of August, everyone's restless. We've been more than two months on Hispaniola, and even if we only return to New Providence for provisions, that's something. I often watch Captain Bellamy cleverly foment discontent. Even those who sailed with my Captain for what seems a long time begin to grumble.

The days grow hotter and so do the tempers.

Then one day, Captain Bellamy's contempt for Captain Hornigold's leadership becomes apparent. "Parley," demands Bellamy. "Parley! Captain Hornigold refuses to plunder British and Dutch vessels. Me and Captain LeVasseur don't think that's fair. I demand we choose. Those who want to plunder all vessels, regardless of nationality, cross this line and sail with me."

11

At the Mercy of the Sea
August–October 1716

I'M DISCOVERING THAT as a pirate, Captain Hornigold has a surprising moral compass. To my further amazement, I learned pirates have a code and under it, the crew elects the captain.

Captain Hornigold's men gather and each chooses whether to sail with him or with Captain Bellamy. I silently count. At first, the numbers are fairly even, but then Captain Bellamy begins working the crowd, and as he does, every man begins choosing him. I'm not really surprised when Peter Cornelius Hoff and John Brown chose Bellamy. Hoff sailed with Bellamy during Bellamy's periagua days in the Gulf of Honduras, and Brown sailed with Captain LeVasseur for months and the transition from LeVasseur to Bellamy was easy because they sailed in consort. I am, however, disappointed when Richard Noland chooses to go with Bellamy.

He has sailed with Captain Hornigold for a very long time and I thought he'd show some loyalty. I'm pleased when Mr. Howard, Smithy, Scotty, Cooky, and Stewy don't desert the Captain.

John Julian and I are the last to be asked. John chooses Bellamy and that saddens me. I thought we're friends and we'd sailed together. He must think sailing with Bellamy will be more exciting.

Finally, it's my turn to choose. "Well?" says the Captain, "You're free to go with Bellamy." I shake my head "no," and he gives me an ever-so-small wink. The final count is eighty for Bellamy and only twenty-six for Captain Hornigold.

Over the next couple of days, Captain Bellamy's eighty men prepare what had been our vessel, the *Benjamin*, to sail. Then one morning LeVasseur in his *Postillion* and Bellamy and Williams in our *Benjamin* set sail, leaving Captain Hornigold and our twenty-six loyal men with the small Spanish prize sloop, seized a few months before. I thought that's an insult because this was the sloop the Captain had kindly let Bellamy sail on our way to this island.

With both the *Postillion* and the *Benjamin* at sea, an eerie peace settles over our camp. We take a few days to prepare, and then the day comes when we raise anchor and set sail for Nassau—our small sloop and our small crew.

Bellamy's and Williams' absences also come as a great relief to us all. Neither had contributed to the chores around the vessels or the camp. Smithy and I think Bellamy is impatient and wants to be the captain of a great vessel all too soon. Smithy's comment is, "No good will come to him."

Smithy thinks we will be at sea for a couple of weeks. We have time to gather fresh provisions for our small crew, and what we gather will stay fresh for this short cruise. Cooky and Stewy have the galley well stocked.

One evening as we sit around having supper, the topic of Captain Bellamy comes up. Scotty speaks first, "You heard Bellamy talk about his girlfriend on Cape Cod. I for one don't think she's real." That brings great laughter from the group and everyone has an opinion.

With the winds calm and sailing easy, the men often sit around the deck after supper, drink, clean their weapons, chat, play cards, listen to the fiddler, sing, and carve. To pass the time one evening, I find an old copy of *The Boston News-Letter* in my chest, the chest Charlie had left behind, and find a place by the rail to read. No sooner have I sat down than a small group gathers around. "Sir, would you mind reading your paper to us?" asks a sailor I know as O'Brien. So as I read, we talk about events that occurred months ago as if they happen today.

The voyage proves uneventful. The Captain's more relaxed now that he no longer is sailing in consort with Captain LeVasseur. I can see that LeVasseur's decisions can get us all in trouble and possibly hanged. Captain Hornigold is a much more cautious leader.

Shortly after our arrival back in Nassau, Smithy and I discuss what, if anything, has changed during our absence.

"Did you see that French sloop, the *Marianne* of Domingue, the one painted blue and yellow, the one Jennings abandoned?" I ask.

"I was told Bellamy sent several men to pick her up after Jennings abandoned her," comments a sailor who is standing nearby.

"Did you see the *Betty*? Perrin should have brought her to Nassau, shouldn't he?" I ask.

"That's right. Almost forgot about the *Betty*," Smithy answers. "I'd assumed the Captain's agent sold her cargo and then her. Wonder what her cargo was and what it brought? You know the men will each get a share, that's the men who stayed with the Captain."

"Yes, twenty-six, not eighty," and we both smile.

Meanwhile, Captain Hornigold is busy parlaying the small Spanish prize sloop into a larger sloop, the *Delight*.

September is spent in the harbor while the *Delight* is fitted for piracy. We have time to frequent The Lion and the Unicorn to catch up on the news. The Captain's friends report that King George had sent a warship from London with orders to arrest Governor Hamilton and return him to England in irons. Some think he'll be tried as a Jacobite sympathizer; others believe the charge will be consorting with pirates. The word is that Peter Heywood will be the acting governor of Jamaica. He has the king's ear and was instrumental in having Lord Hamilton arrested.

The Captain finds Hamilton's arrest very interesting. His response is, "Hamilton has friends in high places, so he'll avoid punishment. I'm wondering what'll happen to Jennings now that he won't have Hamilton to protect him?"

The answer to the Captain's question comes a few days later when one of the Captain's friends comes over at The Lion and the Unicorn. "Read this, Captain. It's about your friend Jennings. These notices are posted all over Jamaica."

"Well, well, well," is the Captain's response. "The king's declared Jennings, Ashworth, and Carnegie to be pirates and they're subject to being arrested and hanged, if caught."

One of the sailors adds, "I hear they fled Jamaica."

Another wonders, "Think they'll set up camp here?"

And another adds, "Jennings bragged about his land in Jamaica. I wonder whether the king will confiscate it? Hmm!"

All the Captain can say is, "I think business at The Killie-crankie Tavern will pick up."

A few days later, I'm at The Lion and the Unicorn with the Captain, who's busy hiring crew. A sailor comes to our table. Captain Hornigold looks up. "Perrin, where have you been and where's my *Betty*?"

Perrin looks a little pale through his tan and slowly begins to speak. "We're sailing here as you instructed when we're seized by Captain Matthew Musson. He said he had a commission to seize pirate vessels. No, not one commission, but two, one from Governor Archibald Hamilton and one from Robert Daniell, the governor of South Carolina. I told him that we weren't no pirates and I'd bought the *Betty* from you. He wouldn't listen, had his mind made up. I had no choice but to turn the *Betty* over to him. He put one of his sailors, Joseph Carpenter, in command and arrested the rest of us. After Carpenter sealed the hold, we all sailed to Charles Town. You know if I'd told them we're all pirates, we'd been hanged.

"When we put in at Charles Town, an awful dispute arose. Who had the authority to unseal the hold, offload, secure the cargo, and preserve the king's interest? The governor, the marshal of the admiralty, the attorney general, the captain of the militia, and the commander of the forts of Charles Town were all on one side, and Richard Wigg, the harbor's tax collector, Colonel William Rhett, and Thomas Howard, captain of the *Shoreham*, were on the other. The dispute grew heated. Threats were made against the governor. Swords drawn, shots fired, and the militia called out.

"With all the commotion over who had the authority over the *Betty* and her cargo, we seized the opportunity to slip away. Our escape took a while but here we are."

"Hmm!" is all the Captain says as he shakes his head.

It's early October and the crew of the *Delight* is now ninety strong. Captain Hornigold's getting edgy and ready to set sail even tho' he knows it's hurricane season and the weather might turn at any time.

We sail for a while and capture a few vessels. One afternoon I visit Smithy, who is taking his watch at the helm.

"Mighty still, she is. Not a good sign," he mumbles to himself.

I hadn't noticed but now that Smithy has called my attention to the weather, I feel the eerie stillness. The sea's absolutely calm and the wind still. The beautiful sky from moments ago is suddenly black. Day looks more like night.

At that moment, the wind picks up and changes direction. Rain begins to fall. The wind keeps building, now it's howling loudly. I can hardly hear Smithy. The rain's driving in sheets.

A huge wave hits the *Delight*. She teeters unpredictably, going left. She's now right. I lose my balance, and fall. I'm sliding across the wet deck. I grab for something—anything, everything's sliding too. *I'm following Charlie into the sea.* I hit the rail.

"IT'S STORMING, CAPTAIN!" shouts a sailor.

That's evident, I think to myself.

"ALL ON DECK!" yells Mr. Howard. "SMARTLY!"

Peters blows his brass whistle tho' his effort seems unnecessary.

I finally manage to get to my knees and then with the help of the rail, stand. The deck's crowded with wet, gasping men. The driving rain pelts us as our vessel tosses violently from big wave to bigger wave. Smithy fights to keep the *Delight* heading into the waves. We all know that if a wave catches her sideways, she will roll over and we'll all drown. Oh, how loudly she creaks and groans as each wave finds us. Up one wave she rides, drops into the canyon below with a thud, then up another. The rain and wind hit us harder and harder. We stand on deck, dripping wet, disoriented. We're in open water and not near land. That's our good fortune. The waves would certainly push us into a reef or a sandbar and the *Delight* would be destroyed.

Several sailors pull at the line that holds the mainsail to the top of the mast, but the block and tackle are jammed by the wind and the rain. A quick-thinking sailor darts from among the group, up the mast he climbs, and with one powerful slice, cuts the line. The *Delight* rocks as the wet sail hits the deck. The mast and sail are saved, at least for now.

We grab anything and everything we can. What can't be lashed down is stuffed down into the hold.

Mr. Howard yells to Smithy, "Heave to!"

Smithy and another sailor lash themselves to the wheel and fight as best they can to head the *Delight* into the waves. They struggle against the relentless swells. I fear a wave will carry them—and the wheel—away.

The *Delight* suffers every time she's hit by a wave and her creakings are heard throughout the vessel. Each blow dealt by the sea causes her more pain than the blow before. My mind darts to dark places. Will she spring a leak, or just burst apart and cast us into the very angry sea? We are at the mercy of the storm.

Everyone will die. Goodbye Mother, Father, my brothers. I pray for us all that we may rest in peace.

12

**The Ultimate Risk of Being a Pirate
October–November 1716**

"STRIKE THE SAILS!" shouts Mr. Howard. This is no easy feat seeing as the *Delight* has several sails and they are heavy with rain. The deck is slick from the hungry sea lapping at us. Each gust of wind threatens to pitch each of us into the sea. "Smartly!" Mr. Howard yells between the storm's punches. "Smartly or we'll lose the mast!"

One by one, the sails come down. I wonder whether the effort is for naught because the storm grows more violent minute by minute. It's only a matter of time before we'll all be in the water, clinging for dear life to whatever splinter of our vessel washes by, just waiting for the sharks. I'd heard stories about sharks and they weren't good.

Meanwhile, the wind and the waves play their games, tossing us at will, first the wind, then the waves, sheets of rain, blinding rain. I can no longer see the mast, let alone whether the sails are struck.

The storm tosses us every which way. We counter by lashing ourselves to the *Delight* with lines tied around our waists. Uncontrollably, however, I slide as if I am on the side of an icy hill. Only my line keeps me from tumbling into the sea.

When we think the storm can't get worse, it does. Above the thunder, lightning, and rain, the Captain and Mr. Howard shout, "All hands below!" I hear the shrill call of the boatswain's brass whistle: "All hands below!" What is not lashed down will be lost to the sea. All that could be done, has been done.

One by one, the men scramble down the ladder to the hold below. I'm reminded of rats fleeing a garbage dump as they seek shelter from a soaring hawk. I can't help but laugh.

"What you laughing at, boy?" Mr. Howard's standing behind me. He's not amused.

"Sorry, sir!"

"Get below before the storm takes you down to Davy Jones' locker."

I don't know who Davy Jones is and why he has a locker, but I follow Mr. Howard's command.

I'm so anxious to escape the wind and the rain, I miss a rung on the ladder and fall with a loud "thud." I'm embarrassed tho' no one seems to notice or care. Well, at least I'm out of the storm.

I find myself in the hold where everything from the top deck's being stored. Except for the short time I was locked in a cabin by Spanish pirates, I've never been below deck. It's dark, damp, and crowded. The smell of black powder fills the air. The stink of bilge water rises up from below.

The *Delight*'s being consumed by the storm—and the night.

"Where's the Captain?" I ask.

A voice mutters, "His quarters, I guess, unless washed overboard."

I see Mr. Howard, who warns me, "The Captain said you shouldn't leave my side. You go up that ladder, boy, and we'll never see you again."

"The Captain'll understand," chimes in another voice. His comment's followed by "good riddance." I ignore that the best I can.

The hatch is sealed and at least for now, that gives us a reprieve from the rain, the wind, and the waves. I squeeze into a spot between Cooky and Stewy.

The *Delight* is thrown around relentlessly. The crew, me included, would be tossed from bulkhead to bulkhead if we weren't so tightly packed. Hours pass. Some men doze off. Their snoring becomes deafening. Some find a barrel of rum and drown their misery. One by one, they too begin to doze off. All becomes quiet except for the sea bashing against our hull, the beating rain, the howling wind, the incessant snoring of our men, and the painful crying of the *Delight*. I don't remember much of the night for I, too, must have dozed off.

I wake. A few slivers of lighter darkness appear around the hatch. Is it morning? Cooky and Stewy haven't moved and show no intention of leaving for the galley. Anyways, who could be hungry at a time like this?

We all continue to sit, just sit. The silence, except for the wind, the waves, and the rain, is broken by the snoring, the cursing, and a few praying. The storm hadn't loosened its grip during the night nor is it releasing us during the morning. It's as fierce as ever. We sit in a state of tension for what feels like hours upon hours.

As suddenly as the storm appeared, it departs. The hatch is swung open and rays of sunlight brightens the hold. I'm unsure if the hatch is opened to check whether it's safe to venture on deck or to clear the stench created by the sequestered crew. The smell is too much for even the strongest of men.

Mr. Howard's the first on the deck. One by one, the men follow. Captain Hornigold is surveying the damage. "Howard, we'll need a safe haven for repairs."

"Aye, Captain."

"Assess the damage. Find me in my quarters with my maps. Where's my boy? Becoming fond of him."

I'm standing behind Mr. Howard. The Captain doesn't see me.

"Here, sir!" I reply, stepping out from Mr. Howard's shadow.

"Come with me, boy, and be useful," the Captain says.

I follow him to his quarters and smile thinking back to what he said, "Becoming fond of him." The Captain has a strange way to show his fondness, I think.

A short time later, Mr. Howard reappears. "Damage substantial, Captain. Lost most of the sails but the mast held. Repair needed badly, about a week's work if we can find the materials and the carpenters."

"Count the men. Who's missing?"

"Aye, Captain!"

Mr. Howard's gone again.

After the violent storm, silence overwhelms the Captain's quarters. He pours over his maps. When Mr. Howard appears again, the Captain exclaims, "Tortuga!"

"Aye, Captain, I'll prepare the men."

Mr. Howard vanishes only to reappear to announce, "Abrams, Daniels, and Walters missing. Sea claimed them."

I can hear the Captain distantly exclaim under his breath, "Rest in peace, rest in peace," before he orders, "Set sail for Tortuga, best you can."

Mr. Howard immediately sets off again.

Daniels, I knew, the curse got him. I'd seen him in the cavern with the Captain and Mr. Howard and later I overheard him telling Abrams about the cavern. The curse got Abrams too. Daniels should have listened to the Captain's warning. Now both gone. The word about Daniels, Abrams, and the curse will soon spread among the crew. I'm not going to be the one to say a word.

My thoughts are cut short when I hear the Captain, "Now, boy, you've work to do. Can you count?"

"Yes, sir!"

"Well, you may be useful after all," he mutters. "Go find Howard."

Mr. Howard is working at a large round table in the middle of his quarters. "Get a sack," he says as he brushes his maps aside. He points to a dark corner, a corner I haven't noticed before.

I find eight sacks and strain to lift one, but it's too heavy. Mr. Howard laughs. "Cooks need to put some muscle on you, boy."

Mr. Howard carries a sack to the table and spreads its contents. Silver with a little gold! There's so many pieces, an unimaginable number! I recognize the sacks from the vessels we've recently captured. Mr. Howard continues to spread the contents on the table. "Now sort and stack."

There's a few English gold guineas and silver crowns, shillings, and pence but they are few and far between. They're perfectly round, nicely minted with clear imprints.

"What's this?" as I hold up a piece of silver.

"Piece of eight, Spanish."

I'd heard about pieces of eight but hadn't seen one. They're roundish but not round.

"Why aren't they nice and round like the English coins?"

"They're not cast in molds like English coins. The silver's mined here, smelted here, and the coins minted here: Peru, Bolivia, Mexico. Ingots of silver are heated red hot and hammered into flat strips, then cut into one-ounce pieces. The coins are valued by weight. Each one-ounce coin is a piece of eight and almost pure silver. Each piece of eight's stamped with a hammer and a die that has the seal with the cross of the Catholic Church on one side and the Spanish coat of arms along with the number eight on the other. A piece of eight's called "cob" because of its irregular shape.

"A piece of eight can be divided eight ways and each eighth is one-eighth of an ounce. One eighth of a piece of eight is called a reale and is one-eighth of an ounce of silver."

I stack pieces of eight. When the stack reaches ten, I return the coins to the sack and make a mark on the scrap of paper Mr. Howard has given me.

"What are these gold coins?"

"Escudos. One escudo's two pieces of eight or sixteen reales. Put them aside."

Mr. Howard and I work silently, sorting and stacking, noting what we count, and returning the coins to their sacks. As we refill all eight sacks, time passes quickly.

We're working on the final sack when Mr. Howard asks, "Boy, can you divide?"

"I can, sir."

"When we finish this sack, need the total number of pieces of eight. Then subtract one hundred for the galley for provisions and one hundred for repairs to the *Delight*."

"Yes, I'll have that number for you, sir."

"Good. Take that number and divide by three. The Captain owns the *Delight*, so he gets a third as owner."

"Done, sir."

"Then every man gets a share of what's left. That's eighty-two shares less the shares for Abrams, Daniels, and Walters. They left no wives or children so no shares need be saved back for them. Add an extra share for the Captain and for me, and an extra half share for each of the other officers. How many's that?"

I pause for a moment. "Eighty-four."

"Good, divide by eighty-four."

That evening, Mr. Howard calls the men together and distributes their shares. He then announces, "An extra tankard of rum for everyone to celebrate surviving the storm."

A loud Hear! Hear! rings out.

The next day, work begins in earnest making whatever repairs can be made as we sail towards the island of Tortuga off the northern coast of Hispaniola. With what sails are left and a good wind, Tortuga is three or four days out.

After breakfast, I find Smithy at the wheel. "Why Tortuga?"

"Hah! Tortuga, one of the original pirate safe havens in these parts. The Spanish claimed the island and then French and English settlers arrived. The Spanish came back and kicked the settlers out and then left. The settlers kept coming back and the Spanish kept returning to kick them out. Finally, the French prevailed, built a fort, and divided the island between the French and the English settlers. Pirates and privateers of all countries were welcomed at the harbor. Over time, the use of the harbor faded.

"Tortuga's a small, out-of-the-way island, not near the Spanish Main or Cuba. The north side of the island faces the ocean and is mountainous—uninhabitable. But around the southeastern end, between Tortuga and Hispaniola, there's a nice harbor. Might be a good place to hide for a few days while we make repairs. The town's Basse Terre, small but it'll do."

On the fourth day, "Hispaniola!" is the cry. Captain Hornigold turns to me, "Won't be long now, boy. Have work to do."

I don't know what he means, but I'll soon find out.

We follow the northern coast of Hispaniola for a time and come to the island of Tortuga. We sail between Hispaniola and Tortuga till Smithy finds the secluded harbor where the *Delight* drops anchor a distance from shore.

"Why so far from shore?"

"Tortuga's not a safe harbor no more. Can't tell what'll happen," is the reply from one of the men standing near.

"If a British warship happens to snoop around, must be able to escape."

That's the first I heard that we were the hunted and not just the hunter.

Mr. Howard alerts the men that each will have one day and one night ashore. We'll sail by the fourth day, assuming the *Delight* is seaworthy. "Stay too long, word'll spread and the British will know we're here."

The longboats are lowered into the water. I follow Captain Hornigold down the ladder, careful not to make a fool of myself again. He and I take our places at the bow. We make for shore, the oars rhythmically propelling us forward.

We approach the wharf and the Captain growls to the oarsmen, "Come back at dusk!"

I soon learn that the Captain will hire more crew including carpenters, sailmakers, and a doctor, if one can be found. He also will replace those lost at sea and those who have had enough and want to stay ashore. The storm's frightened many. The risk's too great for some.

Mr. Howard and the boatswain, Peters, are in the second longboat and will find the material to make the *Delight* seaworthy again.

The Captain, Mr. Howard, and those who want to return to the ship that evening will meet at the wharf at dusk. The longboats will be there.

Cooky and Stewy wait for our longboat to return to the *Delight* and then they will take it to shore to buy provisions to restock the galley. They know a hungry crew will lead to trouble.

We dock at the wharf and the Captain grabs my arm, sharply pulling me up. I feel my arm coming out of its socket.

He admonishes, "No matter what, boy, stay by my side at all times. Tortuga's lawless and unforgiving. No one knows or cares who you are here."

I don't know what he means but I'm not interested in finding out.

Captain Hornigold keeps a brisk pace. It takes all I have to keep up with him. Within minutes, we come to a tavern, The One-Eyed Jack. We enter, the Captain nods to the tavern keeper and we make our way towards an empty table. Captain Hornigold sits with his back to the wall so he can survey the unsavory bunch who patronize Jack's tavern.

Jack comes to our table. "What brings you to Tortuga, Ben?"

Ben? I have never heard anyone call the Captain, Ben.

"Storm," replies the Captain.

"Thought you'd come to see me!" Jack laughs at his own joke. "British snooping, be wary. Didn't know you had a kid."

"Not mine, found him at sea."

Jack looks at me and just shrugs, "Scrawny!"

The Captain shrugs back.

"What'll it be?" Jack asks.

"Two tankards."

"Aye, Aye," replies Jack and soon returns with our order.

"Drink up, boy, drink up!"

I can hardly lift my tankard, let alone "drink up." Whatever it is, tastes awful!

Soon a rather burly sailor approaches our table, early twenties and looks down on his luck. The sea's taken its toll on him.

"Heard you're looking for a few good hands."

"How'd you know?"

"Word spreads fast around here."

The sailor stands while the Captain sits eyeing him, "Sailed before?"

"Royal Navy during the war."

I knew he meant the Queen Anne's War. My Father had said the war's end had put many good sailors ashore with nothing to do. I'm finding that out firsthand.

"A year on *Garland*."

"Captain?"

"Ellis Brand."

"Know him, skills?"

"Carpenter."

"Family?"

"Wife left me when I was at sea."

After a few minutes, I can tell that the Captain has made up his mind about this sailor. "Be at the wharf at sunset, there's work to be done. If you're as good as you say, sail with us."

This process goes on for what seems to be hours. Some, the Captain tells to be at the wharf, others he tells they're not what he needs. They go away grumbling.

"Not a good way to make friends," I think.

Time passes and I try to anticipate when the Captain will say "yes," and when "no." It's clear that now's not the time for me to say anything.

Halfway through the afternoon, I notice several men rolling dice. As they play, they become more animated. Shouts breaks through the usual din.

"You cheated!"

"No, you cheated!"

"Saw you!"

"When?"

"Saw loaded dice!"

Both quickly get to their feet. One pulls a cutlass from its scabbard, the other shows a flintlock pistol.

Jack's quick to intervene. "Now, boys, none of that in here, settle your dispute outside. Don't need to mop the floor. Did that last week."

The men sit down, still snarling at each other. Muffled voices break the silence.

"Buy them a drink," Jack orders someone at the table as tempers slowly cool.

The Captain smiles, "Jack always had a way."

The afternoon comes to an end when the Captain mumbles, "Had enough, boy?" and gets up from the table. "See you, Jack," and with a short wave towards the bar, we amble out.

We're soon on the path to the wharf where our long-boat waits.

"Need to get back," is all the Captain says.

On the *Delight,* repairs are underway. Cooky and Stewy were successful in their buying, and dinner will soon be ready. They're having a special treat for the men because we're not at sea—a meal without salted beef and hardtack. Cooky says what he prepared is salmagundi. He gives me a taste. I stir around in my bowl and find meats, seafood, vegetables, fruit, leaves, nuts, and flowers. The rancid flavor is partially hidden by the oil and spices. I think, "It's not steak and kidney pie." I'm starving, so I'll eat it when supper is served. But the more I taste, the more I long for Mother's cooking.

That evening, as I'm leaning on the rail surveying the harbor, Smithy joins me. We're each lost in our own thoughts when Smithy breaks the silence. "If the harbor could talk, it'd have some interesting stories to tell. Henry Morgan, the Welsh privateer, then lieutenant governor of Jamaica, used this harbor when he was hired by the French to prey upon the Spanish.

"Before Morgan, a French engineer named Jean La Vasseur built that fort up there on the bluff, Fort de Rocher. From the fort, he controlled the harbor and could drive off the Spanish. Built a residence above the fort. In the fort's an iron cage for his prisoners. Two of La Vasseur's men killed him for stealing away one's mistress and abusing her.

"After La Vasseur's death, the Spanish reclaimed the harbor and demolished the fort, never been rebuilt. That's what you see up there."

"Do you think we could go up there tomorrow?"

"Doubt it. No road, not even a path, all overgrown. Would take weeks to cut through all that growth."

"Thanks, anyways. Just a thought,"

I leave Smithy and head for my hammock to get some sleep. La Vasseur's prisoners keep me awake. I find myself looking out at the stars, searching for the constellations, anything to get my mind off La Vasseur's prisoners.

The next morning, the Captain and I return to The One-Eyed Jack. He spends the day recruiting a few more men and tells each to meet our longboat at the wharf at dusk. Late in the afternoon, we head to the wharf to return to the *Delight*.

The town, Basse Terre, if you call it a town, is filthy with drunken sailors loitering wherever you look. As we make our way down the dirty, overgrown path to the wharf, peddlers run up offering to sell this and that, nothing of real interest. The clothing offered looks discarded and the utensils half-broken. The Captain brushes the peddlers aside.

We make an interesting duo walking towards the wharf: the Captain with his long strides and me, running alongside trying to keep up. The bluff and the ruins of Fort de Rocher capture my interest. I call ahead, "Could we stop for a moment and look up at the fort?"

The Captain waits and points up to the ruins, "Great location, guards the harbor, once drove the Spanish away."

I listen attentively and turn to the Captain. Between the sound of the waves lapping the shore and the calling of the gulls, I hear La Vasseur's prisoners screaming in their iron cage. A chill goes up my spine.

"Gulls," the Captain says, "gulls."

"No! Between the cries of the gulls, I distinctly hear screams!"

The Captain looks at me, "gulls," shrugs and walks towards our waiting longboat.

On the third day, I tell the Captain I can't pass the ruins of the fort, I'll stay behind.

Oddly, the Captain and Mr. Howard come back at midday. They're clearly disturbed. Their mood makes me very uneasy.

"Send the longboats to pick up the others. No time to lose. Two hours—everyone must be on board or be left behind."

Mr. Howard leaves quickly to have the Captain's orders followed.

Within the hour, the longboats begin returning; they're sent back for stragglers.

Meanwhile, the Captain, Mr. Howard, and several other officers are in the Captain's quarters. One says with alarm, "The British will have the harbor blockaded within the hour."

"Give the order. *Delight* must be ready to sail, if necessary, at that time," barks the Captain to Mr. Howard.

Mr. Howard leaves in a hurry.

The Captain's voice booms, "Find a plan to get by the British!"

Within a few moments, Mr. Howard reappears. "The *Delight*'s at your command. Scotty sighted a British frigate and a sloop-of-war on the horizon. We don't know whether they know we're here."

I take my seat in the corner. I've a strange feeling that something's around my neck. My neck's getting hot and sweaty. The rope's getting tighter and tighter. I can hardly breathe.

Would they hang a girl?
Why wouldn't they—if she is a pirate?

13

Evading the Enemy
November–December 1716

CAPTAIN HORNIGOLD HAS decided not to sail that evening but to wait till morning. He's instructed his men to rest, for tomorrow will be stressful. Getting a good night's sleep will not be easy with two British warships between the *Delight* and the open sea.

In my sleep I hear eight bells. Eight bells, it must be the end of the second watch—eight in the morning. I've overslept. I rub my eyes and open them to darkness. I think again. Eight bells, the end of the second watch? That can't be right, I think again, eight bells, more like the end of the first watch—four in the morning. Now more awake, I hear the men preparing our escape from the British warships. Even tho' there're just two, a frigate and a sloop-of-war, they're capable of blocking the harbor's entrance. I climb out of my hammock and look over the rail. These warships are real. Their lanterns sway gently in the breeze.

I soon discover everyone has eaten breakfast. Feeling abandoned, I wonder why no one has awakened me. I'd better hurry to the galley or I'll face the day on an empty stomach.

"Where you be, boy?" exclaims Cooky. "Breakfast served hours ago."

"Sorry! Anything left?"

Cooky returns with a bowl and thrusts it at me. "Here, this will tide you over." With the bowl in hand, I make my way back to the open deck. I'm starving, but the best I can do is to poke suspiciously at my bowl: grain, rice, and jerky. It looks bad and smells even worse.

My mind wanders to the soft gray mornings at home with my family. I'd wake up to the aroma of the hot breakfasts Mother would make: perfectly fried eggs, a rasher of bacon, sausages, black pudding, baked beans, grilled tomatoes, mushrooms, warm crisp toast with melting butter, thick marmalade, and tea.

Suddenly, I snap back to reality. Orders ring out, "Shade the lanterns!"

The sun breaks the horizon and the harbor comes to life. The *Delight*'s not the only vessel preparing to raise anchor. Mr. Howard calls out, "Hoist the red ensign," the flag flown by all British merchant vessels.

With our flag raised, the boatswain blows his brass whistle and calls, "Weigh the anchor! Set the mainsail!"

The *Delight* rocks in the waves and meanders forward. Smithy, now at the helm, points the *Delight* towards the harbor's entrance and the British warships.

Captain Hornigold, looking taut, shouts commands. He has a plan, he always does. I need to stay out of his way till he calls.

Even with all the activity onboard, it will be a good while before the *Delight* approaches the harbor's entrance. Still hungry, I donate my dubious breakfast to the fish and head back to the galley to find something to call breakfast.

"We're leaving Tortuga," I announce, stealthily picking a slice of jerky from under Cooky's nose and dropping it in my boot. Luckily, he takes a moment to notice it missing.

"Hey!" Cooky exclaims, "Where's the jerky I's eating? Had one more slice."

Before his suspicions can turn to me, I frown and feign ignorance. "A rat or our cat must have taken it. You know how that cat can be."

"Why did you miss breakfast, boy?" Cooky asks again while returning to his work.

Without directly answering, I mumble a quick "overslept" and flee the galley.

I pick the jerky from my boot for a bite. Remembering the British warships blocking the harbor, my mind returns to that worrying phrase "Pirates be hanged." How's the *Delight* going to get out of Tortuga? What's the Captain's plan?

I head back to the open deck and make my way towards the helm. Our cannons are rolled back and our gunports fastened closed. The crew has thinned to only a few, the others have gone below. Even more surprising, no weapons are in sight. What's the plan?

Smithy guides the *Delight* so she's third in line. The plan now becomes clear. The *Delight* is disguised as a harmless British merchant vessel. I still find it impossible not to worry. How can we not be detected?

The first vessel passes the British, followed by the second. The *Delight* is next. My nerves make each moment feel longer than the last.

Slowly, Smithy guides the *Delight* past the port side of the frigate. Some of her crew are still busy with breakfast. Others tend to early morning chores. No one seems to pay us much mind. We ease by, stand at attention and salute. They salute half-heartedly in return.

Smithy eases the *Delight* past the starboard side of the sloop-of-war. We salute again. The tense silence is broken by commands and responses about duties.

The *Delight* clears the harbor after what seems like an eternity and Smithy sets our course eastward. He then turns to me and whispers, "Too close, not something I'd want to do every day."

Once past the island of Tortuga, we sail north to the open waters of the Atlantic. Captain Hornigold orders the red ensign lowered. No more the hunted, we are, once again, the hunter.

By now, Smithy has finished his watch, and he's at the rail gazing at the sea.

"Smithy, where are we headed?"

"Back to Nassau to finish repairs," he replies, staring forward as if in a trance. I can see he's still rattled from our very close call with the British warships.

Slowly, the *Delight* returns to normal. Some men sit by the rail chewing tobacco, others dip snuff. I take my diary from under my belt and find an open spot along the rail.

"What you doing, boy?" asks a sailor I know only as McCarthy.

I mumble something.

"Leave the boy alone," another admonishes McCarthy.

"Oh, he's not bothering me," I assure him. Truthfully, I'd just been thinking about "Pirates be hanged." Now that we had an encounter with the warships, hanging was on my mind once more.

McCarthy asks, "You can write?"

"Yes, sir."

"Write me a letter to me mum?"

"All right," I reply as he fishes a somewhat clean page from his pocket.

McCarthy begins to talk and I write, correcting his grammar as best I can.

Dear Mum,

Doing well sailing with Captain Hornigold. Don't worry about me none. Doing fine, likely to be back sometime but can't say when. Take care of my little sisters while I'm gone, and don't let my absence keep you from running Dad's shop while he's away.

"How will you deliver your letter?" I ask before handing it over to McCarthy.

"I'll leave it with the tavern keeper at the next port. I'll tell him where we live and he'll pass it on so mum will get it," he answers, gripping his prized possession tightly.

Towards the end of November, the *Delight* leaves Nassau and sets sail for the northeastern coast of Cuba. The repairs have taken longer than expected. A week later, the *Delight* is trolling the waters around the Windward Passage.

On about the third of December, the *Delight* captures a merchant ship, a galley, bound from Jamaica to Bristol, England. John Quarry's the captain. We send over a boarding party and they return with provisions. Quarry's ship's released and sent on her way.

About a week later, the tenth of December, the *Delight* captures a Spanish brigantine with forty guns. She looms over our eight-gun sloop, but she's not a fighting vessel and she surrenders rather easily. Mr. Howard leads our boarding party and they return with more provisions. Because she makes no attempt to flee or fight, Captain Hornigold sends her on her way as well. Boardings like this have become routine, even for me.

Three days later, the thirteenth of December, around eight in the evening, we're off Cape Donna Maria on the western end of Hispaniola when we come upon the *Lamb*, another brigantine. She's sailing from Boston to Jamaica and is the end of her journey. Captain Hornigold orders several warning shots. Being a merchant vessel and not a fighting vessel, she's in no position to refuse to surrender.

The *Lamb*'s captain, Henry Timberlake, and two of his crew lower a rowboat and come over to the *Delight* with her papers.

"Aye, boy!" I hear a voice behind me calling. When I turn around, I see one of our crew, they call him "Squint," motioning to me. "Want to join the boarding party? Captain and Mr. Howard say you can."

I soon find myself in a longboat along with Captain Hornigold and about a dozen of our crew. We row over to the *Lamb* and climb aboard. I stay with Squint as we systematically search the vessel, selecting provisions and carrying them to our longboat.

An hour after we board, we're joined by another sloop, about the same size as the *Delight,* eight guns, about ninety men. The captain of that vessel sends a canoe with several men over to the *Lamb*. They too gather provisions and ferry them back to their vessel.

I ask Squint, "Who has joined us?"

"Captain's old friend, Thache, Captain Edward Thache. We thought he might show up. Thache often trolls these waters. When he served on the *Windsor* during the Queen Anne's War, his frigate frequently patrolled these shipping lanes between Cuba and Hispaniola. He's extremely familiar with these waters."

Four hours or so later, it must be two or three in the morning, we return to the *Delight*.

I'm standing near our Captain when Captain Timberlake asks, "Why did you take us?" Captain Hornigold answers, "Provisions, only provisions. You're free to go."

Captain Timberlake prepares to row back to the *Lamb* when Captain Hornigold calls out, "Need a favor. Hear Captain Quarry's arrested and in jail in Port Royal, arrested as a pirate. When you get to Jamaica, tell the authorities that it was me and not Quarry who took the provisions from that Spanish brigantine. Don't want Quarry hanged for something he didn't do."

Later in the day, I'm in the galley with Cooky and Stewy. "I'm curious. What did we take?"

"Provisions, only provisions: barrels of pork, beef, peas, mackerel, onions, crates of oysters. Oh, and all their clothing. Left them enough biscuits and meat to get back to Jamaica. Timberlake's a good man, he is. He's fair and reasonable."

For the next couple of days, we sail in consort with Captain Thache. Together we sail the waters around the Windward Passage and take two more vessels, one English and the other French.

Captain Thache comes over to the *Delight* a couple of times to visit with Captain Hornigold. They seem to enjoy each other's company.

Captain Thache's tall and thin but unlike most men who are clean-shaven, he wears a beard, a long black beard. Makes him look rather sinister. Funny thing is no one's claimed they witnessed him killing or abusing anyone. Some say he's an annoyance to the British rather than the "cutthroat" he's portrayed to be. I've noticed he walks with a spring in his step as if he's living in a world of his own.

Once when I'm chatting with Smithy, who's taking his watch at the helm, Captain Thache comes over. "Where're you from, lad?"

"A small town in England," I reply.

"Why's a good lad like you sailing with the Captain?"

I explain that Captain Hornigold rescued me from some particularly barbaric Spanish pirates and he now treats me like one of his crew.

I can tell Captain Thache's educated, but I'm in no position to ask where and how.

"What did you do before you became a pirate?" I manage to ask.

"Royal Navy, *Windsor*, during the war, and did a little fishing off the Florida coast," he replies quietly. With that answer, I can see that his mind drifts to years gone by. Abruptly, he turns and walks away.

After breakfast, I go to the rail, only to see Captain Thache's sloop sailing towards the horizon. I wonder when I'll see him again.

It's lonely sailing alone. We've roamed the seas for so many months in consort with other vessels and with other captains.

The sea's calm and the breeze fills our sails. "Want to try your hand?" Smithy asks.

Huh, I don't know what he means. He motions again and I step in front of him and take hold of the wheel with both hands. I feel Smithy's hand still on the wheel.

"Watch the compass, keep the needle where it is. I'll be here if you need help." And so we sail in silence. As time passes, I feel Smithy's grip loosen till I find myself alone with the wheel.

We sail for a while, The sea's calm. Suddenly, there's a slight twist in the wheel, then a stronger tug. I try to focus on the compass. "What's that?" I ask.

"Oh, a wave, a wave struck our rudder."

The rhythm repeats again and again. I feel my arms becoming heavy from keeping the course.

Finally, Smithy comments, "Getting tired? Hard work, huh? Maybe you should see what Cooky has to eat."

I had not thought about food but now that Smithy has mentioned eating, I feel very hungry. Gladly, I accept Smithy's offer and seek out Cooky and Stewy. My time at the wheel has left me famished.

December was a good month for the *Delight,* and Captain Hornigold instructs Smithy to set sail for Port Royal, Jamaica. Although our vessel's a sloop, a small vessel, the Captain has made the best of each opportunity. We've seized some fifteen vessels and have filled our hold with a rich assortment of goods. Our cargo can be sold at the port and the men can spend Christmas ashore with a little silver in their pockets.

A week later, I'm standing with Smithy who is guiding the *Delight* into the Port Royal Harbor. I look around and can't believe my eyes. I expect to see a thriving port but no. Sections of the town look to be in ruins. "What happened?"

"About twenty-five years ago, an earthquake followed by a great wall of water struck the harbor. Much of what remained was consumed by fire and hurricanes. Pretty unbelievable. Port Royal was built on sand. Vibrations from the quake created quicksand, and in the end, the land couldn't support the buildings. Half of Port Royal was just swallowed by the quicksand; it sank into the harbor. Almost everyone died. Those few who survived moved to a small farming village a few miles away, Kingston.

"You see the half that remained. Some buildings were rebuilt but Port Royal will never be the same as it was."

Smithy thinks for a while and then adds, "Once Port Royal was called the storehouse and treasury of the West Indies. Before my time, she was known as one of the wickedest places on earth. People called the destruction retribution for her wickedness. Well, I don't know much about that."

I watch for a while as our cargo is taken ashore. I'm told it's being delivered to our agents and will be sold for a nice price.

Later, I help Mr. Howard divide the proceeds from the sale. He welcomes my help and even gives me a few pieces of eight to spend.

The crew collects their shares and leaves for shore. They look different and then it dawns on me. They're dressed in their finest clothing and jewelry taken from the passengers of the vessels we've seized. I chuckle, thinking that there's no need to dress up for the high seas or for Nassau, but Port Royal must be different.

Later, the Captain and I go ashore. I'm pleased to have this opportunity because my family was headed for Port Royal and they planned to board a coastal merchant vessel to Charles Town. I ask whether anyone has heard about the Pennyworth family.

My inquiries prove fruitless. With every day, the ache I feel inside from missing them becomes a little less unbearable. All I have tangible from my past life is my grandmother's locket. Still, I won't give up hope of seeing them again.

We stop at the tavern. The Captain greets some friends and has a tankard or two. I nurse a pint of rum as I listen to the fiddler and watch the men dance.

On our way back to the wharf, we come upon a large, noisy group of men milling around.

"What draws their attention?"

"Slave trader's galleon arrived in port and her cargo—men, women, and children from Africa—being sold, being sold to the highest bidder."

I'm horrified by the thought but my curiosity gets the better of me. I stand riveted in place. I've never seen a slave auction, only heard of them. Witnessing the actual auctioning of men, women, and even their children is simply unbearable. I watch in horrid fascination. The Captain, seeing I'm extremely upset, takes my arm and leads me away.

14

Facing Reality
December 1716–April 1717

WE ARRIVE BACK on the *Delight* just in time for supper. All's quiet. Most of the men are ashore and won't return for a few days. They know the Captain wants to sail soon after the New Year, so they're making the best of their time away.

With almost everyone ashore, we can feast in leisure. No food out of a barrel for us. Cooky and Stewy bring out oysters, clams, turtle soup, fresh fish, fresh fruit, and fresh water. I eat as if I have never eaten before. I see Cooky give Stewy a quick glance. I'm not sure who enjoys the feast more, me or them watching me eat. Finally, Stewy exclaims, "Poor child, we'll fatten him up."

The men begin to return to the *Delight* and many look as if they had too good a time. They know Captain Hornigold will be anxious to hoist anchor and set sail, so regardless of how they feel, they prepare for the open sea. The rumor around the vessel is that the Captain is selling the *Delight* and buying another sloop, the *Adventure.* We'll transfer vessels soon after the New Year.

A few days later, we celebrate the New Year: seventeen hundred seventeen. I can't believe I have been sailing with Captain Hornigold for over a year. In some ways, I feel sorry for him because he seems not quite satisfied. Maybe being a pirate is getting to him. Everyone knows that the rich landowners and merchants are pressuring the new king to curtail the activities of pirates. When we are on land, I hear rumors that King George changed the governor of Jamaica so the new governor will bring "law and order" to the West Indies. What has been easy pickings for the Captain will now carry more risk. As if that's not enough, the king's increasing the number of Royal Navy warships on patrol. Our game of cat and mouse is losing its appeal.

To me, the Captain's constantly swapping vessels is evidence of his uneasiness. When I first joined him, he was changing to the *Mary.* A few months later, he returned the *Mary* to her owners in Jamaica and refitted a Spanish prize, renaming her the *Benjamin.* After losing the *Benjamin* to Sam Bellamy, Captain Hornigold was forced to sail a small Spanish prize. He then acquired the *Delight,* and now the *Adventure.*

At first, I found sailing with pirates exciting. *What would my friends back home say if they only knew?* But after a while, drinking in a tavern with all those pirates and searching for Spanish merchant vessels has become nothing but ordinary. During the past year, we must have boarded well over twenty vessels and the boarding has become routine. The merchant captains know by now that if they do not try to escape, they can resume their voyage with a minimum of loss and delay. We'll take only the provisions we need and a little something to sell when in port.

With the New Year, we prepare to leave Port Royal in our new sloop, the *Adventure*. I work on the porridge I'm carrying around for my breakfast and make my way to the helm to ask Smithy where we're heading.

Mr. Howard is standing nearby and answers, "Shipping lanes between Havana and Cartagena."

"Cartagena, where's that?" I ask curiously as I swallow the rest of my porridge.

"Do you know nothing, boy? Have you grown another head, boy?" Mr. Howard asks staring at me.

"Sorry, sir."

"Well, it's on the Colombian coast. Silver from the Peruvian and Bolivian mines comes through Cartagena." Mr. Howard's eyes grew big as he imagines chests filled with silver.

"Oh," I say, not wanting to display any more of my ignorance.

"But first," explains Smithy, "we'll stop at the Isle of Pines to careen this vessel. Don't know her condition below the waterline and her hold's empty except for provisions. Perfect time to check her."

After spending a couple of weeks on the Isle of Pines, we sail to the shipping lanes between Cartagena and Havana. From his vantage, Scotty spots sails and cries out, "Sail ho!" When she comes closer, Captain Hornigold identifies her as English, the *Charles Galley*, a ship we'd seen when we're at Port Royal.

"Follow her," orders the Captain. "Don't capture her, just follow her. I hear she's sailing to Charles Town with some sugar and rum. Aren't interested in that right now."

We follow the *Charles Galley* for a couple of days. She approaches the Bay of Campeche, and the Captain orders Smithy to change course and head back to the shipping lanes between Cartagena and Havana.

"Why's the Captain changing course?"

"Too close to the Bay of Campeche. Spanish warships are trying to wipe out the log cutters. Sailing alone's too dangerous. The *Charles Galley*'s heading into trouble."

As the days wear on, Smithy guides the *Adventure* towards the shipping lanes between Cartagena and Havana.

At last, we see our prey, a merchant vessel flying the Spanish flag. Her captain knows she can't outrun us.

"Hoist our flag!" shouts Mr. Howard. "Run a shot across her bow!"

The tranquility of the day is interrupted by the explosion from our cannon. The Spanish vessel strikes her colors, furls her sails, and turns into the wind.

Smithy brings the *Adventure* alongside. I can hear Mr. Howard order, "Grappling hooks now, boys!" Matthews and a few others throw the grappling hooks, tying the two vessels together.

Mr. Howard selects nine men to board the Spanish vessel. Soon, sacks of silver coins are loaded onto the *Adventure*. Then comes sacks of ground corn and sugar and a few barrels of rum. The grappling hooks are returned to the *Adventure* and the Spanish vessel is released to resume her voyage.

That evening, our crew celebrates. The fiddler, whom we always enjoy, is in rare form. As he starts playing, he's joined by several of the crew, one who plays a penny whistle and another a concertina. They play into the night and as the rum flows freely, the men begin singing and dancing. The music concludes with a hornpipe dance that grows faster and faster. When the music and the dance reach a feverish tempo, one of the dancers throws his hat up in the air and it's caught by the breeze and carried into the sea. One hat follows another and then another till no hat remains on board.

The next day, the men pay an exorbitant price for their jubilance. The hot, tropical sun is relentless and unbearable.

To our good fortune, a vessel comes over the horizon. Her captain must think we're just another merchant vessel because she approaches without hesitation. We see she's a coastal merchant sloop that carries passengers as well as goods. She's not large but large enough. Mr. Howard orders some sails struck as we wait for her to catch up to us. Once she gets near, we hoist our pirate flag, and her captain knows she can't escape. She strikes her colors and her sails and heads into the wind. She knows we'll take her, so she makes boarding convenient. We hear later that her crew was surprised when all our boarding party took were their hats—every single hat.

After sailing the Cartagena-to-Havana trade route for a few days, Captain Hornigold decides to head closer to home. The *Adventure* is now cruising the Florida coast when we come upon a snow from Jamaica. Being a snow rather than a sloop, she's square-rigged with two masts. A trysail is attached to the mainmast. Although she's faster, her small crew, no more than thirty-five, will be an easy match for us. The *Adventure* has eighty seasoned fighting men, and the snow has only merchant seamen who have little interest in fighting to protect their cargo.

Mr. Howard leads our boarding party. He finds the cargo to be typical of similar vessels, but she has one thing that all pirate captains crave, a surgeon. Over the vehement objections of the snow's captain, Benjamin Blake, and the surgeon, our crew relocates Dr. John Howell along with his medical chest and his personal items to the *Adventure*.

We pull away from the snow while Captain Blake is still yelling, "Hornigold, I'll get even. I'll get even with you someday!"

So Dr. John Howell becomes our surgeon, tho' admittedly unwillingly.

Dr. Howell couldn't have joined the *Adventure* at a better time. He finds one of our men desperately ill. His death is rumored to be imminent. After examining him, Dr. Howell opens his medical chest and mixes what proves to be a magical elixir. Within days, the sailor recovers and is back at his post. From then on, the doctor's good reputation is beyond question.

After Dr. Howell joins the *Adventure,* a Dutch vessel comes along and we seize her. She's being plundered by our boarding crew when a second Dutch vessel comes upon us. We seize her too.

Our boarding parties will not be back for several hours and that gives me time to visit with Smithy, who is at the helm. "I'm surprised the Captain would attack those vessels. I thought he wouldn't attack British or Dutch vessels."

"Well, the Captain learned a lesson when he lost the *Benjamin* on Hispaniola last August. He now knows he won't be able to keep either his men or his vessel if British and Dutch vessels are not fair game."

After these vessels are sent on their way, Captain Hornigold orders Smithy to sail northeast.

"How long before we get to New Providence?"

"Not going to New Providence. We're going to Harbour Island."

"Why there?"

"Well, after the Captain left Jamaica and moved to New Providence, the Spanish threatened to attack, so he moved to Eleuthera Island. Harbour Island's off the northeastern tip of Eleuthera Island. When the Spanish threat subsided, the Captain moved back to New Providence."

"There must be more to the story," I blurt out.

"There is. The Captain first moved to New Providence with John Cockram and John West to sail periaguas, and he moved to Eleuthera when Cockram married the daughter of Richard Thompson, a well-established fencing agent for pirated goods. Cockram went into business with his father-in-law. They deliver goods to Charles Town and carry sugar and provisions back to Nassau. Old man Thompson has lived on Harbour Island for a long time. He's well connected. Cockram now makes good money. He and his father-in-law even own a vessel together, the *Richard & John*. Captain Hornigold went to visit them."

The *Adventure* sails into Harbour Island's harbor and I'm overwhelmed by its sheer beauty. The beaches are a dazzling pink. "You've been near here before. Don't you remember?" Smithy asks.

"Hmm. Does look familiar."

"Remember when you first joined us? We'd captured the *Mary* of Jamaica and you're found locked in a cabin. A month or so later, we went to careen the *Mary* and you violated the Captain's orders and followed us into that cavern."

"Oh, I remember all too well. I thought the Captain would leave me somewhere or throw me overboard."

"You're lucky! He came pretty close," Smithy adds with a smile.

"Why's it so quiet here?" I ask, trying to change the subject.

"Small island, only about thirty families living here."

I could see that with so little traffic in the harbor, the beaches had remained pristine. When we drop our anchors, only two vessels are there purchasing supplies.

Smithy and I watch our men go ashore. "There goes William Howard, our quartermaster. He appears to be leaving with his chest. Where's Mr. Howard going with his chest?"

"Oh, forgot to tell you, we're changing quartermasters. The new quartermaster's John Martin. You'll meet him soon."

Smithy points, "There, see there! Dr. Howell's pleading his case to the Captain."

"Let me leave the *Adventure* and go ashore," he's saying.

Dr. Howell is unlike others on the vessel because his doctoring skills can't be easily replaced. While the *Adventure* is in port or near other vessels, the good doctor must be constantly guarded to prevent his escape. He's tried on more than one occasion. Has to be guarded—constantly—sometimes by up to nine men.

I'm surprised when Captain Hornigold relents, "All right then. I'll arrange for you to stay with William Pindar while we're here at Harbour Island. He's a merchant in Nassau and a friend of mine. Go pack what you'll need for a couple of weeks."

Smithy's quick to point out, "The Captain knows the *Adventure* will be in Harbour Island for a while because all her plunder needs to be offloaded and sold. Maybe he's getting tired of Dr. Howell's begging to be released, or maybe he thinks Dr. Howell can't escape from Nassau. Who knows?"

Smithy turns his attention back to the Captain. "Over there's the new quartermaster talking to the Captain. If you listen carefully, you'll hear what they're saying. You know, the Captain doesn't speak softly."

"John, take a few men and go over to Nassau and get another rowboat. When you go, take Dr. Howell with you. Make sure he gets to Pindar's. Tell Pindar that the doctor will be staying for a few weeks. Pindar will be happy to have company."

And so it is. Dr. Howell gets his wish to leave the *Adventure*, at least for a few weeks.

Harbour Island, a sleepy little place with not much to do, is a welcoming break from our usual activities. Our men spend their days at the local tavern while I explore the beaches, picking up treasures washed ashore from sunken ships.

Several days after we arrive, a French ship, the *Mary Anne*, drops anchor nearby.

A couple of days later, I'm surprised to see Dr. Howell is back on Harbour Island. I'm standing by the rail and can hear the doctor arguing with Captain Hornigold.

"Get on the *Adventure*!" the Captain orders.

"I'll mix some medicines for you but I'll stay here!" Dr. Howell answers.

The Captain's losing patience, "*Get you on board, you dog, or I'll mix your soul!*"

With that, Dr. Howell rejoins the *Adventure*.

I wait for the doctor to get resettled and then pay him a visit. "I didn't expect to see you on Harbour Island so soon."

"Long story. It's like this. Me and Pindar had just finished dinner when there's this loud knock on his door. Pindar got up from the table and opened the door. I glanced over his shoulder and saw a group of menacing half-drunk French seamen standing there cursing in French. I shan't repeat what they're saying. Fortunately, they couldn't see me. One shouts, 'Captain Bonadvis from the *Mary Anne* sent us. We came for the doctor, hear he's here! Came for a hogshead of rum, too!'"

Pindar was quick to reply. "Don't have the rum and you can't have the doctor unless Captain Hornigold says so."

"Bonadvis' men were becoming irate. I thought this was no place for me here, so I headed out the back door and over to Benjamin Saunders', who worked for Richard Noland, Hornigold's agent. Saunders hid me till the Frenchmen left, and then he had Noland arrange for me to sail back over here where I'm safe. So here I am."

A few evenings later, Jean Bonadvis, the *Mary Anne*'s captain, and several of his men appear at the tavern where the Captain and I are passing the time. I'm sitting next to the Captain as Bonadvis approaches our table. The Captain motions for me to move away. He and Bonadvis engage in a heated argument. Bonadvis demands Dr. Howell for his vessel.

Captain Bonadvis is several years younger than Captain Hornigold. I can tell Bonadvis had a little too much to drink. He insists that he's taking Dr. Howell to his *Mary Anne* as his surgeon. Frustrated, he yells, *Pas de si ni de mais.*

Captain Hornigold looks puzzled.

"No ifs, ands, or buts, you English dog," Bonadvis repeats, but this time in his drunken, broken English and he then lapses back into French.

Several of our men hear Bonadvis and come stand threateningly behind our Captain. We wait to see what Bonadvis will do next. Will he draw a weapon? Fortunately, he doesn't. He only becomes louder. As he does, the Captain becomes quieter and finally says, "If Dr. Howell says he'll go with you, you can have him."

The next day Mr. Martin asks Dr. Howell if he'd like to sail with Bonadvis. Dr. Howell's reply is emphatic, "I would rather sail with the English than with the French!" To say the least, Bonadvis is not happy.

We stay at Harbour Island for a few more days and then sail to Nassau to prepare the *Adventure* for her next cruise. Naturally, the Captain and I go to The Lion and the Unicorn. We're enjoying our tankards in familiar surroundings when a sailor approaches our table. "Hornigold, that you?"

The Captain looks up and a large smile crossses his face. "Napping? Haven't seen you in years. Where've you be?"

"Sailing the coast of Africa," the sailor Napping replies.

"West coast of Africa? What's going on there?"

"Not much. Slave trade and all that. Once in a while, a spice ship comes back from the East. Lots of Portuguese, but I'd rather have Spanish silver than Eastern spices."

"I'm sailing in a few days. Want to sail in consort?"

"Why not?" answers Captain Napping. "Safer together."

And so arrangements are made for Captain Napping to sail in consort with the *Adventure*.

Captain Napping's an intriguing fellow because no one seems to know much about him, not even his first name, except he's the Captain's friend. Cooky, Stewy, and I have fun making far-fetched guesses about this mysterious Captain Napping.

In mid-March, the two sloops set off for the shipping lanes around Porto Bello. I'm not familiar with the destination, so I inquire about it. Mr. Howard explains, "Porto Bello is on the Isthmus of Panama where silver's shipped to Havana and then to Spain."

We sail towards Porto Bello and approach Friends Islands off Panama. On the first of April, Scotty spots the sloop *Bennet.* We approach and Captain Hornigold orders, "Hoist our flag." Our black flag is raised. I'm surprised to see the uniqueness of Captain Napping's flag, a white death's-head and an hourglass on a black background.

The *Bennet* is seized without resistance and Mr. Martin leads our boarding party. I'm standing by the rail with Smithy when they return with a chest of gold belonging to the current asiento company.

"What's the asiento company?"

"Asiento contracts, very nasty business," comments Smithy. "We need to go back two centuries to the Treaty of Tordesillas between Spain and Portugal where a line was drawn from pole to pole down through the Atlantic Ocean. Land east of the line would belong to Portugal and land west of the line would belong to Spain. What this meant was Spain could not go to the ports of West Africa to get slaves for its plantations and mines in the Caribbean and the Spanish Main. Spain had to get a third party to get the slaves and bring them to the Spanish islands and the Spanish Main. Every few years, the Spanish crown allows countries and companies to bid on the exclusive right to supply slaves in Spanish America. This chest of gold belongs to the company that has the asiento and has just sold a galley full of slaves. It represents Spain's percentage of what's received from the sale, and is being shipped to Spain in payment for that exclusive right, nasty business, very nasty business."

In addition to the gold, Captain Hornigold likes the *Bennet*. He negotiates a trade with her captain, Captain Hickinbottem: the *Adventure* and freedom for Captain Hickinbottem and his men in exchange for the *Bennet*. Captain Hickinbottem can hardly refuse. Once our guns, black powder, provisions, and personal items are transferred to the *Bennet*, we set sail east towards Jamaica.

Six days later, the *Bennet*, in consort with Captain Napping's sloop, is in Bluefields Bay, Jamaica. We capture a vessel whose captain is Captain James. Captain Hornigold learns from Captain James' men that a rich Dutch ship is trading on the southern coast of Cuba.

I'm surprised we stay at Bluefields Bay rather than sail to investigate the "rich Dutch ship." Captain Hornigold appears in no hurry to leave Jamaica.

His decision to stay is not without merit. Three days later, the *Bennet* captures another vessel, the *Revenge*.

We now sail towards the southern coast of Cuba. On the twelfth of April, Scotty spots the twenty-four-gun Dutch ship. She's alone and we're two vessels. After a brief discussion, Captain Hornigold and Captain Napping decide to attack.

The *Bennet* runs a shot across the Dutch ship's bow, but she shows no sign of surrendering. The chase is on. For two days, Captain Hornigold and Captain Napping engage in a running battle with this Dutch ship. We're gaining when Scotty spots a ship coming over the horizon. The chase continues, but as the newcomer draws closer, we discover she's a British warship, the twenty-gun frigate *Winchelsea*. If the chase continues, we'll need to take on not only the Dutch ship but also the *Winchelsea*. Captain Hornigold signals Captain Napping to end the pursuit.

The *Winchelsea* follows us for some time. Luckily, she's a frigate and we're sloops, so eventually we outsail her. Not wanting to tangle with a British warship, we head for the safety of Nassau and the pirate colony.

Between our two vessels, we've taken four hundred thousand pieces of eight and the chest of gold. Even without any plunder from the twenty-four-gun Dutch ship, our men celebrate a successful April.

When we return, we find conditions in Nassau still deplorable. The filth and stench have become worse since we last were here. Garbage and human waste are everywhere. Cows, pigs, goats, chickens, and other livestock roam freely. The paths are overgrown. What's most disturbing is the amount of illness. Many sailors have either come down with something while at sea or have caught disease from the women they visit. Both doctors and medical supplies are scarce.

The few families, who stayed in Nassau after the French and Spanish burned the town, fled as the pirates invaded. The pirates, as a group, staked out a permanent presence, but pirates are transient. A pirate is in Nassau only as long as his vessel is in the harbor.

The town also suffers from a lack of government. Pirates are not interested in creating a government. All they want is a safe haven where they can rest and resupply without the constant threat of the Royal Navy. With no government, there'll be no services. Without services, the filth and disease will only get worse.

From the beginning of the resurgence of the pirate colony, the leadership was basically in the hands of Captain Hornigold and Captain Jennings, both well known and well respected within the pirates' isolated world. Through various rumors and rantings, I learned that the animosity between the two was legendary. Captain Jennings' a landowner, educated, a Catholic, a Jacobite, a Tory, and from Jamaica. He believes King James, a Catholic Stuart, was wrongly deposed and the Stuarts should be returned to the British throne. Captain Hornigold, on the other hand, is a seaman, an Anglican, an anti-Jacobite, a Whig, and someone who now lives in the Bahamas. He supported Queen Anne and now supports King George, a Protestant Hanover. Although both Jennings and the Captain are considered members of "The Flying Gang," a name ex-privateers and naval men give to themselves, they'd never consider sailing in consort.

Captain Hornigold's ability to find medical supplies for the stricken sailors is complicated by his relationship with Thomas Walker, who was judge of the vice admiralty court of the Bahamas before the Queen Anne's War, and one of the few men who remains from the time when Nassau once thrived. Although Walker pretends to be anti-pirate, he's known to buy goods from the pirates themselves. Walker's double-dealing is an open secret in the Bahamas and Captain Hornigold poses a special threat to him. Walker wants to be the only leader in the Bahamas. Even tho' Walker moved his family from New Providence to nearby Great Abaco Island last June and then to Charles Town, he still acts as if he has authority in New Providence and that makes the procurement of medical supplies difficult.

I can tell the Captain realizes his dream for a pirate republic is in jeopardy. I have come to have a strange respect for the man who keeps me from my family. I know he's a good leader, but I can only wonder if his hope for a prosperous, democratic pirate republic is on the wane.

15

The Next Generation: Sam Bellamy and Stede Bonnet May–September 1717

MAY PASSES UNEVENTFULLY and for some unknown reason, the *Bennet* stays at anchor in the harbor. Although the hurricane season in the Bahamas will not begin for another month and the shipping lanes remain busy, Smithy says the *Bennet* will not sail for a while and when she does sail, she will not sail for very long or for very far.

The men are restless, shuttling back and forth between the *Bennet* and shore. Nassau is small, dilapidated, filthy, and just plain uninviting. Only prostitutes, tavern workers, merchants, carpenters, sailmakers, blacksmiths, ammunition dealers, smugglers, and pirates are the able-bodied people here. Often, five or more pirate vessels and an equal number of merchant vessels are anchored in the harbor at any one time, and that means four hundred to six hundred men.

Sometimes, the number increases to eight hundred, nine hundred, or even a thousand. Only the number of sick on shore grows; the healthy return to their vessels. Without an occasional vessel to plunder, there's no pay, and Nassau's not a place where seamen without money want to spend time. Without money, even the tavern becomes off-limits. And the rats, the rats are beyond mentioning! Even our cat and ratter dog can't keep them at bay on the *Bennet*.

Dr. Howell and I talk about the conditions. He has one word for them: "deplorable!" He says, "I'm doing what I can, but without adequate medicines, even I'm helpless. I know the Captain visits other ports in search of medical supplies but they're just plain scarce, even there. The Captain has told me he's notified when a vessel with a medical chest is brought into the harbor, but even these supplies don't go far enough. What frustrates me the most is that some illnesses are contagious and just incurable."

I commiserate with the good doctor and assure him that I see for myself that the sailors' living conditions make the spread of disease inevitable. I tell him he's doing his best and that's better than nothing.

When in port, Smithy and I spend a great deal of time together. He likes to chat at length about the war.

"During the war, everyone knew the Royal Navy was thousands of miles away. Only a few warships were spared for the West Indies. We rarely saw a navy ship at sea or in port.

"Privateers were essential! Really an extension of the Royal Navy. Rich merchants and plantation owners encouraged privateers. We disrupted the Spanish and the French traders and their trade routes. The way the merchants and owners saw it, the less Spanish and French competition, the higher the prices they could charge and the greater their profits would be. Remember, it all comes down to profits.

"Privateers prevented the Spanish King Philip's fleets from bringing the silver and gold from the mines to Spain. His treasury was running dry and he couldn't keep financing his wars.

"Queen Anne supported the privateers by granting commissions, you know, letters of marque, to encourage them to harass Spanish and French shipping. Her plan was for the government to share in the profits from the captured vessels. Well, hah! Profits that rightly belonged to the government went into the pockets of local officials. Fraud was out of control. The privateers were good business for all.

"The letters of marque expired at the end of the war. With no war, those merchants and those plantation owners who once needed the privateers turned on them. With nothing else to do, privateers had no choice but to continue doing what they were doing before the war ended. Once they called us privateers, now they call us pirates. Huh! Navy seamen who'd been discharged, stranded, and found no work, joined us. Tell you what, that's no way to treat those who served their country! No way!

"We're more than a nuisance. We affected profits. They couldn't tolerate us no more. Rich merchants and plantation owners needed a way to end piracy and they found a receptive ear in the new king, and what's more frustrating, those who're complaining the loudest are still buying pirated goods and making nice profits."

"What hypocrites!" I sharply sympathize.

I leave Smithy and join the men in a longboat who are going ashore. When in town, I always look for a newspaper even tho' they generally are weeks old. Every once in a while, I'm lucky to find *The Boston News-Letter* or two that carry stories about what's happening in the colonies, and once in a while, a story about the West Indies. The tone of these stories has changed over time. Stories about pirates now use the words rogue, abominable, wicked, ruthless, notorious, barbarous, evil, untrustworthy, cruel, villainous, vile, blood-thirsty, inhuman, and my personal least favorite, cutthroat. It's obvious with whom the newspaper's loyalties are.

I know the Captain had great hopes of creating a pirate republic on the island of New Providence. He anticipated the actions of the rich and the increase in naval ships, but the West Indies is a big place and pirates have an advantage by sailing sloops rather than frigates. Sloops are faster, with less draft, and with a single mast, they can easily hide in the shallow coves.

The Captain should have known that Jennings and his Jacobite sympathizers would try to oppose everything he did. Jennings has no interest in the republic. He's a landowner in both Jamaica and Bermuda and is only interested in another Jacobite rebellion. To make matters worse, the islands in the Caribbean, especially Jamaica and Barbados, are great places for the king to exile Jacobite troublemakers.

Rumors float around Nassau that the British Admiralty gave orders "to burn, sink, or destroy pirate vessels." The ante is raised.

In early July, Captain Thache makes one of his rare appearances in Nassau. I chat with Scotty, who says, "Did you notice Thache was speaking with our former quartermaster, Mr. Howard? Wonder what they're talking about. You know, Captain Thache doesn't stay long in Nassau, never does. Something's on his mind."

"I've noticed Captain Thache's appearances are brief. Never does stay long, never mingles much, very restless, very restless," I reply.

True to form, in a few days, Captain Thache's sloop is no longer in the harbor. I comment to Scotty, "Captain Thache is gone, suppose you're not surprised."

A few days later, I take a longboat ashore and make my way along with the others to The Lion and the Unicorn. I enjoy the tavern because I'm somewhat of a novelty. Even when I enter with crew members other than the Captain or Smithy, I receive a warm welcome. This day is no different. "Join our table, Sam," or "Sam, have a place for you," or "Have some stories for you, Sam."

They don't know my name is really "Abby" and I'm a girl. I'm not about to tell them. So "Sam" I am.

I always learn something new during my tavern visits and I hope today will be no different. I join a group I had sailed with. They now sail for other captains. That's not unusual. Seamen constantly change vessels and captains.

"Tavern keeper, a tankard for me friend," someone at the table calls out.

The conversation soon turns to Captain Bellamy and his friend Paulsgrave Williams.

"You know them?" A sailor asks me.

The incident with the *Marianne* of Domingue and the *St. Marie* of Rochelle flashes through my mind. I also remember their taking our *Benjamin* right from under us and disrespecting Captain Hornigold. "Oh, yes. They sailed with us as our guests for a couple of months."

"Well, have you heard about the *Whydah*?"

Before I can answer, the sailor next to me speaks up, "Aye, you mean the *Whydah Gally*? The slave ship?"

"What I hear is when the *Whydah* was on the last leg of her voyage back to England after delivering a galley full of slaves to the slave market to Jamaica, it was February, well, Captain Bellamy in the *Sultana* and Captain Williams in the *Marianne* spotted her heading towards the Windward Passage. They just couldn't resist. Fully rigged, three hundred tons, eighteen six-pound cannons with room for more, not to mention her three masts and crew of one hundred fifty. She was built for passengers, cargo, and slaves. I hear she's quite a beauty. Who'd turn down that sorta ship?"

"So what happened?"

"I hear it was quite a chase. Captain Bellamy in the *Sultana* and Captain Williams in the *Marianne*."

"Paulsgrave Williams?"

"Aye, that's what I hear."

"Thought they sail with La Buse," interrupts one of the men at the table.

"The Frenchman?" inquires another.

"Aye, the Frenchman, the buzzard. What happened to him?"

"Cut out around New Year's. I hear he talks about sailing to Brazil or the African coast and then to Madagascar. Too many British warships around here, he said."

"So what happened with the chase?"

"Aye, so Captain Prince of the *Whydah* got off a couple of rounds from his pursuit guns and the chase was on. Three days later, Bellamy and Williams drew alongside the *Whydah* and their men displayed their weapons: cutlasses, muskets, and grenades. You know, the usual stuff. Captain Prince thought better of trying to resist and gave up, was in the Windward Passage between Cuba and Hispaniola, exhausted, I guess."

"Poor Captain Prince."

"Then what?"

"Bellamy took the *Whydah* and did the gentlemanly thing, gave Prince the *Sultana* so Prince and his men could get home."

"Well, Bellamy and Williams discovered the *Whydah*'s a real treasure trove. Her hold's piled high with elephant tusks for ivory, cinchona wood for quinine, and sacks and barrels of sugar, molasses, and indigo plants. I hear they discovered silver and gold in the hold, sacks of silver and gold, bags of gold dust, African jewelry, and a box of East Indian jewels. Twenty to thirty thousand pounds worth of silver and gold. Enough for fifty pounds a man.

One sailor says, "I hear a few men left the ship along the way with their shares. Don't know what happened next."

Another adds, "Hear Captain Bellamy took the *Whydah* to his safe haven, Blanco Islet in the Virgin Islands, and had her cannons increased from eighteen to twenty-eight. Understand that he in the *Whydah* and Williams in the *Marianne* sailed north so Bellamy could see his girlfriend, Maria Hallett, on Cape Cod."

"What about Williams?"

"Well, Williams wanted to see his mum and sisters on Block Island off the Rhode Island coast. You know he lived on Block Island before turning pirate. His stepfather lived there too before he was lost at sea. Williams' wife still lives in Newport, I'm told. He didn't want to see her or his kids."

"Hmm. I heard about the girlfriend. Wonder where Bellamy and Williams are now?"

I couldn't wait to get back to the *Bennet* so I could tell Cooky and Stewy, "Fifty pounds a man! Wow!"

When I return to the *Bennet,* I hear our boatswain's brass whistle and watch our men raise the anchors and hoist the sails. The *Bennet* passes through the western entrance of the harbor and Smithy hears my usual question, "Where're we going?"

"Captain wants to sail around Cuba to see what's going on. Hear there's more navy activity.

"You've met the new quartermaster, John Martin. Howard left with Thache when Thache was in Nassau. I told you something was up when we saw them talking."

We sail between Cuba and Jamaica and encounter one of the king's warships, the *Winchelsea.* "Not a good sign," I think to myself. We saw the *Winchelsea* earlier in the year when the Captain and Napping were pursuing a fine Dutch merchant ship.

Once again, our sloop is faster than the *Winchelsea* and she soon disappears over the horizon. The Captain feels uneasy with the increasing Royal Navy presence and tells Smithy, "Think it wise to head back to Nassau. Seen what we came to see."

The *Bennet* drops anchor and Smithy comments to me, "Did you see? Thache's sloop, the *Adventure*, is back in the harbor. Wonder what he wants and how long he'll stay this time?"

A week or so later, it must be early September, I'm standing by the rail with Smithy when a sloop sails into the harbor. Smithy turns to me, commenting, "Strange, she's flying a black flag. Never seen her before."

We take a closer look. "See, she's once a beauty, a real beauty, an about eighty-ton sloop, I guess. Pretty new, built up north, possibly Newport, can see from her design and her beams. Looks like she was changed from a merchant vessel to a working pirate vessel. Someone put serious money into her. But now, she's pretty much beaten up, aye, pretty much beaten up. Looks like she's in a battle and got the worst of it. Wonder what happened? Real shame, aye, real shame. Was a real beauty."

I quickly finish my chores, grab a bite of breakfast from the galley, and give Cooky and Stewy a quick account of what we just saw. I brush off their questions with, "Need to catch the longboat leaving for shore," and dash off.

The longboat's waiting, "Quick, boy, quick!"

And so I'm on my way to The Lion and the Unicorn for the second day in a row.

When I enter, everyone's talking about the pirate captain who's just arrived. I join a group to listen.

"Seen that gentleman captain?"

"Gentleman captain? Hah! Sails into harbor standing on his battered deck in his dressing gown, a dressing gown, no less." Everyone at the table roars with laughter. Their comments and questions follow rapidly.

"Sure's a dandy. I hear his name's Bonnet, Steve Bonnet."

"No, not Steve, Stede!"

"Major Stede Bonnet."

"Major, huh?"

"Major in his island's militia in the last war, I guess."

"His island?"

"Aye, Barbados."

"Where's Barbados?" a voice in the group asks.

"Isn't Barbados one of them small southern Caribbean islands, British, down near the coast of Colombia?"

"Aye, think you're right. Sixteen to seventeen days sailing from here," someone answers.

"Stede, hmm, strange. Sure it's not Steve?"

"I hear he inherited his father's estate, a sugar plantation. His family's been in Barbados for generations. Must have money to burn."

Then one of the more seasoned sailors speaks up, "He's a wealthy landowner from Barbados, all right. Under Barbados law, Bonnet got the title of major by being a landowner. I doubt he spent a day in the local militia." And that brings a laugh from the others at his table.

"Major, hah!

"I'm told a nice-looking sloop sailed into Bridgetown Harbor one day from Charles Town. Bonnet liked her looks and bought her, paid out of his own pocket. Her captain, Captain Malbone, was happy to sell at the price Bonnet offered. Bonnet liked her name too, *Revenge*, and said he'd keep it, a slight at Queen Anne. Bonnet's one of those Jacobite sympathizers, you know."

Another at the table pipes up, "Hmm? Too rich to steal a vessel!" And everyone laughs.

"He don't know much about sailing, I hear. Wants to be a pirate for the adventure."

"Well, Bonnet commissioned a local shipyard to fit out the *Revenge* for pirating. Wanted her to be able to sail with at least a dozen guns and a crew of over one hundred. I heard he wanted the captain's quarters fitted for a gentleman of his stature and to include his most precious library.

"Then he hired a crew and paid them out of his own money."

Another of the seasoned sailors couldn't wait to finish the story. "Then one spring night in April or May, under the cover of darkness, the *Revenge*, outfitted with six cannons, a crew, and provisions, slipped out of Carlisle Bay. They tell me Bonnet left behind his wife and three small children, including a baby. Escaping from his wife . . . marital problems, so they say."

One of the younger sailors adds, "Should've shown her who's boss, he should."

"Nah, he's a gentleman. Just run." That brings more laughter.

"As you say, name of his ship's *Revenge*. His revenge's leaving her," someone jokes.

"I hear Captain Thache's looking for him."

"Someone needs to tell Thache that Bonnet's not able to leave his sloop. Too banged up. Convalescing."

"I didn't know pirates have the luxury of convalescence, con-va-les-cence. Big word. Thought us pirates just got hurt and either got better or died. Convalescence, hah!" And they all laugh again.

The next day, I head back to the tavern in hopes of hearing more sensational news. I join the group I sat with the day before. A few men who sailed with Bonnet on the *Revenge* have joined the group and share their story.

"After the *Revenge* leaves Barbados, we sail north for a couple of months and wind up off the Virginia Capes. We take a sloop under Captain Joseph Palmer of Barbados. The Major puts a prize crew aboard and they sail her south to an inlet in Carolina, the Cape Fear River, and she's used to careen the *Revenge*. Then she's burned. The Major says she's burned because she's from Barbados and he don't want word to get back to Barbados that he's a pirate. Now calls himself Edwards, Captain Edwards."

Another at the table picks up the story. "After the *Revenge's* careened, we sail back north, past the Virginia Capes, to New York. Off the eastern tip of Long Island, we seize a sloop, forgot her name, bound for the West Indies, then on to Gardiner's Island where the Major releases our captives and purchases supplies. Then sail south, down the coast."

His friend continues, "It's late August when the *Revenge* takes a brigantine from Boston and then a sloop from Barbados. The Major orders both to sail back up to the Cape Fear River where they're used to careen the *Revenge*. He lets the brigantine go but burns the sloop because she's from Barbados.

"We sail south again, this time to the coast of Florida and the Spanish wrecks. On the way, the *Revenge* encounters what the Major thinks is a merchant ship. Turns out she's a Spanish warship guarding the wrecks. The Major orders us to engage her. Big, big, big mistake! Thirty to forty casualties, including the Major. He's in pretty bad shape. He's in no condition to captain the *Revenge* so his quartermaster takes over.

"You can see she's damaged pretty bad. Decide to sail here for repairs. With the remaining men who're able and our vessel's condition, sailing took four to five days. So, here we are. Pretty sad state, pretty sad state we're in."

I go back to the *Bennet* and tell Cooky and Stewy what I learned at the tavern the past few days. Stewy thinks for a moment and then comments, "Neither Bellamy nor Bonnet has experience as a privateer. They are unseasoned, hotheaded, don't know pirate ways. That don't bode well for either, don't bode well for either."

16

One Premonition Comes True
September–November 1717

ALL IS QUIET around Major Bonnet's *Revenge* for the next day or two and then everything changes. The carpenters and the sailmakers arrive and begin making the necessary repairs. The arms dealers increase her cannons to twelve.

"Smithy, what's going on?" I ask.

"Well, shortly after Bonnet arrived, Thache rowed over to the *Revenge* and saw that Major Bonnet was in no condition to captain the *Revenge*. What they talked about, I don't really know. I'm sure we'll find out one of these days. All I know is Bonnet's *Revenge* is being repaired."

Over the next few days, we watch as Thache hires more men and resupplies the *Revenge*.

A week or two later, both Bonnet's *Revenge* and Thache's old sloop, the *Adventure*, leave the harbor. "Hmm, looks like they're sailing in consort. Wonder where they're going?" Smithy mumbles.

"Probably north, if they're smart," Scotty replies. "Avoiding the hurricanes. If this Bonnet character sails with Thache for a while, Thache will teach him a thing or two about sailing and about being a pirate. Maybe when Bonnet comes back, that's if he comes back, he'll be better for it."

With Thache and Bonnet gone, the harbor takes on an eerie quiet except for activity around the *Bennet*.

Scotty and I make our way to the tavern and find a group who are in animated conversation concerning Major Bonnet.

One fellow calls out, "Have a tankard, boy!"

"Mighty obliged," I politely reply.

One of the men remembers I was at the tavern when Major Bonnet's *Revenge* first dropped anchor. He knows I've been away from the tavern for a few days. "Well, here's what happened while you we're gone. Captain Thache rowed over to the *Revenge* and had a chat with the Major. Thache says he'll sail Major Bonnet's sloop for him and Bonnet can rest in his quarters and read. Bonnet had little choice and agreed. The matter was brought to the survivors of Bonnet's crew and they voted that Thache should captain the *Revenge* till the Major recovered from his wounds. Bonnet's happy with that. He can stay in his library and read his books. Thache's happy. He has a more impressive sloop and by sailing in consort with his old sloop, he can make a name for himself. Funny how things work out. Thache's real savvy.

"Aye! Captain Thache had the *Revenge* repaired and refitted before she left the harbor. He increased her guns to twelve and her crew to over one hundred. He moved Hornigold's former quartermaster, William Howard, from his sloop, the *Adventure*, to the *Revenge* and promoted his quartermaster, Richards, to captain the *Adventure*. Then they sailed off, north, I'm told."

A few days later, Scotty reports that Captain Napping's vessel isn't in the harbor. I finally spot Smithy, "Where's Captain Napping?"

"Napping is out sailing with Thomas Nichols for awhile. He may be back."

I'm occupied catching up on the gossip at The Lion and the Unicorn while Captain Hornigold's busy changing vessels again. He's leaving the *Bennet* and moving to a larger vessel, the *Ranger*. No longer will he be sailing a cramped sloop. His new vessel will be a two-masted square-sailed brigantine with thirty guns.

A few days later, Captain Hornigold decides to venture out again. Smithy's excited because he hasn't sailed the *Ranger*.

We prepare to sail, and Captain Hornigold orders Smithy to head north rather than south.

Around the seventeenth of October, Captain Hornigold and our brigantine, *Ranger*, are off the North Carolina coast in the shipping lanes between the Caribbean and the small colonial cities of Philadelphia, New York, Boston, and Newport. The *Ranger* captures two merchant vessels, plunders what provisions that are needed, and sails on north.

The next day, the *Ranger* is off the Virginia Capes when we meet Major Bonnet's *Revenge*. Captain Hornigold's former quartermaster, William Howard, is still Thache's quartermaster. Major Bonnet's in his quarters enjoying his library. Captain Thache's sloop, *Adventure*, under the command of Richards, sails nearby.

Shortly after we arrive, the *Revenge* and the *Ranger* sail in consort and capture Captain Prichard's vessel from St. Lucia.

That evening, Mr. Howard joins Smithy and me on the *Ranger*. I can see that he's envious. Captain Hornigold sails a brigantine while Captain Thache still sails a sloop. Mr. Howard makes a point to tell us how busy they'd been.

"Well," he begins, "after leaving Nassau in mid-September, Captain Thache took us up the coast. The current and the prevailing winds made sailing easy. By the end of September, I would say, we're here off the Virginia Capes. Must have been around the twenty-ninth of September when we captured the sloop *Betty* of Virginia. We plundered some pipes of Madeira wine and some goods that could be sold. Thache wanted to show the Major that he's tough, so he had me drill holes in the *Betty*'s hull and we watched her sink with what cargo was left in her hold.

"We sailed up the coast to Delaware Bay. All the vessels sailing to and from Philadelphia go through there. Stayed a week or so and must have captured a dozen vessels. Don't remember them all. Do remember one that's sailing from Liverpool and Dublin. Captain Codd's her master. She had one hundred fifty passengers, mostly indentured servants going to their new life in America. They'd never seen a pirate vessel or a pirate before, they're terrified, real terrified. What should we do with all those terrified indentured servants? After Thache took some goods from the vessel's hold, he told Captain Codd to continue on to Philadelphia. Seems funny now, all those terrified indentured servants.

"Captured two snows, double-masted square-sail vessels, as they're leaving the Delaware River. One's the *Spofford* and the other's the *Sea Nymph*. The *Spofford*'s loaded with staves for Ireland. Captain Thache ordered the staves thrown overboard and then let her sail off. The *Sea Nymph* was sailing under Captain Budger of Bristol and was loaded with wheat for Oporto, Portugal. Thache kept her and converted her into a pirate vessel.

"The Delaware River's a great spot but we needed to keep moving. Don't want to be an easy target. Captain Thache won't stay in one place for too long. After a week, we sailed down to the Virginia Capes.

"The week when we're waiting for you gave us time to capture a couple of vessels bound for Virginia. One's Captain Peter Peters' sloop sailing from Madeira Island off Africa. Took twenty-seven barrels of Madeira wine and thirty indentured servants. Thache ordered her mast cut down and left her to run aground.

"Then there's Captain Grigg's sloop from London. Took thirty indentured servants. Thache ordered her mast cut down and she sank.

"Then there's another sloop, this one's sailed from Antigua and belonged to New York. Don't remember what happened to her.

"Then there's Captain Farmer's sloop. Poor Captain Farmer, he'd been looted by pirates already. Thache took her mast and anchors and put the thirty indentured servants we got from Captain Grigg's sloop on board. Without a mast, she drifted ashore.

"The last vessel I remember was Captain Sipkins' sloop. Converted her into a twelve-gun sloop."

As Mr. Howard rows back to Bonnet's *Revenge*, Smithy asks me, "Well, what do you think, boy? Hmm?"

"With all those vessels, what did they get? Didn't hear any mention of silver or gold, did you? So, what did they get?"

The next day, Captain Hornigold gives Smithy orders to sail for home, Nassau.

We sail south. That gives me time to visit with Smithy. "What do you think about sailing all the way up north to meet Thache? What's that all about?"

"Not sure, not sure at all" is Smithy's reply, shaking his head. "Maybe the Captain's concerned that Thache's taking too many risks. We all hear that Spotswood, the lieutenant governor of Virginia, wants Thache bad, real bad. Thache's disrupting trade in Delaware, Virginia, and the Carolinas. Spotswood's not one to be trifled with. So maybe the Captain's concerned for Thache's safety. Or maybe the Captain thinks Thache is stirring up trouble for all us pirates. Or maybe the Captain just wants to show off the *Ranger*. She's certainly more impressive than the sloops the Captain and Thache been sailing. The *Ranger*'s fit for the leader of the pirate republic. I'll bet Thache'll get a more impressive vessel."

We arrive back in Nassau and find the harbor unusually quiet.

Several days later, the *Marianne,* the French sloop we captured in April a year ago at Port Mariel, now under the command of Paulgraves Williams, drops anchor in the harbor. She's still painted blue and yellow. Captain Williams' subdued and asks whether we've heard about the *Whydah*.

A few days later, a snow, the *Ann,* under the command of Richard Noland, Captain Hornigold's old friend, drops anchor in the harbor.

Smithy's excited. "Have you seen the *Ann*? She's in terrible shape. Looks like she's been beaten up by a terrible storm. Noland and the Captain go back to their periagua days, and Noland was Hornigold's agent in Nassau when Dr. Howell went to stay with William Pindar. Noland became one of the Captain's crew when we sailed to Hispaniola. He deserted when Bellamy took our *Benjamin*. Noland's been sailing with Bellamy and Williams ever since. Wonder what happened?"

I hear that Captain Williams and Captain Noland are at The Lion and the Unicorn and telling what happened after the *Sultana* and the *Marianne* captured the *Whydah*. Smithy is more than willing to go ashore with me. At the tavern, we find a group of sailors gathered in hushed silence around Williams and Noland.

Captain Williams' saying, "Captain Bellamy sailed the *Whydah*."

Captain Noland interrupts, "and I'm Captain Bellamy's quartermaster."

Captain Williams resumes, "I was captain of the *Marianne* and sailed in consort with the *Whydah*. We're heading north, seizing and plundering vessels as we went. Was April and we found ourselves off the Virginia coast. Between us, we must have had one hundred thirty men. The *Whydah*'s still loaded to capacity. Nothing's been offloaded after we seized her in the Windward Passage. She still has everything she received in exchange for the slaves that she sold in Jamaica. Everything in the hold was being shipped back to England. Bellamy wanted to show his girlfriend's parents and the town's naysayers he made good and wasn't just some out-of-work sailor. The only space we had for plunder was in the *Marianne*.

"So, here we're off the Virginia Capes. A violent storm came out of nowhere: four days, three nights. After the storm, a dense fog rolled in. Was a very dense fog. We lost sight of the *Whydah* and spent the next day plugging leaks and pumping water caused by the storm. We were just trying to keep the *Marianne* afloat."

Captain Noland interjects, "On the seventh of April, the fog lifted and the *Whydah* found herself in the middle of the shipping lanes off the Virginia Capes near the mouth of Chesapeake Bay. That morning, we captured a merchant vessel, the sloop *Agnes*. She was sailing from Barbados to Virginia with rum, sugar, molasses, and a variety of European goods. The same day, we captured the *Ann*, a snow, and the *Endeavor*, a pink. Five days later, we captured a vessel from Leith, Scotland. The *Agnes* was damaged and leaking. After she was unloaded, Bellamy ordered her destroyed. He let the *Endeavor* and the vessel from Leith be on their way but added the *Ann* to our growing fleet. Made me her captain."

Captain Williams speaks up, "A few days later, those of us on the *Marianne* spotted the *Whydah* and we resumed sailing north in consort: the *Whydah*, the *Marianne*, and the *Ann*.

"At Block Island off the Rhode Island coast, the *Marianne* left the *Whydah* and the *Ann*, and I set off to visit my mum, sisters, and niece. They live on the island. That was convenient because I have friends who'd fence all the goods in the *Marianne*'s hold. Bellamy in the *Whydah* and Noland in the *Ann* sailed on to Eastham, near the tip of Cape Cod. As I said before, Bellamy wanted to see his girlfriend and to show off the *Whydah*. We planned to meet near Damariscove Island off the Maine coast."

Captain Williams pauses for a time. His mind appears to wander, and he begins to digress. He seems to be trying to understand his own life.

"See, summer of fifteen, Bellamy and I met at a tavern, Boston or Block Island or Newport, can't remember which. As we talked, he told me he's wanting to make some money so he's no longer an out-of-work sailor. I told him I'm wanting to leave my wife and kids and to get some excitement in my life. Well, as we talked, I discovered he had sailing skills and I had access to money, so we decided I'd buy a small sloop and we'd sail together.

"We hired about twenty or so men, bought provisions, and sailed south. We sailed and kept hearing about the hurricane and the destruction of the Spanish plate fleet, so we decided to head to the Florida coast to fish the wrecks. Got there in early January, year last, and found those wrecks were all fished out. Well, sometime towards the end of January, we're chased off by the Spanish. Had no interest in sailing back north, so we sailed down to the Gulf of Honduras and traded our sloop for two periaguas. Several logmen from the Bay of Campeche joined us. Also picked up a Miskito Indian, John Julian's his name. John said he knew how to pilot along the coast."

I can see Captain Noland's restless. "Paulsgrave, let's get back to the *Whydah*."

At this point, Captain Williams takes a long pause. He's getting choked up and I think he can't go on.

"I was there, Paulsgrave. Want me to finish?" Captain Noland asks.

"Give me a minute, I'll be able," Captain Williams replies.

Captain Williams takes a long draw of his beer and then continues, "Dropped anchor at Block Island. After the *Marianne*'s offloaded, a nor'easter rolled in. I've lived in New England all my life and have seen nor'easters, never seen one that bad. I knew the *Whydah* and the *Ann* had a day or two of sailing, and I didn't know whether they made Eastham, anchored in a safe harbor, or were riding out the storm at sea. Worried, plenty worried. Neither Bellamy nor Noland was from these parts and they had no experience with how violent a nor'easter can be. Only could hope they were safe.

"Well, after visiting my family and fencing our goods, the *Marianne* set sail for Damariscove Island off the Maine coast. We stopped at Monhegan Island on the way, maybe around the twenty-ninth of April. Stayed for a few days and sailed up to Damariscove Island and waited and waited for the *Whydah*. Finally, maybe on the twentieth of May, the captain of a whaling boat told us about the wreck of the *Whydah* off Cape Cod. Heard all but two were lost. My friend, Sam Bellamy, dead. With that news, we began to make our way here. Seized a few vessels along the way, but finally made it here."

Captain Noland then begins to speak, "After the *Marianne* left the *Whydah* and the *Ann*, we continued to sail north. On the twenty-fourth of April, while passing Nantucket, just south of Cape Cod, we seized the *Mary Anne*, a pink with a cargo of seven thousand gallons of Madeira wine. She was sailing from Naratasket Harbor on route to New York. Then we seized the *Fisher*, a sloop. Her cargo was tobacco and hides. She was sailing from Virginia to Boston. Now we have four vessels: the *Whydah*, the *Ann*, the *Mary Anne*, and the *Fisher.*

"Two days later, the twenty-sixth of April, the weather deteriorated rapidly. Around four in the afternoon, a very thick fog rolled in. The *Whydah* put a light on her stern.

"Around ten that night, the wind whipped up to about seventy miles an hour and heavy rain squalls began pounding our vessels. The waves were above thirty feet and lightning turned night into day.

"Montgomery, the former captain of my vessel, the *Ann*, told Bellamy he sailed Cape Cod and Eastham before, so Bellamy gave him the helm of the *Ann*. She became the lead vessel. I swear Montgomery intentionally guided *Ann* towards the sandbars and the shore. When Bellamy discovered the *Whydah* was being driven into the shore, it was too late. The *Whydah,* with all her cargo, rode too low in the water and ran aground on a sandbar. The pounding waves ripped her apart. Those who attempted to swim to shore couldn't make it, the water was just too cold.

"The *Ann*, being a snow and smaller and lighter, sailed over the sandbars and turned back to the open sea. She met up with the *Fisher* and they rode out the storm together.

"The *Fisher* had her own problems. She began to leak and was abandoned. Ultimately, she sank."

"The *Mary Anne*. What about the *Mary Anne*?" Someone asks.

Captain Noland replies, "Well, don't rightly know, but I think she was thrown up on shore after taking a beating.

"You can see the storm that took the *Whydah* did great damage to the *Ann* even tho' she rode out the storm at sea. My men patched her up as good as they could. Sailing here was long and arduous. Most of my men either starved to death or deserted. Can't blame them for deserting."

We are dumbstruck. Slowly, in small groups, we leave the tavern in disbelief. I head back to the *Ranger* to tell Cooky and Stewy. A dark mood hangs over the *Ranger* that night.

17

Don't Say You're a Pirate
November–December 1717

W HEN THE *RANGER* arrived back in Nassau the beginning of November after sailing up north to meet Thache, she remained in the harbor. Except for the stories at The Lion and the Unicorn, the days and weeks simply blended together.

One day Captain Hornigold calls me to his quarters. "I'll be away for a few weeks. The *Ranger* will stay here, and John Martin will keep you busy. Have some business to attend to."

One day in early December when Smithy and I are at the tavern, an old sailor enters and calls out, "More news about the *Whydah*." We all gather around.

"After Captain Williams left Captain Bellamy to visit his mum on Block Island, Captain Bellamy captured another vessel, also named *Mary Anne*. Her cargo's wine from Boston to New York. Bellamy sent seven men as his prize crew to sail the *Mary Anne*. Soon, the *Whydah* and her new prize became separated by dense fog. The sky blackened and the winds stiffened. The *Mary Anne,* battered by high waves and ferocious winds, was pushed towards the coast. Finally, she ran aground on a small island south of Eastham. Everyone on the *Mary Anne* found themselves on dry land. Some locals spotted the wreck and Bellamy's men were transported to the mainland."

"What then?"

"Well, they made their way to a tavern and one of them was so drunk he blurted out, "We're pirates." That did it! All seven were arrested and were awaiting trial. That was the end of April. I don't know what happened to them."

After I hear that the survivors of the wrecks were in jail, I'm almost afraid to go to the tavern. All I hear lately is bad news. But when I do venture back a few days later, the talk is about Captain Thache and Major Bonnet.

"News about the twenty-eighth of November," one of the sailors is saying. "Thache and Bonnet captured the slave ship *La Concorde* of Nantes, France, near the island of Martinique. A galleon, forty guns. Thache took her for his flagship and renamed her the *Queen Anne's Revenge*. He kept Bonnet's *Revenge* to sail in consort. Now Thache has three vessels: the *QAR,* the *Revenge,* and his original small sloop, the *Adventure.*

Smithy turns to me as we leave the tavern, "Bad, very bad. Nothing good will come out of that. Thache will be even more reckless and that'll be his downfall."

On my next visit to the tavern, the news is again grim. A sailor is recounting what he heard. "The seven pirates from the *Mary Anne*—Thomas Baker, John Brown, Peter Cornelius Hoff, Hendrick Quintor, John Schuan, Thomas South, and Simon Van Vorst—were all transferred to the Boston jail where they joined Thomas Davis, one of the two survivors from the *Whydah*. The other survivor, John Julian, a Miskito Indian, was sold off as a slave because he had dark skin.

"The seven from the *Mary Anne* were tried first. Thomas South, a carpenter, was found not guilty; he convinced the court that Bellamy had forced him to join his crew. The others were not so lucky. They were all convicted and hanged at Boston's Scarlett's Wharf on the fifteenth of November. Sad day, very sad day. You probably know most of them.

"The court then tried Thomas Davis, the other survivor from the *Whydah*. The court found him not guilty. He too convinced the court that Bellamy had forced him to join his crew."

Upon hearing this news, Smithy and I walk back to the wharf in silence. On our way, he turns to me and quietly says, "John Brown—me and you knew John Brown."

"Oh?" I reply.

"Aye, he sailed with us on the *Benjamin*. Was over a year ago. Captain Hornigold met LeVasseur and we sailed around Cuba to the Isle of Pines to careen our vessels, and then spent three months camped out on Hispaniola during hurricane season. Captain LeVasseur took John Brown off a Dutch ship that carried logwood from the Bay of Campeche. We had left Nassau and as we reached the Cuban coast, John's ship came sailing east. He spent the summer with us on Hispaniola."

With that, it all comes back to me. "I remember Bellamy calling 'parley' and the men choosing between sailing with Captain Hornigold or with him. John Brown chose Bellamy and they took our *Benjamin*. Yes, I remember him very well."

We walk for a while and then Smithy says, "Peter Cornelius Hoff, aye, Peter Cornelius Hoff. Odd fellow. Dutch? Swedish? Old for a working pirate. Wasn't a pirate till Bellamy got his hands on him. Bellamy captured a coastal trader, his captain was Cornelison, I believe. Was in the Gulf of Honduras, Bellamy took Huff off that vessel."

"Yes, I remember Peter quite well. I spent time talking to him when we were on Hispaniola. He talked about wanting to get back to Sweden to see his family. He left home at sixteen and was now in his thirties, that's a long time to be away. He didn't want to be a pirate, so I couldn't understand why he chose to sail with Bellamy. He said he tried to escape but was caught and whipped. Had a better chance to stop being a pirate if he sailed with Captain Hornigold to Nassau. His bad choice got him hanged. Sad. I liked Peter and his interesting stories. Was hoping he'd get home to Sweden someday. I know what it's like to miss your family."

"John Julian—me and you knew John Julian," Smithy whispers.

"Yes, John was only a few years older than I, a Miskito Indian, he said. He claimed to be trained as a vessel's pilot, and joined one of Bellamy's periaguas in the Gulf of Honduras. John and I became friends during those months on Hispaniola. He taught me how to spearfish. Now he's a slave. Hope he'll be alright. I was hoping, because we're friends, that he'd choose to sail with Captain Hornigold rather than with Bellamy. I was wrong. Can't picture John being a slave, not John. He's so proud, so independent. Not good for John, not good at all."

We resume our walk in silence and I keep feeling a tightness around my neck. Then I remember "Pirates be hanged." I feel my neck again, all I find is my grandmother's locket.

We walk and I mentally list some of the people we'd encountered: Captain Bellamy and his crew, dead; Captain Napping sailing off somewhere; Captain LeVasseur sailing off the coast of Brazil or Africa; Captain Thache and Major Bonnet sailing up north; and who knows what Captain Jennings and Charles Vane are up to.

Smithy turns to me again, "As you remember, Bellamy left Hispaniola with ninety men and never returned to Nassau. When Paulsgrave Williams returned sailing the *Marianne*, I recognized some of his men as having sailed on the *Benjamin*. When Noland returned with the *Ann*, I recognized a few more who sailed on the *Benjamin*. I wonder who else sailed with us and went down with the *Whydah*?"

18

Weighing the King's Act of Grace
December 1717–February 1718

*E*ARLY IN DECEMBER, rumors began circulating that King George was offering a pardon to any pirate for his past deeds. I didn't know the terms of the pardon, whether Captain Hornigold would find them acceptable and, if he did, whether Cooky, Stewy, and I would be included. The noble concept of a democratic pirate republic was fading away like a sunset on the sea.

Shortly after Smithy and I return to the *Ranger*, I hear the familiar call, "Sam!" Captain Hornigold has returned from Jamaica. "Tell John Martin to alert the men. The *Ranger* sails in three days. Hurry! No time to lose! Tell him we'll be sailing to the shipping lanes in the Gulf of Mexico."

I hurry off to find Mr. Martin, all the time wondering whether this urgency has something to do with the Captain's visit to Jamaica and the king's pardon.

On the morning of the third day, the *Ranger* is at sea. Although the men had anticipated celebrating Christmas ashore, they're more than happy to be on the hunt again. *No prey, no pay.* Smithy sets our course for the Gulf of Mexico. "Four weeks," he says. "Not a long cruise but that will be long enough."

Around Christmas, the *Ranger* is in the shipping lanes between Vera Cruz, Mexico, and the western tip of Cuba. We capture a few vessels, take what we want but not too much, after all, this is the Christmas season, and let them go on their way. In a few days, the hold of the *Ranger* is brimming with treasures.

Then a day or two before the New Year, a large Dutch merchant ship comes along. She's well-armed with twenty-six guns but she doesn't have a fighting crew. We capture her with ease and make her our prize. Mr. Martin sends over a half a dozen men to sail her. Within a day, she's ready to join the *Ranger*.

A day or two later, we encounter an even larger Dutch merchant ship, the *Younge Abraham*, with thirty-six guns. We seize her as well, and Mr. Martin sends over another half a dozen men as our prize crew. Captain Hornigold's fleet is now three vessels and almost one hundred guns.

On the fifth of January, Captain Hornigold orders Smithy to sail for home, Nassau. The prevailing winds are light and sailing is slow, but neither the Captain nor Mr. Martin seem to be in much of a hurry. Our small fleet drops anchor in Nassau Harbor early in February. The four-week cruise has extended into eight weeks.

After the Captain tells Mr. Martin to have our men offload all three vessels and deliver our cargo to Richard Noland, his agent ashore, he turns to Smithy and me saying, "I'm thirsty, are you?"

The mood is festive at The Lion and the Unicorn. We join several of the Captain's old friends, Francis Leslie, Josiah Burgess, and Thomas Nichols. Captain Hornigold recounts our last cruise and our good fortune.

"So what's been happening around here?" he asks.

Captain Burgess takes a moment to gather his thoughts. "You won't believe it. The king did it!"

"Did what?"

"The king did it—the pardon. We'll all be pardoned!"

"I knew that's coming," the Captain says. "The details, give me the details."

"Well, on the fifth of September, King George issued a royal proclamation. Sent copies to Boston, New York, Bermuda, and Port Royal. Benjamin Bennett, the governor of Bermuda, sent his son here with copies. Knew you were at sea so I saved you a copy. Here."

The Captain gives the proclamation a quick read and then passes it over to me.

Captain Burgess continues, "Young Bennett says a frigate will arrive in Nassau towards the end of February and anyone interested can receive a certificate of safe passage. That certificate will be good till the royal governor arrives later in the year with official pardons."

Captain Leslie takes his turn. "That's not all that's happened. Upon hearing the news of a pardon, all the Jacobite sympathizers met at The Killiecrankie Tavern. Full house I'm told, real general council, it was, lots of shouting. Jennings, as their leader, argued they should take the pardon, but Vane, who, as you know, sailed with Jennings for years, was adamant they should not. They argued and argued but couldn't agree on nothing. Jennings got fed up and stormed out. He went back to the *Barsheba*, packed up, and, with about seven of his men, sailed off for Bermuda to take the king's pardon from Governor Bennett."

Captain Hornigold can't contain his laughter. "Been trying to get rid of Jennings for years. That easy, huh! But laughing aside, Jennings' smart, always was, got to give him credit for that. Didn't do much pirating but got rich when he attacked the Spanish storehouses on the Florida coast after Christmas of fifteen, and when he claimed the *St. Marie* in Bahia Honda and the cargo from the *Marianne*."

"You can be sure that both were with Governor Hamilton's blessing," Captain Leslie mumbles.

Captain Burgess adds, "The French and the Spanish governments were absolutely furious. Supposed to be a time of peace."

"I guess there's a little justice," Captain Leslie remarks. "Captain Jennings lost his land in Jamaica when King George, the German, declared him a pirate over all that."

I can see Captain Hornigold feels no sympathy for Captain Jennings. "He has enough land in Bermuda to make him happy as a country gentleman. One good thing's come from all this, Jennings sees the handwriting on the wall and gives up trying to make James Francis Edward Stuart king. So, we're done with Mr. Jennings!"

Captain Nichols is anxious to add his news. "Jennings' departure, you know how that works, created a lack of leadership. That upstart Vane was more than happy to fill it. He's been biding his time, waiting for this opportunity. He's hot-headed, unpredictable, and cruel, real cruel. He won't care about his men."

"That's right!" Captain Burgess adds. "Word has it, Vane took about sixteen followers with him to some secluded anchorage east of the harbor. We hear he commandeered a small merchant sloop named the *Lark* and made her into a fighting vessel. Sorry to say, we're not done with Charles Vane."

"What about the others?" Captain Hornigold asks.

"Well," Captain Leslie speaks up, "Christopher Winter and Nicholas Brown sailed to Cuba to hide among the Spanish. Edmund Condent and about one hundred of his men headed to Brazil and Africa to continue pirating. We hear a number of others booked passage on merchant vessels for Boston, Charles Town, Newport, and Port Royal. They just wanted to get out of Nassau and find a new life. I guess they're tired of hearing about their friends being hanged and wondering whether they're next.

"You know, many became pirates by accident, not by choice. Some sailed as privateers and their captains and their vessels continued doing what they're doing even tho' their commissions had expired. Others were taken off merchant vessels and forced to join pirate crews. The king's pardon ends their misfortune. If they say they didn't commit acts of piracy after the fourth of January, they can even keep the plunder they received before that date. Nice little nest egg if they had anything and saved some of it."

When we return to the *Ranger*, Smithy, whom I discover can't read well, asks me to read the proclamation out loud to the men who have gather. So I begin slowly because I know there's much to understand. I pause from time to time to add my own explanation.

I begin:

> *A Proclamation for the Suppressing of Pyrates.*
> *Whereas We have received Information . . . .*

"'We' refers to King George," I note.

> *That several Persons, Subjects of Great Britain,*
> *have, since the Twenty-Fourth Day of June, in the*
> *Year of our Lord, One Thousand Seven Hundred*
> *and Fifteen . . .*

"'Twenty-fourth of June 1715 refers to the official date the Queen Anne's War ended. That's the date the privateer commissions expired and seizures of French and Spanish vessels after that date were considered acts of piracy."

*committed divers Pyracies and Robberies upon
the High-Seas, in the West-Indies, or adjoining to
Our Plantations, which hath and may Occasion
great Damage to the Merchants of Great Britain,
and others Trading unto those Parts; And tho' We
have appointed such a Force as We Judge sufficient
for Suppressing the said Pyracies . . .*

"The king's saying he's increasing his navy in the West
Indies."

*Yet the more effectually to put an End to the same,
We have thought fit, by and with the Advice of
Our Privy Council, to Issue this Our Royal Proc-
lamation . . .*

"The king thinks a pardon is a better way to end piracy
in the Americas."

*And We do hereby Promise and Declare, That the
said Pyrates shall on, or before, the Fifth Day of
September, in the Year of our Lord, One Thousand Seven Hundred and Eighteen, Surrender him
or themselves, to One of Our Principal Secretar-
ies of State in Great Britain or Ireland, or to any
Governor or Deputy Governor of any of Our
Plantations or Dominions beyond the Seas . . .*

"You'll need to surrender to a governor or another British
official on or by the fifth of September of this year and
request a pardon."

> *every such Pyrate and Pyrates so surrendering him*
> *or themselves, as aforesaid, shall have our gra-*
> *cious Pardon of and for such his or their Pyracy*
> *or Pyracies, by him or them committed before the*
> *fifth day of January next ensuing . . .*

"And you'll be forgiven for all your acts of piracy committed before the fifth of last January.

"The last part of the king's proclamation deals with rewards, so I'll skip that and just read the very end."

> *Given at Our Court, at Hampton-Court, the fifth*
> *Day of September, One Thousand Seven Hundred*
> *Seventeen, in the fourth Year of Our Reign.*
>   *George R.*
>   *God save the King*

I see that most of the men don't understand what I just read, so I say, "If you get a pardon on or by the fifth of September of this year, you can't be arrested, tried, convicted, and hanged for any acts of piracy you committed before the fifth of January of this year."

When I finish, one of the men asks, "What happens to all the plunder we seized before the fifth of January? Can we keep it?"

"The proclamation doesn't say you can't, so I assume you can because you're pardoned for all those acts."

Another speaks up, "What if I don't ask for a pardon?"

"Well, you're where you are now. You can be arrested, tried, convicted, and hanged." That draws a collective groan.

Another asks, "What if I get arrested before the fifth of September but haven't asked for a pardon. Could I get a pardon then?"

"The proclamation doesn't say you cannot so long as you can find an official who can issue the pardon."

"But what if I commit piracy on or after the fifth of January?"

"Then you can be arrested, tried, sentenced, and hanged for those acts of piracy."

"Even if I have a pardon?"

"Yes, even if you have a pardon because the pardon only applies to acts of piracy committed before the fifth of this past January."

I look over to Smithy. He needs time for the idea of not being a pirate to sink in. Then, being satisfied that he has heard properly, he shrugs, snorts, and leaves again for shore.

The men who gathered walk away in twos and threes. I go to the Captain's quarters to see if he needs anything before I settle in for the night. He tells me he met a British officer early in December in Jamaica and was told about the proclamation.

The king's offer of a pardon weighs heavily on his mind. I know now why he's been preoccupied for the past weeks. He understands that many of his men will be looking to him for advice. In the end, tho', he knows that each must decide for himself. I also now understand why the Captain was so anxious to sail to the Gulf of Mexico and why all our pirating had to end before the fifth of this past January.

I've sailed with the Captain for over two years and have a good idea what he's thinking. He no longer needs to wonder if the rumors of King George's pardon are true and, if so, what will be the terms. But what will he do after he accepts the pardon? What will Cooky, Stewy, and I do? I can tell that, in a way, we've become his family and he feels responsible for our well-being. The members of the crew can take care of themselves, but we're different.

To the Captain, it's obvious that Charles Vane and his Jacobite friends will oppose the pardon and intimidate others to do the same. As Jacobites, or at least Jacobite sympathizers, they hate King George, and the thought of Britain being ruled by a non-Catholic king, a German at that, and not a Stuart, is beyond what they can tolerate. For them, the fight is more than pillaging a few vessels. The fight is about the destiny of Britain.

A few days later when all the crew have returned to the *Ranger* and are eating supper, Mr. Martin asks, "All you know about the proclamation?"

Most nod, but others shake their heads and murmur indistinctly. For their benefit, I recite the gist of the proclamation, which has firmly secured a spot in my mind. After I finish, many look uneasy. Being a part of Captain Hornigold's crew has become natural for many by now.

Harold, one of the newest members of the crew, asks, "What's that mean?"

"Well, Harold, any acts of piracy committed before the fifth day of January of this year will be pardoned. You can't be hanged for those acts. Bygones will be bygones and you can keep what you have.

"Also, you need to get a document from the governor that says you're pardoned for those acts. That must be done on or before the fifth of September of this year. So you've some time."

"But we got no governor," Harold exclaims.

"I hear the king will be appointing one shortly. Don't worry. The Captain will take care of everything."

To escape the discomfort of the moment, I quickly add, "I'll go see if Cooky and Stewy have the Captain's dinner ready."

I hurry to the galley and then to the Captain's quarters with his dinner tray. He looks weary.

"Think most of the men will stay pirates?" I wonder out loud.

"That's unlikely," the Captain mutters, pushing his dinner away. "If they do, they've got to steal to get by. Then they'll risk bad health or getting caught and hanged. I suppose just going along with the king's offer would be safer."

I leave the Captain deep in thought, drumming his fingers on his table.

19

Charles Vane Challenges the Royal Navy
February–April 1718

LL IS QUIET on the morning of the twenty-third of February. The *Younge Abraham*, the twenty-six-gun Dutch ship that Captain Hornigold brought in, guards the harbor's entrance. The smaller Dutch ship that he captured is anchored nearby. The *Mary Galley* of Bristol, an unarmed French wine vessel, a sloop, a number of pirate vessels, and some pirate prizes are also at anchor.

Smithy calls me over to the rail and points to a small Royal Navy frigate entering the harbor. We watch as the frigate drops anchor and launches a longboat with a landing party. One sailor, who appears to be the officer in charge, stands holding a white flag. They reach shore, disembark and are encircled by the crowd that gathers. After several hours, the landing party returns to their longboat and rows back to their frigate. The frigate raises her anchor, sets sail, and leaves the harbor.

I turn to Smithy. "What's that all about?"

All Smithy can do is shake his head.

The next morning, the frigate returns followed by the *Lark*, Charles Vane's small sloop.

I hear "Sam!" and quickly find the Captain.

"Come with me."

We board a longboat and head for shore. Captain Hornigold finds his friends Leslie, Burgess, and Nichols, and we row out to the frigate, which we learn is the *Phoenix*, under the command of Captain Vincent Pearse. The *Phoenix*, with twenty six-pound guns, has sailed down from her station in New York.

We reach the *Phoenix,* and Captain Hornigold and our party are granted permission to board. We're greeted by Captain Pearse. After a brief discussion between the captains, Captain Pearse invites us to his quarters.

Captain Hornigold is the first to speak, "To our great surprise, we saw the *Lark*, Captain Vane's sloop, anchored behind your ship. Vane has seventeen men. Where are they?"

Captain Pearse explains, "When my landing party met with the group on shore, they expressed grave concern about Vane and his men, and they told my lieutenant where Vane and the *Lark* were hiding. You saw the *Phoenix* leave the harbor yesterday and return this morning with the *Lark*. Well, we found Vane, all right. When Vane refused to surrender, we used force and he surrendered along with his men. We captured the *Lark* and had our boarding party sail her here."

"Well," says Captain Hornigold, "seeing you bring in the *Lark*, and with Vane and his men in custody, agitated my men on the *Ranger*. The word's spreading that the king's pardon is only a ploy and worthless. The message you sent is Vane and his men will be hanged. Release them if you want others to surrender and accept the king's act of grace."

Captain Pearce listens quietly. After a few minutes, he orders Vane and all but one of Vane's men released.

"What about releasing the *Lark*?" Captain Hornigold asks.

"Can't do that," Captain Pearse replies. "The *Lark* was involved in an act of piracy after the fourth of January, so she's not free to go."

"Very well then."

With that, we row Leslie, Burgess, and Nichols back to shore and Captain Hornigold and I make our way to the *Ranger*. A short time later, Smithy points out that Vane and his men are being rowed ashore by sailors from the *Phoenix*.

Heavy rain drenches the harbor that evening and continues for two days. The rain continues into the twenty-sixth when Captain Hornigold, Mr. Martin, Smithy, Cooky, and Stewy take a longboat and row ashore. The Captain makes sure I'm not left behind. We pick up Leslie, Burgess, and Nichols again; Richard Noland joins the group. We then row over to the *Phoenix*.

Captain Pearse greets us and shows us to his quarters. He takes a seat behind a long table; we stand in front. One by one, he asks whether we understand the king's pardon and what is required if we accept it. We each answer in the affirmative. He then asks whether we want to accept the terms of the pardon. Again, we each answer in the affirmation. One by one, he asks our name and writes it on a certificate of safe passage. The Captain goes first, then Smithy, Cooky, and Stewy. When he comes to me, I'm ready to reply when I hear Captain Hornigold say, "Abigail."

A range of emotions flows over me. He always calls me either "Sam" or "boy." I was sure he didn't remember my name.

Captain Pearse asks for my family name and I slowly reply, "Pennyworth," a name I haven't used since what seems to be a previous life.

He writes my name on the certificate and pushes the document across his table for me to sign. I sign and stare at it for a few seconds. This document can assure me a normal life, a life I almost can't remember having.

I hand the certificate back to Captain Pearse, who signs it, affixes the royal seal in wax, and enters my name in his logbook.

"Keep this safe, Abby," he says as he hands it back to me.

And so it is. We return to the *Ranger* lost in our thoughts and with certificates in hand.

Upon our return, a number of the others, now seeing that no harm has befallen us, feel safe to make their way to the *Phoenix*. The more suspicious take a wait-and-see attitude.

We watch a procession of pirates in their longboats, including, to our surprise, Charles Vane, make their way to the *Phoenix*.

A few days later, Smithy and I visit The Lion and the Unicorn. Most of the conversation is about the king's pardon. The mood's relaxed and the conversation turns to who accepted the king's act of grace. One by one, names of the many captains are repeated: Francis Leslie, Josiah Burgess, Thomas Nichols, Paulsgrave Williams, John Lewis, Richard Noland, Charles Vane, Leigh Ashworth, and our own Benjamin Hornigold.

Some sailors talk about going home; others just wonder whether to stay in Nassau to see what happens. The conversation soon turns to the new royal governor of the Bahamas.

One sailor asks, "Hear about the new royal governor?"

Another pipes up, "Woodes Rogers, I hear. Know him?"

"Aye," says a third, "sailed with him and his brother when he's a privateer. Good seaman. Circumnavigated the globe. Seemed impossible! Hard taskmaster but good to his men. Injured in battle twice. Still recovering, I hear. Brother's killed in one of those battles."

Some of Smithy's friends call us to their table, and one asks, "Haven't seen Henry Jennings. Anybody seen him?"

Smithy replies, "Sailed before Captain Pearse arrived. I'm told he's heading for Bermuda to accept a pardon from the governor there. Too uppity to accept a certificate from Captain Pearse. I understand he's family and land there—wealthy—giving up sea life. He's not interested in having his neck stretched, I guess." That comment is followed by an uneasy chuckle from the group.

I pipe up, "I noticed a few of his friends are gone as well. Did they sail with him?"

"Aye! About seven. I understand business at The Killiecrankie Tavern is slowing down."

Another at our table speaks up, "Good riddance to Captain Jennings and his Jacobite friends. Three cheers!" and they all raise their tankards. "To King George!"

All is quiet till the seventeenth of March, I believe. I'm following my usual routine by visiting the galley for breakfast before I make my rounds. Cooky looks up from what he's doing and asks, "Seen or heard anything strange last night, late last night?"

"No, why? What happened?"

"Well," says Cooky, "a couple of our men just told me that late last night, Vane and about sixteen of his men rowed from shore past the *Ranger* and the *Phoenix* and out the harbor's west entrance. They rowed so quietly as not to break the silence of the night. Didn't want to arouse suspicion on the *Phoenix*."

"Very interesting. I'll let the Captain and Mr. Martin know when I make my rounds."

That night, the Captain, Mr. Martin, Smithy, and I make a point to keep watch over the harbor. The evening passes and one by one they fall asleep. I'm determined to stay awake. Sure enough, it's late when I see some men on the beach. I quickly wake the Captain, who wakes the others. We watch in silence.

The Captain whispers. "Over there, I count twenty, no, twenty-four men in a longboat!"

We watch as the men quietly row past the *Ranger* and the *Phoenix* and out the harbor's west entrance.

"Vane's up to no good again. Be assured of that," is all the Captain says.

Mr. Martin asks, "Anyone we know with him?"

"Edward England," mutters the Captain. "Hmm! I thought he's too smart and too reasonable to sail with Vane."

"Calico Jack," Smithy whispers.

"You mean Jack Rackham?" Mr. Martin asks.

"Uh-huh. Picked up the name Calico Jack by wearing clothes made from brightly colored calico. Got to be him. Can see those clothes clearly in the moonlight. No one else would dare be seen in those clothes. England's keeping bad company."

For the next several nights, we watch. The eighteenth, nothing, the nineteenth, nothing, the twentieth, nothing. Then on the twenty-first, in broad daylight, Vane and his men come sailing into the eastern entrance to Nassau Harbor in a small trading sloop. They drop anchor just to the east of Potter's Cay, the small island that divides Nassau Harbor into two basins. They go ashore and begin loading cargo.

We watch and Mr. Martin turns to the Captain, "Pearse must be beside himself. Can't do nothing. Too shallow on either side of Potter's Cay for the *Phoenix* to cross into the eastern basin. Vane's going too far. Taking enough rope to hang himself. Give him time! Give him time!"

"Vane's gone pirate again," is all Smithy can say.

That evening, the harbor is quiet except for the celebration on Vane's sloop. Captain Hornigold watches and mutters, "Vane's enticing others ashore to join him. Poor Pearse. Can't do nothing about it. No one likes being taunted, especially if you're a captain in the Royal Navy."

By around midnight, the harbor is absolutely quiet. We assume that Vane's men have drunk themselves to sleep. I go to my hammock, and no sooner have I dozed off than I'm awakened by gunfire coming from the direction of Potter's Cay and the eastern basin. In the darkness, the silhouette of a longboat makes her way around Potter's Cay and heads our way. The men from the longboat board the *Phoenix* and all is quiet again.

The next morning, I ask Smithy, "What's all the gunfire last night?"

"Well, Captain Pearse couldn't stand being humiliated so he sent a boarding party to capture Vane's vessel. Figured Vane's men were too drunk to fight. He thought wrong. Vane stationed a lookout, and Pearse's plan unraveled. Now poor Pearse's even worse off than before."

The next day, the twenty-third of March, the *Phoenix* raises her anchor, sets sail, and leads a convoy of four sloops out of the harbor. One, the *Lark*, was refitted back as a trading vessel and is now manned by sailors from the *Phoenix*.

A few nights later, we awake to see the *Younge Abraham* ablaze. She's the Dutch merchant ship the *Ranger* captured near Vera Cruz and the Captain stationed near the harbor's entrance. The *Mary Galley*'s also ablaze.

On the twenty-ninth of March, Captain Pearse and the *Phoenix* return to the western basin of the harbor only to find the smoldering hulls of the *Younge Abraham* and the *Mary Galley*. The smaller Dutch ship escaped the torch but was run aground on Hog Island. Charles Vane is gone but he has left his mark.

Two days later, the thirty-first of March, Vane returns to the eastern basin. He's no longer sailing the small merchant trader he captured a few weeks earlier but is now sailing his former sloop, the *Lark*.

I find Smithy. "I thought Vane left in a small merchant trader and Captain Pearse had the *Lark*. How did Vane return in the *Lark*?"

Smithy paused for a moment. "It's complicated. When Captain Pearse seized the *Lark*, he changed her back to a trading sloop. When she left the harbor, she was on a private trading mission for Captain Pearse up the Florida coast to St. Augustine. She was sailed by a half-dozen sailors from the *Phoenix*. On the way back, three of the sailors mutinied and took her over. They sailed down to Vane's little encampment behind Buskes Cay and had her refitted as a pirate vessel. Now Vane has two vessels and over seventy-five men.

On the fourth of April, we watch as Vane sails out of the eastern entrance in the *Lark* with a black flag flying.

On the eighth of April, the *Phoenix* sails out of Nassau Harbor. Smithy says she's returning to her home port, New York.

Much has changed after young Bennett's visit to Nassau with copies of the king's proclamation. All's quiet for now, but we all know Charles Vane will be making life difficult for everyone.

20

Life After the King's Pardon
April–September 1718

ALL IS QUIET, at least for the next few weeks. With many of the Jacobites and Jacobite sympathizers no longer in Nassau, business at The Killiecrankie Tavern falls off dramatically. Two hundred or so pirates, mostly non-Jacobite sympathizers, sign up for pardons. Many leave Nassau to begin new lives. Even in the good years, no more than five hundred to a thousand pirates were in Nassau at any one time. Now only a few pirate vessels come into the harbor to trade their pirated goods.

Several weeks after Vane and the *Lark* left Nassau, rumors begin circulating at The Lion and the Unicorn that Vane was trolling the shipping lanes off the Bermuda coast and behaving in a most unorthodox and barbaric manner.

On the twenty-eighth of April, three and a half weeks after Vane sailed, he's back. He left with just the *Lark* but has returned with a four-vessel fleet. His men are now going around Nassau bragging about capturing a dozen vessels, seven from Bermuda alone. They seem pleased Vane has a grudge against Bermuda. Those of our crew who spoke with Vane's men thought his grudge is due to Governor Bennett's son bringing news of the pardon to Nassau. Others thought Vane's trying to establish himself as independent from his mentor, Henry Jennings, who sailed to Bermuda for his pardon and was now living there.

Vane himself brags that he plans to stifle legitimate trade around Bermuda and in the Bahamas. He laughs when people accuse him of unleashing a reign of terror on shipping coming to and from Bermuda. He sneers and snarls, "Good!"

The discussion at The Lion and the Unicorn focuses on Vane's brutality. They describe how he selects one member from a captured vessel for especially brutal treatment. The details make me so physically ill that I flee the tavern and return to the wharf to wait for a longboat to the *Ranger*.

We hear Governor Bennett has had enough of Vane and has commissioned Henry Jennings to track Vane down and bring him back to Bermuda for trial.

A few days after Vane's return, I watch a four-vessel fleet sail through the western entrance into Nassau Harbor. The flagship is very large, twenty-two guns and one hundred fifty men.

"Smithy, would you tell me about that ship?"

"Aye, she's a slave ship, alright, a galleon, built in Bristol, England, and named *Concord*. She was captured by French privateers and sailed under the name *La Concorde*. Nasty bit of business there, slave trade. After Thache captured her, he changed her name to the *Queen Anne's Revenge*, an insult to our late Queen Anne. Many just call her the *QAR*. I won't be surprised if Major Bonnet's on that ship. He's still sailing with Thache, I'm told. Thache probably even made Bonnet a library. Wonder if Bonnet's in his dressing gown?" The thought brings a broad smile to Smithy's face.

"Is Bonnet's old sloop *Revenge* sailing with the *QAR*?"

"Aye, she is, see, that's her over there. Wonder who's her captain?"

A few days later, I watch as Thache and his fleet sail out of the harbor. I think he stays just long enough to show off the *QAR* and his fleet. Wants everyone to know he graduated from an eight-gun sloop and now's the captain of a galley and the commodore of his own fleet.

"Smithy, where do you think Thache's going?"

"With spring turning into summer, wouldn't be surprised if he's sailing to the Florida Straits and then north up the coast."

I changed the subject to John Martin, our quartermaster. "I was looking for Mr. Martin this morning, but I couldn't find him."

"Humph!" grunts Smithy. "Sailed off with Thache. First it's Howard, now it's Martin."

"But I thought Mr. Martin went with us to the *Phoenix* and received a certificate of safe passage. Didn't he say he's giving up being a pirate?"

"So he did. He'll be sorry he's sailing with Thache. Thache's reckless and has it in for British shipping. Must have had a really bad experience with the Royal Navy during the war. John Martin won't last long. Thache'll get him hanged. Mark my words."

For the first weeks of May, Vane and his fleet stay at anchor in Nassau Harbor. He appears to be waiting for something or someone. Finally, around the twenty-second, Vane and his flagship, *Lark*, followed by his small fleet, raise anchor and sail away.

Around the fourth of June, the Captain, Smithy, and I visit The Lion and the Unicorn when the Captain's friend Josiah Burgess joins us. "Haven't seen you in a while," Captain Hornigold comments.

"Trying to make a little money sailing back and forth between here and Charles Town." Captain Burgess pauses and then adds, "You're not going to believe what happened to me and my sloop, *Providence*."

"Well, tell us," Captain Hornigold prompts.

"It's like this. I sailed from Nassau early in May with a shipment for Charles Town. Went up the Florida Straits and then into Charles Town Harbor, a difficult harbor that harbor is. You need to sail over a shoal and enter through the harbor's narrow mouth. Treacherous, very treacherous if you don't know your way.

"I made my delivery and put in for a couple of weeks to enjoy my friends. You know some of them. They all signed certificates with Captain Pearse and were waiting in Charles Town for their official pardons from the governor. When I'm ready to return to Nassau, I pick up my cargo, bottles of ale and a few plates. There's always a market for them in Nassau.

"On my way back through the Florida Straits, minding my own business, I get stopped by Thache and his little fleet. Thache wants to know whether I was familiar with the Charles Town Harbor. I tell him I've just come from there. Well, Thache says he'd buy what I'm carrying if I'd show him how to sail into the harbor. So I did.

"Then he wants me to wait ashore to be 'his eyes and ears.' I'd little choice, so I said I would. I sail into the harbor, and he in his galleon and his three sloops set up across the mouth of the harbor so no vessel can come or go. They stay there for about six days. All he wants is a chest of medicine. After he receives the medicine chest, he frees the vessels and passengers he's holding and sails away. He takes some clothing, money, and jewelry from the passengers but not much else.

"Once I see he's gone, I get another load of bottled ale and sail back here. So, that's the story. Pretty strange, six days for a medicine chest. Thought he'd do much better. Did have four vessels, including a galleon. What do you make of that?"

"Must need that medicine real bad. Must have some very sick men," is all Captain Hornigold can say.

"Which way did he sail?"

"North, up the coast. Aye, north, up the coast."

A few days later, the men at The Lion and the Unicorn are talking about Vane again. One asks, "Do you think Vane's hanging around the harbor expecting something to happen?"

"I hear from one of his men that he's expecting Jacobite reinforcements. Vane wants to take over New Providence and make Nassau a Jacobite republic."

"Guess he gave up when Jacobite forces didn't arrive. Impatient, always impatient," another comments.

A third adds, "Want to hear what Vane did after he left on the twenty-second?"

"What!"

"Well, a day later, the twenty-third, he captured the *Richard & John* near Crooked Island, two hundred miles southeast of here."

The name *Richard & John* silences the crowd. Captain Hornigold, who's seated at a table nearby, breaks the silence in uncontrollable laughter. So Vane's done it! He knows the *Richard & John*'s off-limits. She's owned by Richard Thompson and his son-in-law, John Cockram, our agents on Harbour Island. The *Richard & John*'s about fourteen tons and has been bringing supplies to Nassau Harbor from Charles Town and Jamaica and trading them for pirated goods. She's been doing that from the time we've been here.

The sailor who first talked about the *Richard & John* then adds, "I hear Vane dumped her crew, including her captain, Cockram's brother Joseph, on an island and kept the vessel."

Captain Hornigold can't resist and comments, "Not good for Vane. He'll pay for this. That won't help him make friends. Mark my words, he'll pay plenty!"

A week or so later, this must be the end of the third week of June, Captain Hornigold and the men of the *Ranger*, who'd accepted a certificate of safe passage, sail for Bermuda to exchange their certificates for pardons from the royal governor, Benjamin Bennett. The voyage seems strange because we're not searching for vessels to plunder or the Royal Navy to avoid.

I ask Cooky, "Why did the Captain choose Bermuda rather than Jamaica?"

"Safer, when we're a fighting vessel and sail in consort, the Cuban *guarda costas* wouldn't engage us. They know what will happen. But now we're just a merchant vessel, and they've the advantage and they'll stop us to search for Spanish coins. Any Spanish coin will do. They'll say it's stolen. We'd be arrested and held for ransom. So, by sailing to Bermuda, there's no need to sail around Cuba on our way to Jamaica."

We arrive in Bermuda and go to the governor's house where Governor Bennett greets us. We exchange our certificates for royal pardons and are soon on our way.

A month later, mid-July, we return to Nassau only to find several sloops blocking the harbor's entrance. Each flies a black flag. They recognize Captain Hornigold's *Ranger* and allow us to enter and drop anchor.

"Smithy, what's happening?"

All he can say is, "Hmm, don't see Vane's *Lark*, not in the harbor. Seems strange, this has all the markings of Vane."

Later in the day, the Captain, Smithy, and I head for The Lion and the Unicorn. We join Captain Burgess.

"Well, Josiah, what do you make of all this?" Captain Hornigold asks.

"All Vane's doing, as you can guess. Remember late in May? Vane called on his old crew for one last cruise before the new governor arrived. About seventy-five were willing, including Edward England and Calico Jack Rackham. Vane left Nassau around the twenty-second of May. Sailed in the *Lark*. Was really nice around here after they left.

"Well, all that changed on the fourth of July when Vane returned. He traded the *Lark* for a large French vessel, two hundred to two hundred fifty tons. Made her his flagship. Also captured a two-masted vessel and made Edward England captain. Captured the *Richard & John* near Crooked Island and a brigantine, the *St. Martin* of Bordeaux, near Hispaniola. Sailed both with prize crews and that gave him a fleet of four. But that wasn't all. On his way back to Nassau, he sailed near Harbour Island and came upon a group of small trading sloops. Took three, the *Drake* and the *Eagle*, both of Rhode Island, and the *Ulster* of New York. Now with a fleet of seven, he entered Nassau Harbor. Thought he was pretty important but he wasn't done yet. Seized two more sloops. They were already in the harbor, the *Dove* and the *Lancaster*. They brought his fleet to nine. You impressed?"

Captain Hornigold chuckles, "What can he do with nine vessels? So he decides to block the harbor entrance. He says he's the governor, and no vessel can enter or leave without his permission. Hmm! All I know is nine vessels means a lot of mouths to feed, especially just anchored in the harbor. No prey, no pay, just mouths to feed."

Captain Burgess gives Captain Hornigold a hard look. "True, so what are you going to do about Vane?"

"Me? Nothing, just nothing," laughs Captain Hornigold. "I hear Governor Rogers left London this April past. Should arrive any day now. Vane's his problem, not mine. Let Vane think he's governor for a few more days."

"One more thing," adds Captain Burgess. "Thomas Walker and his family are back."

"Not surprising, not surprising at all. Let Rogers deal with Vane and Walker."

We return to The Lion and the Unicorn a few days later and the talk is about Woodes Rogers.

"I hear the governor'll be living in Nassau, the old governor's house," comments a sailor at a table near us.

Another asks, "Arriving soon?"

"Sailed from London April last," is the reply. He's quite a fleet, seven vessels. Three Royal Navy warships. The frigate *Milford,* that's his flagship. Commodore Peter Chamberlaine's in command. Then there's the frigate *Rose* and the sloop-of-war *Shark.*

"That's not all. Woodes Rogers and his business partners paid for the other four. Rogers' sailing the *Delucia,* a private man-of-war. Rounding out his fleet's the *Willing Mind,* a transport, the *Buck,* a private sloop-of-war, and the *Samuel,* a supply ship. Soldiers and settlers are also on his ships."

"I'm told over one hundred guns."

"Some firepower, some firepower, quite impressive," is all Captain Burgess can say.

After taking a breath, the sailor continues, "That's not all. Bringing soldiers and settlers' just the beginning. Supplies to feed and clothe them for over a year, all them tools and materials to build a fort and houses and to plant crops. Guess the governor plans to make Nassau a respectable place. What's more, he's bringing some, what would you say, 'gentlemen' to help him run this place."

And everyone around the table groans.

Several days later, late afternoon on the twenty-third of August, the first sighting is made. A lookout shouts, "First ship of the fleet, the *Rose,* the *Rose.* Governor Rogers' fleet's approaching the western tip of Hog Island."

Smithy and I choose to watch from the rail as the frigate sails into the harbor and drops anchor just inside the entrance. A short time later, we see the *Shark* enter, sail around the *Rose,* and drop her anchor. The *Buck* and the *Willing Mind* enter and anchor near the *Rose.* Smithy points, "See, off in the distance, about three miles, the *Delicia* and the *Milford,* sailing back and forth in the open sea."

"Do you see the supply ship, the *Samuel?*

"No, can't see her."

"Smithy, what do you think the *Delicia* and the *Milford* will do?"

"Probably stay at sea. They have too deep a draft to take a chance entering the harbor this late in the day. They'll wait for the high tide in the early morning. Vane and his fleet are pretty well bottled up. Think we've seen what we'll see. Need some supper!"

Stewy greets us with, "What's been keeping you two?"

Everyone's quiet as they eat and anticipate the events of the next day: the confrontation between Vane and the new governor for control of Nassau. One by one they leave to perform their chores before turning in. We go to sleep thinking about tomorrow.

It's the middle of the night, running boots are in my dream, followed by voices. A voice is calling Abby.

"Captain?" I mumble an answer in my grogginess.

"Shake a leg, Abby! Shake a leg!"

I open my eyes and there stands the Captain. "Hurry, hurry, Vane's trying to escape!"

But how? I thought. Governor Rogers' warships have the entrance blocked. Vane and his flagship are trapped. Vane's flagship's too large to sail around Potter's Cay. He's no way out.

Quickly I throw on some clothes and join the Captain at the rail. The moon lights the sails of Vane's flagship. They're unfurled and her anchors raised.

Captain Hornigold's shaking his head, "What does Vane think he's doing sailing directly into the teeth of Governor Rogers' fleet?"

Vane doesn't hear Captain Hornigold and even if he did, he wouldn't care.

We watch and wait. We're spectators, there's nothing we can do. Vane's flagship draws closer to the governor's fleet, then suddenly, she erupts into a bright orange fireball, followed by the explosion of her cannons. We can't avoid the heat and the smell of black powder.

Vane's flagship makes straight for the *Shark*, the *Rose*, the *Willing Mind*, and the *Buck*. The governor's vessels panic, cut their cables, set sail, turn, scatter, and make for the harbor's entrance.

Several hours later, calm settles back over the harbor. The smoldering remains of Vane's flagship block the entrance. No vessel may enter or leave.

The sun has risen. We look around. When we went to bed, a small sloop, the *Katherine*, Captain Charles Yeats' vessel, was anchored near Vane's flagship. Now the *Katherine* and another small sloop are sailing around Potter's Cay and heading towards the east entrance of the harbor. The *Buck* and another sloop are in pursuit.

Captain Hornigold turns to Smithy, "Didn't know Yeats and Vane were friends."

"What happening? Why's the *Katherine* leaving?" I ask.

"Old, old trick," the Captain replies. "Vane caused a diversion with his fireship at the western entrance and sailed out the eastern entrance in the smaller *Katherine*."

A few minutes later, cannon fire echoes in the distance. "Vane's mocking the governor," Smithy chuckles. "He'll get what's coming to him in due time, in due time."

A couple of hours later, the *Buck* and her consort return through the eastern entrance and around Potter's Cay, empty-handed.

The next day, Smithy and I return to The Lion and the Unicorn. The conversation turns to the new governor, Woodes Rogers.

"I hear the governor received a letter from Vane threatening both him personally and Nassau," reports one sailor.

"No way to make friends with the new governor," is all another has to say.

His friend questions, "What's he expecting to gain?"

"Rogers will be happy to see him swing from the gallows. Rogers will be happy to do the job himself." They all laugh.

"Aye," comments Smithy, "Vane's laying down a challenge."

Back on the *Ranger*, word circulates that the *Delicia* and the *Milford* will enter the harbor the next day and that everyone's expected ashore to welcome the new governor.

The next morning, the twenty-seventh of August, Smithy, Cooky, Stewy, and I join the crowd along the road from the harbor to the fort. Governor Rogers is rowed ashore and is met by Captain Hornigold and Thomas Walker. As the three make their way to the fort, those along the road discharge their muskets into the air as a sign of welcome.

For the next few days, all is quiet. The *Samuel*, the governor's supply vessel, arrives and Woodes Rogers moves into the governor's house. Two hundred or so pirates use the opportunity to accept the official king's pardon. The few who are willing and able make an effort to clean up the town.

Two weeks into September, the fourteenth to be precise, Captain Hornigold receives word that Governor Rogers wants to see him at the governor's house. The Captain asks us to join him. So the Captain, Smithy, Cooky, Stewy, and I row over to the wharf, walk to the governor's house, and are escorted into the governor's office.

Governor Rogers greets Captain Hornigold. "I asked for you, Captain, but who are the others?"

The Captain introduces each of us to the satisfaction of the governor. We seat in front of the governor's desk while the Captain says he's more comfortable standing behind us.

"I've a special request," Governor Rogers begins solemnly.

"Oh?" the Captain's replies.

"As you know, the date to surrender for the king's pardon has passed. Many have accepted his terms. King George would like you to accept a commission to hunt down the pirates who have not accepted his Act of Grace. Specifically, he wants you to bring Charles Vane to justice. I recently received information that Vane is at Green Turtle Cay at Abaco Island, a day or so sailing from here. You know the place. The king also asked Captain Cockram, your old friend, to sail in consort with you. Will you do that for your king?"

I see Captain Hornigold's taken aback, but as a British subject. He believes he has no choice.

"Well, fine then," says the governor. "Will the others be sailing with you?"

For some reason, attention focuses on me. I swallow hard and say, "I've not seen my parents for almost three years. I need to try to find them." I feel a sharp disappointment in myself because I consider myself a member of Captain Hornigold's family. Then I realize I can't live with myself if I don't search for my real Mother and Father.

"As governor, I may be able to help."

Smithy, Cooky, and Stewy in turn say they will join me on my quest.

We spend a moment hugging each other and do not notice that the Captain has taken his leave. We didn't hear him go.

Several days later, we met again with the governor.

"I have made inquiries and the Pennyworth family landed in Jamaica almost three years ago. They spent days looking for their daughter, but ultimately left for the Carolinas. I think they're expected there. I've made arrangements for you to sail on the next coastal trader to Charles Town. I wish you all well."

A wave of homesickness comes over me. Over time, I've forgotten how I missed my previous life. Despite the people I met and the adventures I had, I was eager to put my days as a pirate behind me and to see my family again.

And so, I bring to a close my story about sailing with my friend, the notorious pirate Benjamin Hornigold.

Epilogue

September 1719

A YEAR HAS PASSED since Captain Hornigold and I parted ways in Nassau. Much has happened during that year.

Woodes Rogers, the royal governor, continued to struggle to bring British rule to Nassau and the Bahamas.

Lord Archibald Hamilton was tried and acquitted by a board of trade in London, as Captain Hornigold had predicted.

Edward Thache, after scuttling the *Queen Anne's Revenge* and abandoning Major Stede Bonnet, was killed in a battle by Lt. Robert Maynard and several members of his crew in November at Ocracoke, a Province of North Carolina. Lt. Maynard and his small force had been sent by Alexander Spotswood, the lieutenant governor of Virginia.

Major Stede Bonnet was captured, tried, and hanged in December here in Charles Town, at White Point Garden.

Charles Vane was marooned by his crew on an uncharted island in February. The captain of a passing vessel recognized Charles Vane and refused to take him aboard. He was picked up by another passing vessel. By chance, the two captains were meeting for dinner when the captain of the first vessel noticed Vane working in the hold of the second vessel. He told his host, who immediately had Vane put in chains. Vane is now in Port Royal awaiting trial.

As for me, I often remember with fondness how Governor Rogers kept his promise and made arrangements for Smithy, Cooky, Stewy, and me to sail to the Carolinas. Upon arriving in Charles Town, Smithy and Cooky left to meet friends. Stewy and I made our way to Stewy's sister's house, where Stewy surprised his daughter.

"Papa! Papa! You're here! Please stay here with me, Papa! Papa! Please!" she pleaded.

"Aye, dear. I'll always be here with you, my sweet little one. Aye, my sailing days are over."

After Stewy explained that we had left Nassau for good, his sister and brother-in-law invited me to stay with them till I found my family.

A few days after I've settled in, Stewy offers to show me Charles Town. We walk past a shop and I happen to look in the open doorway. The young man who is working there, looks up and our eyes lock. "Abby! Abby!" He's my own brother! Tears begin streaming down his face. "I thought I would never see you again, but Mother and Father never gave up hope. They prayed every night that someday you'd come back to them."

"Are they here? In town?"

"No. They're in the country serving the church, they'll be back within a fortnight."

"And little brother?"

"Little brother's grown since you seen him and he's with them."

A week or so later, I'm helping Stewy's sister churn butter and pay little attention to the woman who enters and greets Stewy's sister. Without warning, I feel arms engulfing me. I'm overwhelmed by visions of that Spanish pirate abducting me. "Who's this white-haired woman and why is she doing this to me?"

"Abigail Margaret Mary Pennyworth" is all she can whisper through her tears.

"Mother" is the last word I remember saying.

My next thoughts are of lying on a bed with Mother and Stewy's sister pressing cool compresses to my forehead.

Many months later, I happen to glance at a copy of *The Boston News-Letter* and my eyes are drawn to the following story:

MEXICO Reports have been received of a disaster in the Gulf off the coast of Mexico. The hurricane that terrorized the coast destroyed the brigantine, Ranger. The vessel could not escape the hurricane's winds and waves that dashed her upon a reef. The vessel split in two and went down with all her crew, except two. The vessel's captain, Benjamin Hornigold, who was a privateer during the Queen Anne's War, a notorious pirate after the war, and a pirate hunter after he accepted the King's Pardon in 1718, went down with his vessel.

Although Captain Hornigold, as a pirate hunter, was unable to bring the notorious pirate Charles Vane to justice, he was successful in bringing other pirates to the gallows.

I read and tears stream down my cheeks. Thinking my eyes are deceiving me, I read the story again and again. Once my tears subside and my initial shock lifts, a slight smile comes to my face. I know the sea was in the Captain's blood and that if he had a choice, he would have chosen to pass in no other way.

/s/ Abigail Margaret Mary Pennyworth
Charles Town, South Carolina
September 1719

End

Glossary

Aft

The back part of a vessel.

Anchor

The anchor's weight was determined by a vessel's tonnage—1/5000 of the vessel's tonnage. An anchor was hung on both sides of the vessel's bow.

Anchor Buoy

A small, wooden, waterproof barrel was attached to the anchor cable that identified the location of the anchor.

Articles

The terms and conditions agreed upon by the crew of a pirate vessel such as no women onboard, no fighting onboard, equal division of the plunder.

Asiento

Under the Treaty of Tordesillas, which divided the world between Spain and Portugal, the Spanish were unable to sail to West Africa for slaves. Therefore, Spain devised a plan called Asiento de Negros (Asiento) whereby every few years, the Kingdom of Spain would award an exclusive contract to a government or company to sell slaves in Spanish America. This created a triangular system whereby a ship would leave a European port with a cargo that could be sold in West Africa, a shipload of slaves would be purchased and transported to a slave market in the Caribbean (known as the middle passage), and the proceeds from this sale would be used to buy sugar, rum, and other commodities that would be transported back to the European port.

Bahamas	A group of over seven hundred islands, cays, and inlets in the Atlantic Ocean that, along with the islands of Turks and Caicos, form the Lucayan Archipelago. The Bahamas are north of Cuba and Hispaniola (now Haiti and Dominican Republic), northwest of the Turks and Caicos Islands, southeast of Florida, and east of the Florida Keys. Nassau on New Providence Island is the capital. Although Columbus landed in the Bahamas in 1492, the Spanish saw no commercial value in the Bahamas, so the British controlled the Bahamas during the Golden Age of Piracy.
Battle of Killiecrankie	Killiecrankie, located in Perthshire, Scotland, was the scene of a battle that took place on July 27, 1689, during the 1689 Scottish Jacobite uprising. A Jacobite force defeated a superior government army.
Bay	A small body of water that is smaller than a gulf and opens to a larger body of water.
Bell	A vessel's brass bell that is rung every half an hour or as a warning to other vessels during storms.
Bilge	The lowest level of the vessel where the bottom curves under the vessel and where the wastewater is collected and ballast stored.
Bluefields, Jamaica (18.1742° N, 78.6295° W)	A remote harbor on the southwest coast of Jamaica. Bluefields was named after Abraham Blauvelt, a Jewish, Dutch pirate, privateer, and explorer of Central America (Honduras and Nicaragua) and the western Caribbean. In 1644, he commanded his own vessel raiding Spanish shipping from a base in southwest Jamaica, later to be named after him.
Boarding Party	When a vessel was seized, the small group of men who were sent over to plunder that vessel.
Boatswain (bosun)	The officer in charge of maintaining a vessel's hull that included the sails, riggings, and anchors.
Bow	The front end of a vessel.

Bowsprit
: The spar that projects forward from the vessel's bow to which triangular sails were attached. Lines were also attached to the bowsprit to keep the mast from falling backwards.

Brig
: The brig and brigantine were two-masted vessels that had similar hulls although different rigging. The masts on the brig were square rigged, with three square sails on each mast.

Brigantine
: A two-masted vessel—a foremast and a taller mainmast. Three triangular sails were attached to the bowsprit and the foremast and looked similar to the sails attached to the bowsprit of a sloop. The foremast had three square sails. The mainmast also had three square sails plus a triangular sail that was attached to the foremast. The mainmast also had a gaff-rigged sail and possibly a triangular sail above that.

British Naval Ships

Ship of the Line
: A large square-rigged warship with at least two gun decks. The ship was designed to be lined up in battle, side by side with other ships of the line.

Frigate 1st Rate
: Ship of the line with 100+ guns, three gun decks, 850–875 men, and 2,500 ton.

Frigate 2nd Rate
: Ship of the line with 80–98 guns, three gun decks, 700–750 men, and 2,200 ton.

Frigate 3rd Rate
: Ship of the line with 64–80 guns, two gun decks, 500–650 men, and 1,750 ton.

Frigate 4th Rate
: Ship of the line with 50–60 guns, two gun decks, 320–420 men, and 1,000 ton.

Frigate 5th Rate
: 32–44 guns, one or two gun decks, 200–300 men, and 700–1,450 ton.

Frigate 6th Rate
: 20–28 guns, one gun deck, 140–200 men, and 340–550 ton.

Sloop-of-War
: 16–18 guns, one gun deck, 90–125 men, and 380 ton.

Bulkhead The partitions (walls) within a vessel.

Cabin Boy A young boy who carried out various low-level jobs such as helping the cooks, running messages between officers, and carrying meals to officers and crew.

Canary Islands (28.2916° N, 16.6291° W) A Spanish archipelago off the coast of northwestern Africa. Tenerite is its largest island. Vessels sailing from Western Europe to the West Indies in the Americas would sail south with the clockwise current and then follow the westward current, which is the strongest around 30° N, across the Atlantic to the Caribbean.

Cape Land that is connected to the mainland on two sides. The other two sides border water.

Careening The process by which the accumulation of sea creatures and vegetation was removed from the underwater hull of a vessel and the gaps between the vessel's planks sealed with oakum, tar, and pitch to make the vessel watertight. The vessel was tilted on its side to expose its undersides for cleaning and repair.

Carriage Gun A cannon mounted on a wheeled under-assembly.

Cartagena, Colombia (10.3932° N, 75.4832° W) Founded in 1533, Cartagena gained importance as a port on the Caribbean from which silver mined from Potosi was shipped to Spain.

Caulk Sealing the gaps between a vessel's planks with oakum, tar, and pitch.

Charles Town (South Carolina) (32.7765° N, 79.9311° W) Founded in 1670, Charles Town was the capital of the Province of Carolina, a proprietary colony. In 1716, the population of Charles Town was almost 3,000.

Chesapeake Bay (37.5214° N, 76.1050° W) The entrance to Chesapeake Bay is Norfolk, Virginia. Near the northern end of Chesapeake Bay is Baltimore, Maryland.

Cob	The Spanish coin that was irregular in shape because it was cut from strips of silver and struck by hand.
Colors	The flags flown at or near a vessel's stern to show its nationality.
Commission (Letter of Marque)	Written authority granted by a government to a private person to seize foreign vessels and their goods. A commission granted an individual a license to plunder enemy vessels.
Cooper	A person trained to make wooden casks and barrels from timber staves.
Courses	The lowest square sails (fore and main) of a vessel.
Cove	A small inlet or bay that usually has a narrow, restricted entrance and often is circular or oval.
Crew	The personnel on a vessel were divided between officers and seamen (ordinary hands). The specialized crew members included the cooks, carpenters, sailmakers, coopers, and gunners.
Delaware Bay	The entrance to Delaware Bay is defined by Cape May to the north (38.9435° N, 74.9090° W) and Cape Henlopen to the south (38.8032° N, 75.0946° W). Delaware Bay is the entrance to Wilmington, Delaware, and Philadelphia, Pennsylvania.
Dowse canvas	Strike a sail. To quickly lower a sail.
Drake, Francis, Sir	An English explorer, sea captain, privateer, slave trader, naval officer, and politician who circumnavigated the world in a single expedition, from 1577 to 1580.
Drop the Sail	Lowering the sail. The opposite of hoisting the sail.
Dry Goods	Merchandise ranging from clothing to jewelry to accessories.

Earl of Mar

The Earl of Mar who raised James II and VII's standard was John Erskine, the 23rd, the 6th Earl of Mar (1675–1732). He was the Jacobite commander during the Second Jacobite uprising (1715) and fled to France when the uprising failed.

Eleuthera (24.9314° N, 76.1900° W)

Eleuthera refers to both the single island in the archipelagic state of The Commonwealth of the Bahamas and to its associated group of smaller islands. Eleuthera forms a part of the Great Bahama Bank.

Eleuthera Island, Bahamas

A long, narrow island (110 miles long and as little as 1 mile wide) located 50 nautical miles east of Nassau. Its eastern shores face the Atlantic Ocean and its western shores face the Caribbean Sea. Its beaches are pristine white and pink sand. Eleuthera Island incorporates Harbour Island, a small island located off its northeast tip.

Ensign

The national flag flown by a vessel at or near the vessel's stern.

Exuma (23.6193° N, 75.9695° W)

About 124 nautical miles from Nassau, Exuma consists of over 365 islands (cays), the largest being Great Exuma (62 square miles), and joined to another, Little Exuma (11 square miles).

Fathom

Six feet deep of water.

Firth of Forth

The estuary of several Scottish rivers including the River Forth. It meets the North Sea with Fife on the north coast and Lothian on the south.

Fish the Wrecks

Treasure hunting around sunken shipwrecks.

Flags

The flags used by the lookout of a pirate vessel to communicate with the lookouts of other pirate vessels.

Flagship

The vessel in a fleet commanded by the ranking officer of the fleet.

Florida Strait (23.3825° N, 82.3886° W)

A strait located between the Gulf of Mexico and the Atlantic Ocean, and between the Florida Keys and Cuba. It is 93 miles at its narrowest (between the Florida Keys and Cuba) and carries the Florida Current (the beginning of the Gulf Stream) from the Gulf of Mexico.

Fore	The front part of a vessel.
Fore-and-aft	Fore is the front of the vessel and aft is the back. A sail running fore-and-aft runs parallel to the vessel rather than perpendicular.
Fore-and-aft Rigging	The sails that parallel the length of the vessel (usually triangular sails).
Forecastle	The short deck built over the front of the main deck.
Fortnight	Fourteen nights or two weeks after that date.
Frigate	A square-rigged warship that was less heavily armed than the ship of the line.
Furl the Sail	On a square-rigged vessel, bind the sail to the yard.
Gale	A strong wind used in a nautical context that is 34–47 knots of sustained surface winds.
Galleon	A large three- or four-masted vessel that was used to transport passengers or cargo. The *Queen Anne's Revenge* was a galleon.
Galley	The cooking area aboard a vessel.
Galley	A ship propelled by sails and by oars and used to transport passengers and cargo. The oars could be used when the winds were less favorable and when navigating harbors.
Glorious Revolution	The Revolution of 1688 replaced King James (James II of England and Ireland and James VII of Scotland) with his daughter, Mary II, and her husband, William III of Orange. James was Catholic; Mary and William were Protestant. With the birth of James' son, the thrones would have passed to him rather than to Mary and would have remained Catholic.
Going "on the account"	Becoming a pirate.
Grapeshot or Grape	Small balls secured in a canvas bag that scattered over a wide area when fired from a cannon.

Grog　　Rum mixed with water.

Guarda Costa　　The Spanish coast guard. They patrolled around Cuba.

Gulf Stream　　A warm ocean current that originates in the Gulf of Mexico, flowing up the East Florida coast and turning eastward off the coast of North Carolina and continuing northeast across the Atlantic.

Gunner　　A member of the crew who fires a cannon.

Gunweale　　The upper planking along the sides of a vessel.

Halyard　　A line for raising and lowering a sail or yard.

Harbour Island, Bahamas (25.5001° N, 76.6341° W)　　(East of Nassau). An island in the Bahamas located off the northeast coast of Eleuthera Island. Harbour Island is part of the Out Islands of the Bahamas. The island's only town, Dunmore Town, was named for John Murray, the Fourth Earl of Dunmore, who was the governor of the Bahamas from 1787 to 1798, long after the Golden Age of Piracy.

Harbour Island is about 47 nautical miles from Nassau and 4.3 nautical miles east of the tip of Eleuthera Island.

Harbour Island is known for its pink sand beaches that are found all along the east side of the island. The pink comes from foraminifera, a microscopic organism that has a reddish-pink shell.

Head (Toilet)　　An area located at the bow of the vessel with planks with holes as seats so human waste could be deposited directly into the sea.

Heave Down　　To tilt a vessel on its side for careening.

Heave To　　To turn the vessel into the wind and bring it to a standstill.

Helm　　The tiller or wheel that is attached to the rudder that steers the vessel.

Hog Island An east/west island that forms the northern edge of Nassau Harbor. It has been renamed Paradise Island.

Hoist our colors A black flag (black ensign) indicated a pirate vessel; a red flag (red ensign) meant take no prisoners.

Hold The hold is the deck for storage of provisions, black powder, and plunder. On a sloop, the hold is the deck below the top deck and above the bilge.

Hurricane A tropical storm where the winds have reached a sustained speed of at least 74 miles an hour.

Isle of Pines An island south of Cuba that is a part of Cuba. It is the seventh-largest island in the West Indies and has been renamed Isla de la Juventud.

Killiecrankie See Battle of Killiecrankie.

Land Legs Adjusting one's legs and balance after being at sea.

Lateen Sail A triangular sail that is mounted on a spar that is attached to a mast.

League Three statute miles on land and three nautical miles, or 3.452 statute miles, at sea.

Lee The side sheltered from the wind. Backside.

Lee Shore A sailing vessel will be blown onto this shore.

Leeward In the opposite direction from which the wind blows, that is, away from the wind. The side of an island or a vessel that is sheltered or away from the wind. For example, if a sailing vessel is heading east and the wind is southerly (out of the south), the leeward side would be the north side of the vessel.

Letter of Marque (See Commission)

Lines A vessel's ropes are called lines. The main categories of lines are anchor lines and ground tackle, docking lines, standing rigging (holds up the masts and spars), and running rigging (move the sails).

Log, logbook — The journal kept by the navigator where the vessel's location, speed, and course are recorded along with notes as to wind direction, weather, sail changes, flag signals, and the vessels met along the way. The captain and other officers may also keep logbooks.

Longboat — The largest boat carried by a vessel. An approximate length of a longboat was the square root of the length of the vessel on which it was carried times two.

Main (Master) Gunner — The crew member who oversaw the gunners who fired the cannons.

Mainsheet — The rope at the lower corner of the mainsail that was used for regulating the position of the mainsail.

Mast — A tall vertical spar to which sails, spars, and derricks were attached. A vessel could have one (sloop), two (brig and brigantine), or three (galley or galleon) masts.

Foremast — The first mast if the vessel had more than one mast.

Mainmast — This mast was usually located near the center of the vessel and was the taller if the vessel had two masts and the tallest if the vessel had three masts.

Misenmast — The mast behind the mainmast if the vessel had more than two masts.

Mizzen Sail — On a three-mast ship, usually the triangular lateen fore-and-aft sail.

Mona Passage (18.5000° N, 68.0000° W) — About an 80-mile-wide channel between Hispaniola and Puerto Rico, and was an important shipping lane between Panama and the Atlantic Ocean.

Morgan, Henry, Sir — (1635–1688) A Welsh privateer, plantation owner, and later lt. governor of Jamaica. From Port Royal, Jamaica, he raided settlements and shipping on the Spanish Main.

Nassau, Bahamas (25.0443° N, 77.3504° W) — Nassau, the capital city of the Bahamas, is located on New Providence Island, an island 21 miles long and 7 miles wide. Nassau Harbor on the north side of the island was the Pirate Republic during the years following the Queen Anne's War.

Nautical Mile	1,852 meters, or 1.853 kilometers, or 6,076 feet or 1.151 statute miles.
Newport, Rhode Island (41.4901° N, 71.3128° W)	Founded in 1639 and located on Narragansett Bay, approximately thirty-three miles southeast of Providence, Newport was an important trading center and had a rich history as a pirate safe haven.
Oakum	Twisted jute fiber that was used to caulk between the wooden planks of a sailing vessel to make the vessel watertight.

Officers

Captain	The leader on a vessel, although the quartermaster was in charge unless the vessel was in battle or giving chase. Pirate vessels were a democracy, so the members of the crew had a vote and elected the captain.
Quartermaster	Except when in battle, the quartermaster was in charge of the day-to-day operation of the vessel. He saw that the captain's orders were carried out. The quartermaster led the boarding parties, controlled the plunder, and distributed the rations, powder, work, prize, and punishment.
Boatswain (Bosun)	The person responsible for seeing that the vessel was fit for sailing and battle. He was in charge of the vessel's anchors, cables and lines, colors, deck crew, boats, and rigging.
Helmsman (Navigator)	The person responsible for steering the vessel. The helmsman needed to know the vessel's draught, the vessel's width, and how sharply it could turn. In shallow waters, the crew would take soundings to check the water's depth and report to the helmsman.

Peninsula	Land attached to the mainland on one side with the other three sides bordered by water.
Periagua (Sailing canoe)	A large canoe made from a hollowed-out tree trunk that was rowed or paddled and had a single mast. A periagua may be built in two sections with a plank inserted between the sections for extra storage.
Piece of Eight (Peso)	A Spanish coin with the weight of 25 grams of silver. One-eighth of a peso was a reale. In 1707, Parliament set the value of a piece of eight at 4s6d plus a premium when in the American colonies. The buying power of a piece of eight, however, varied from place to place.
Pink	A small sailing vessel with a narrow stern and a flat bottom. A pink had a cargo capacity and was generally square rigged. The flat bottom resulted in a shallow draft that made this vessel useful in shallow waters.
Plunder	Stolen goods, loot.
Pope Alexander VI	Pope from 1492 to 1503. The Spanish-born pope who issued bulls setting up a line of demarcation from pole to pole 100 leagues (about 320 miles) west of the Cape Verde Islands, giving Portugal the rights to land to the east and Spain the rights to land to the west.
Pope Clement XI	Head of the Catholic Church and the ruler of the Papal States from 1700 to 1721.
Port	The left side of a vessel when facing the bow.
Porto Bello, Panama (9.5489° N, 79.6530° W)	Founded in 1597, Porto Bello gained importance as a port on the Caribbean from which silver mined from Peru was shipped to Spain. Now named Colon.
Port Royal, Jamaica (17.9363° N, 76.8411° W)	Located on the southeastern coast of Jamaica and the capital of Jamaica prior to the earthquake and fires of 1692.

Powder Monkey — A young boy who carried black powder from where it was stored (usually the hold) to the gunner for his cannon.

Prevailing Winds — Winds that blow constantly in a given direction over a particular region of the Earth. In the Atlantic, the North-easterly Trades blow westerly below 30° and the Westerlies blow easterly above 30°.

Privateer — A privately owned vessel that had received a letter of marque to capture enemy vessels and their cargo.

Prize — An enemy vessel captured by a privateer.

Prize Crew — After a vessel was seized, a few men were sent to sail the captured vessel.

Quartermaster — Second to the captain. Generally elected by the crew and was in charge of the crew and saw that the captain's orders were carried out.

Queen Anne's War (*1702–1713*) — A territorial war fought in North America on three fronts and involving England, France, and Spain and their respective Native American allies.

Red Duster (Red Ensign) — The flag flown by British merchant vessels after 1707. This ensign was red and showed the Union Jack in the upper-left quarter.

Reef — A ridge at or near the surface of a body of water. Naturally formed reefs are stone or skeletons of small animals (corals).

Reef — The area of a sail is reduced by rolling it up or bundling part of it and securing that part with short lines.

Rigging — The rigging on a pirate sailing vessel were the ropes, wires, and chains used to support and operate the masts, sails, booms, and yards of the vessel.

Running Rigging — Lines that operate the sails. Differs from standing rigging.

Sail ho! The call by the lookout that the sails of a vessel have been spotted.

Sail in Consort When two or more vessels intentionally sail together.

Sails The three configurations of sails are the triangular, the rectangular, and the gaff rig. A gaff rig sail is a four-cornered sail, fore-and-aft rigged, controlled at its peak and, usually, its entire head by a spar (pole) called the gaff. Its bottom is attached to a spar (pole) called a boom.

Saint Lucie (27.4992° N, 80.3422° W) Location on the east coast of Florida that marked one boundary of the Spanish plate fleet wreck.

Sandbar A long narrow sandbank often found by the mouth of a river.

San Sebastian Inlet (27.8164° N, 80.4706° W) The location on the east coast of Florida where the Spanish were storing the silver, gold, and other objects fished from the Spanish plate fleet wreck in 1715. Location is ten miles south of Melbourne Beach and six miles north of Vero Beach.

Scottish Thistle A weed that blooms across the Scottish landscape and is an early symbol of Scotland. The legend that dates back to the mid-thirteenth century concerns a surprise invasion by the soldiers of the Norse king at one of the western Scottish coastal towns. After coming ashore, the Vikings removed their shoes so they could creep up on the sleeping Scottish Clansmen and Highlanders. One of the soldiers stepped on a Scottish thistle and cried out in pain, thus waking the sleeping Scots and negating the surprise of the attack.

Sea Legs After being on land, the ability to adjust one's balance to being at sea.

Sea Worms Any type of worm living in the sea that burrows into the wood of sailing vessels.

Ship A vessel with three or more fully square-rigged masts.

Ship of the Line   A warship large enough to take its place in the line of battle.

Shipping Lanes   The sea route followed by vessels sailing from one place to another.

Shorten the Sail   On a square-rigged vessel, the sail could be shortened to reduce its size or part of the sail could be taken in.

Show a Leg!   Get a move on! Get out of bed!

Sloop   A sailing single-masted vessel with fore-and-aft rigging. Often three triangular sails were attached to the bowsprit and the mast. A gaff-rig sail was attached to the mast and pointed to the stern. A headsail may have been attached to the top of the mast. Sloops could range up to 80 feet with a crew of 60–80.

Sloop-of-War   A sloop-of-war may have one, two, or three masts. A Royal Navy warship with a single gun deck armed with up to eighteen guns.

Snow   A two-masted square-rigged vessel with an additional trysail mast raised close behind the mainmast on which there was a set of fore-and-aft sails.

Sound (to take a sounding)   To measure the depth of the water by dropping a lead weight at the bottom of a line that was marked at regular intervals.

Spanish Armada   In 1588, a Habsburg Spanish fleet of 130 ships sailed from Lisbon to escort an army from Flanders to England. The army's purpose was to: (1) overthrow Queen Elizabeth I and her establishment of Protestantism in England; (2) stop English interference in the Spanish Netherlands; and (3) stop the English and Dutch interference with Spanish shipping in the Caribbean. The armada failed due to inadequate leadership, poor weather, and illness.

Spanish Plate Fleet   A fleet of eleven Spanish ships and a French frigate escort left Havana in late July 1715 laden with silver for the king of Spain. All the Spanish ships wrecked in a hurricane near San Sebastian Inlet, Florida.

Spanish or French Prize	A Spanish or French vessel seized by a privateer who was given authority to do so by a commission (letter of marque) by a British official.
Spar	A strong wooden pole that was attached to a mast or to a yard that was attached to the mast.
Spyglass	A portable telescope (monocular) that magnified a distant object for the viewer. It was called a "bring 'em near." The spyglass was invented in the early 1600s but did not come into common use by mariners until the second half of the 1700s.
Square-Rigged	When the principal sails are square (rectangular) and at right angles to the vessel's length. Square-rigged is the opposite to fore-and-aft rigged.
Square the Sail (Square the Yard)	On a square-rigged vessel, the primary driving sails are perpendicular or square to the keel of the vessel. To square the sail is to lay the yard at right angle to the line of the keel.
Standard of James	The personal banner of James Francis Edward Stuart, the son of King James II and VII, that promoted the Jacobite cause.
Standing Rigging	The rigging that supports the masts and spars and that is stationary when the vessel is sailing.
Starboard	The right side of the vessel when facing its bow.
Stem	The main timber that forms the leading edge of the vessel.
Stern	The rear of the vessel.
Strike Her Colors	Lower the flag that signified the vessel's nationality.
Strike Her Sails	Lower the sails on a fore-and-aft rigged vessel.

Swivel Gun — A small piece of artillery that was attached to the top of a vessel's rail, stern, or bow and that was rotated side-to-side and up-and-down to direct its fire.

Tack (Tacking) — To sail in the direction of the wind by working the sail back and forth so the wind catches one side and then the other thus propelling the vessel forward.

Take It In — The fastest way to stop using a sail.

Tender — A supply vessel.

Thistle — See Scottish Thistle.

Topsails — The square sail set above another sail.

Trysail — A small triangular or square fore-and-aft rigged sail hoisted in place of a larger mainsail when the winds are very heavy.

Vera Cruz, Mexico (19.1810° N, 96.1342° W) — The Mexican port founded in 1513 that was used by the Spanish to ship silver mined in Mexico to Spain.

Vero Beach, Florida (27.6386° N, 80.3973° W) — The present-day location of wrecks of the Spanish plate fleet of 1715. Wreckage was strewn along the ocean floor from San Sebastian Inlet (27.8164° N, 80.4706° W) to Saint Lucie (27.4992° N, 80.3422° W).

Virginia Capes — The entrance to the Chesapeake Bay is defined by Cape Charles to the north (37.2679° N, 76.0174° W) and Cape Henry to the south (36.9315° N, 76.0199° W).

War of the Spanish Succession — (1701–1714). A conflict triggered by the death of Charles II of Spain over who would be his successor and therefore which countries would control the balance of power in western Europe. France and Bourbon Spain supported Philip of Anjou, the grandson of King Louis XIV of France, while the Grand Alliance (England, the Dutch Republic, Habsburg Spain) supported Archduke Charles, the younger son of Leopold, the Holy Roman Emperor.

Weigh — To pull up as in weigh the anchor.

West Indies A subregion of North America that is surrounded by the North Atlantic Ocean and the Caribbean Sea, and is composed of numerous islands in three major archipelagos: the Greater Antilles, the Lesser Antilles, and the Lucayan Archipelago. The Bahamas takes up 97 percent of the Lucayan Archipelago.

Wharf A structure built at an angle to the shore where vessels can tie up and load or offload.

Whydah (Ouidah) (6.3717° N, 2.0763° E) A port in southern Benin, West Africa, known for its role in the slave trade.

Windward Facing the wind. Then your back is leeward.

Yard A cylindrical spar, tapered at each end, that is attached to a vessel's mast for a sail to be attached. The term is usually used to describe horizontal spars on a square-rigged vessel.

Sources

Books

Brooks, Baylus C. *Dictionary of Pyrate Biography: 1713–1720*. Lake City, FL: Poseidon Historical Publications, 2020.

Ashworth, Jasper & Leigh (Gentlemen of Jamaica. Jasper and his partner, Daniel Axtel, loaned fitted-out vessels to privateers.

Leigh left Charles Town Harbor just after Josiah Burgess left for the first time and before Thache's blockade.)

Augur/Augier, John (Surrendered to Captain Vincent Pearse in February 1718, but when sent out by Governor Woodes Rogers as a pirate hunter, he returned to pirating. He and twelve of his crew were captured on November 15, 1718, by Hornigold and Cockram at Exuma Island. Three died before trial. Ten were tried and found guilty. Nine, including Captain Augur, were hanged at Fort Nassau on December 12, 1718. One was released.)

Axtell, Daniel (Part owner of the *Barsheba*, commanded by Henry Jennings, and the *Eagle*, commanded by John Wills. Axtell was involved in the storage and sale of pirated goods.)

Baker, Thomas (One of six pirates from Bellamy's *Mary Ann* that was thrown up on the shore during the nor'easter. Hanged at Scarlett's Wharf in Boston.)

Bellamy, Samuel (Nicknamed Black Sam Bellamy, sailed with his partner Paulsgrave Williams. Bellamy was captain of the *Whydah* when she wrecked on Cape Cod.)

Blackbeard (See *Thache.*)

Bonadvis, Jean (French pirate, captain of the *Mary Anne*, who attempted to pry Dr. John Howell away from Captain Hornigold.)

Bonnet, Stede (Landowner from Barbados who purchased the sloop *Revenge*, hired a crew, and sailed north. Near Florida, he attacked a Spanish warship and he was wounded. His crew sailed to Nassau for repair and while there, Edward Thache convinced Bonnet to let him be the captain while Bonnet could recuperate and spend time in his onboard library. Sometime after Thache seized *La Concorde* (*Queen Anne's Revenge*), he abandoned Bonnet. Bonnet was captured, tried, and hanged in Charles Town on December 10, 1718.)

Bostock, Henry (Deposition, December 19, 1717) (Captain of the sloop *Margaret* that was captured by Thache on December 5, 1717.)

Brown, John (Taken from Captain Kingston's vessel in April 1716 by Olivier LeVasseur. One of the six pirates from Bellamy's *Mary Ann* who was thrown up on the shore during the nor'easter. He was tried and hanged at Scarlett's Wharf in Boston.)

Buck, Samuel (Details a lease from the Lord Proprietors and the financing of Governor Woodes Rogers' voyage to New Providence Island.)

Bunce, Phineas (Leader of the mutiny aboard Captain John Augur's sloop *Mary*, at Green Key, Bahamas, October 6, 1718. He was killed when Captain Hornigold's pirate hunters attempted to take him into custody.)

Burgess, Josiah (Captain of the *Providence* of the Bahamas who left Charles Town in May 1718. This probably was just before his encounter with Thache, who made Burgess return to Charles Town to be his lookout during Thache's blockade.)

Carnegie, James (Captain of the *Discovery*, who was involved with Captain Jennings as they seized the *St. Marie* in Bahia Honda. He traded the *Discovery* for the *St. Marie*, April 1716. Does not go into detail about the seizure of either vessel.)

Clark, Robert (Captain of a pink, the *Crowley* of London, that was taken by Thache in May 1718 at Charles Town Harbor.)

Cockram, Jonathan (Sailed one of the three periaguas out of Nassau along with Hornigold and John West in late 1713. Left to marry a daughter of Richard Thompson, a merchant on Harbour Island. Later sailed with Hornigold as a pirate hunter.)

Cockram, Joseph (Brother of Jonathan Cockram and was the captain of the *Richard & John* until it was seized by Charles Vane.)

Cunningham, William (Gunner for Thache. Joined John Augur as a pirate. Was captured, tried, and hanged at Nassau on December 12, 1718.)

Darvell, Jonathan (Merchant who lived in Eleuthera as early as 1671. Father-in-law of Daniel Stillwell. Owned the sloop *Happy Return*.)

Davis, Thomas (When the *St. Michael* was captured by Bellamy and LeVasseur on December 19, 1716, he was taken to Blanco Island, then forced aboard the *Sultana*, and after that forced aboard the *Whydah*. Davis, a carpenter, and John Julian, a pilot, were the only survivors of the wreck of the *Whydah*. Davis was tried and acquitted.)

D'Escoubet, Jean (Memorial of Monsieur Moret, captain of a company of infantry at Saint Domingue, and Extract from a letter by Captain D'Escoubet to Lord Hamilton concerning the capture of the *St. Marie* in Bahia Honda.)

Dossit, George (Quartermaster for Carnegie on the *Discovery* and then on the *Marianne*, April 1716. The names of the vessels have been mixed up. The vessel was the *St. Marie* rather than the *Marianne*.)

Dowling, William (Sailed with John Augur; captured, tried, and hanged in Nassau on December 12, 1718.)

Dunavan, James (Captured aboard the pink *Mary Anne* of Dublin, on April 20, 1717, off the Virginia Coves, and survived the wreck of the *Mary Anne*. Dunavan described their capture and some events leading up to the wreck.)

Edwards (Possible alias for Bonnet.)

Eels/Eales, Joseph (Deposition, December 20, 1716) (Quartermaster on Ashworth's *Mary*. Eels said that Ashworth, Jennings, Carnegie, and Liddell all met up at Bluefields, Jamaica. This contradicts the statements of others who said only Jennings and Ashworth sailed from Bluefields and met Liddell at the Isle of Pines and Carnegie at Cape Antonio (near Cape Corrientes). He also said that outside of Bahia Honda, Carnegie exchanged his sloop with the French for the *St. Marie*, and Jennings, Ashworth, and Carnegie sailed to Nassau together. Carnegie actually arrived at Nassau a few days after Jennings and Ashworth.)

Fitzgerald, Thomas (Deposition of Thomas Fitzgerald and Alexander Mackonochie, May 6, 1717) (Fitzgerald was a mate and Mackonochie was the cook of the *Mary Anne* and the deposition detailed Bellamy's seizing the *Mary Ann*, the nor'easter, and the arrest of the pirates who were on the *Mary Anne*. One interesting statement differed from the tavern scene when the survivors were identified as pirates. The deposition describes what happened as "[T]wo men came over in a canoe, namely John Cole and William Smith, who carried the seven pyrates over to the mainland, and then Cole came again to Fitzgerald and Mackonochie and inquired who they were (meaning the seven he just took to the mainland) and Mackonochie answered they were pyrates and had taken the said pink, and soon after the said John Cole informed Mr. Justice Done of Barnstable thereof, by virtue of whose warrant the said seven pyrates were apprehended . . . .")

Fletcher, John (Served aboard Captain Abraham Lamb's *Blackett* that was captured in October 1715 by Hornigold before the capture of the *Mary* of Jamaica. The *Blackett* had sailed from Jamaica and was captured before it reached the wrecks off the Florida coast. Neither Fletcher nor Higgins was permitted to return to the *Blackett*, but they were forced to join Hornigold's crew. Subsequently, Fletcher sailed with Bellamy, who made him quartermaster of the *Marianne*, November 1716.)

Godin, Benjamin (Wealthy South Carolina merchant who gave a detailed account of Thache's blockade of Charles Town beginning about May 22, 1718. He noted that Bonnet visited Charles Town the summer before Godin.)

Hamilton, Lord Archibald (Governor of Jamaica. Between November 21 and December 20, 1715, he issued ten commissions, including a commission to Henry Jennings, John Wills, and Matthew Musson. Letter from Don Juan de Acuna to Hamilton, January 1716, and Letter from Hamilton to the Governor in Council Jamaica, August 24, 1716, concerning his request to Jennings for the return of his commission, and a letter from the governor of Cuba to Hamilton concerning Jennings' raid. (The calendar date is the Spanish date under the Gregorian calendar.) Brooks states that Hamilton left Jamaica aboard the *Bedford* on

September 21, 1716, and was back in England by late November 1716 to face Peter Heywood's accusation that he was dealing with pirates. His prosecution was set aside by the king in August 1717.)

Heywood, Peter (Governor of Jamaica following Archibold Hamilton. Discussed the politics involved in the removal of Archibold Hamilton and the increase in pirate activity under his own administration.)

Higgins, Jeremiah (Served aboard Captain Abraham Lamb's *Blackett* that was captured in October 1715, before the capture of the *Mary* of Jamaica. The *Blackett* had sailed from Jamaica and was captured before she reached the wrecks off the Florida coast. Neither Fletcher nor Higgins was permitted to return to the *Blackett*, but they were forced to join Hornigold's crew. Subsequently, Higgins was boatswain on the *Marianne* for Paulsgrave Williams, mid-1717.)

Hipps, John (Forced into piracy by John Augur. Was captured, tried, and acquitted.)

Holmes, Edward (Deposition, April 20, 1709) (Described Lewis Martel's cruelty.)

Hoof, Peter Cornelius (Statement) (Swedish. Member of Bellamy's crew. Survived the wreck of the *Mary Anne* and was hanged in Boston on November 15, 1717.)

Hornigold, Benjamin (Leader of the non-Jacobite pirates on Nassau.)

Howard, William (Quartermaster for Hornigold on the *Bennet*, then quartermaster for Thache on Bonnet's *Revenge*. Testified at the trial of Dr. John Howell.)

Howell, Dr. John (Testimonies at the trial of Dr. John Howell, December 22, 1721) (William Howard was Hornigold's quartermaster and led the boarding party. Pearce Wright was a member of the boarding party. Testimony of Richard Noland.)

Hudson, Robert (One of three Royal Navy sailors who deserted Captain Pearse when he sent them to sail the *Lark* to St. Augustine on a private voyage. Hudson took up with Charles Vane.)

James, Edwards (Deposition, August 16, 1716) (John Wills, the *Eagle*, but not Edward James, was commissioned as a privateer by Governor Hamilton along with Henry Jennings, the *Barsheba*.

James had refitted his vessel for the voyage, but decided not to accompany Jennings and Wills on their raid but rather to invest in the sloop *Eagle*, one-third share, commanded by John Wills. In his deposition, James discussed the division of the silver from the raid and Governor Hamilton's involvement in his deposition.)

Jennings, Henry (Leader of the Jacobite pirates. Led the attack on the Spanish storehouses at San Sebastian Inlet on December 26, 1715, and on the *St. Marie* at Bahia Honda in early April 1716.)

Julian, John (Miskito Indian. Sailed with Bellamy and was one of the two survivors of the wreck of the *Whydah*. Captured and sold into slavery.)

Kentish (Possible alias for Thache.)

Kerr, James (Testimony at the trial of ten pirates at Nassau, December 9, 1718.)

Kingston, Thomas (One of three Royal Navy sailors who deserted Captain Pearse when he sent them to sail the *Lark* to St. Augustine on a private voyage. Kingston took up with Charles Vane.)

Le Gardew/Guardeu (Captain of the French vessel, the *Marianne*, that was captured by Hornigold at Port Mariel. Specifically stated that Jennings took only the cargo from the *Marianne* and implied not the *Marianne* itself.)

LeVasseur, Olivier (French pirate. Sailed in consort with Hornigold and then Bellamy and Williams. Subsequently sailed to Madagascar. He was captured on Reunion Island and hanged on July 7, 1730, leaving an encrypted message on the location of his treasure.)

Lewis, William (Description at his trial. Sailed with John Augur, was captured, tried, and hanged in Nassau on December 12, 1718.)

Liddell, Samuel (Deposition, August 7, 1716) (Joined Jennings, Ashworth, Carnegie, Bellamy, and Williams as they captured the *St. Marie* in Bahia Honda.)

Ling, William (Description of his trial. Sailed with John Augur, was captured, tried, and hanged in Nassau on December 12, 1718.)

Lorraine, Joseph (Deposition, August 21, 1716) (Sailor aboard Jennings' *Barsheba* during the raid on the Spanish storehouses, December 26, 1715.)

Martin, John (Succeeded William Howard as Hornigold's quartermaster. Hornigold instructed Martin, and not Howard, to take Dr. Howell to Nassau to stay with William Pendar. The change must have been by mid-March 1717.)

McCarthy, Dennis (Sailed with John Augur, captured, tried, and hanged in Nassau on December 12, 1718.)

Merry, Ralph (Deposition of Ralph Merry and Samuel Roberts, May 11 and 16, 1717) (Merry and Roberts were mariners on the *Fisher* when it was seized by the *Whydah*, survived the nor'easter with the *Ann*, transferred to the *Ann* before the *Fisher* sank, and sailed on the *Ann* up to Monhegan Island, Maine, to wait for the *Whydah*. They were jailed on Monhegan Island and when released, were taken by shallop to Marblehead where they gave their depositions.)

Middleton, Daniel (Deposition, August 22, 1716) (Sailor aboard John Will's *Eagle* during the raid on the Spanish storehouses December 26, 1715.)

Moret (Captain of a company of infantry at Saint Domingue who requested compensation for the *Marianne* and *St. Marie*.)

Morris, Thomas (Sailed with John Augur, captured, tried, and hanged in Nassau on December 12, 1718.)

Musson, Matthew (Captain. Took a privateer's commission from Archibald Hamilton. Captured the sloop *Betty* and took John Perrin into custody.)

Napping/Napin (Sailed in consort with Hornigold. According to Governor Peter Heywood, Napping captured a small trader near Trinidad, a port in the center of Cuba's southern coast, in early October of 1717. Napping told this trader that he had parted ways with Hornigold two or three days prior.)

Nichols, Thomas (Sailed in consort with Napping around July 1717.)

Noland, Richard (Quartermaster for Bellamy on the *Whydah* but then became the captain of the *Ann* after it was captured off the Virginia Coves. He later became Hornigold's agent in Nassau.)

Oliver, Peter (One of Hornigold's 148-man crew on the *Ranger*.)

Pearse, Vincent (Captain of the *Phoenix* who arrived in Nassau Harbor on February 23, 1718, to grant pirates certificates of safe passage.)

Perrin, John (Appointed by Hornigold as captain of the *Betty*. Captured by Matthew Musson and taken to Charles Town.)

Perry, Micajah (London merchant who encouraged action against the pirates.)

Porter, Thomas (Sailed on the *Bennet* when Hornigold took two Dutch ships, one the *Younge Abraham*, so the date must have been between April and June 1717.)

Rouncifull, George (Joined Augur and Bunce with eight others who on October 6, 1718, took the cargo from Augur's sloop *Mary* at Green Cay. Captured, tried, and hanged in Nassau on December 12, 1718.)

Savage, Abijah (Deposition November 30, 1716) (Captain of the sloop *Bonetta* detailing his vessel's capture by Bellamy.)

Shuan, John (Sailed with Bellamy on the *Whydah* and transferred to the *Mary Anne*. Survived the wreck, surrendered, tried, and hanged in Boston on December 15, 1717.)

South, Thomas (Sailed with Bellamy on the *Whydah* and transferred to the *Mary Anne*. Survived the wreck, surrendered, tried, and hanged in Boston on December 15, 1717.)

Spatchers, James (Captain of the sloop *Dolphin* that carried the pirated goods from the *St. Marie* and *Marianne* to the owners of the *Barsheba*, Daniel Axtell and Jasper Ashworth, in Port Royal.)

Spotswood, Alexander (Lt. Governor of Virginia. Determined to hunt down Thache.)

Stillwell, Daniel (Sailed with Hornigold out of Eleuthera in the *Happy Return*. Captured by Thomas Walker and rescued by Hornigold.)

Terrill, Thomas (Terrill, Ralph Blankenshire, and Benjamin Linn came to Eleuthera Island from Nassau with Hornigold.)

Thache/Theach/Thatch/Teach, Edward (Blackbeard) (See *Kentish, possible alias*) (For a discussion of the vessels Thache captured after leaving Nassau and before Hornigold's arrival, see Konstam,

Blackbeard 69–70 and Brooks, *Pyrate Biography, Thache/Theach/ Thatch/Teach, Edward.*)

Thompson, Richard Sr. (Merchant living on Harbour Island. Supplied Charles Town and Nassau. Thompson's daughter married John Cockram.)

Timberlake, Henry (Deposition, December 17, 1716) (First known record of Thache as a pirate. Captain Timberlake said his brigantine set sail from Boston Harbor on about the sixteenth of November. Therefore, the thirteenth of December was his twenty-eighth day at sea. Had he reached his destination, Jamaica, he would have sailed about 1,480 nautical miles at a speed of two knots.)

Trott, Nicholas (Early governor of the Bahamas.)

Tucker, Richard (One of Hornigold's 148-man crew on the *Ranger.*)

Ubilla, Juan Estaban de (General and commander of the Spanish fleet that left Spain on September 16, 1712, for Vera Cruz, and ultimately joined General Don Antonio de Echeverz y Zubiza's fleet in Havana. The two fleets joined to form the Spanish Plate Fleet that was wrecked off the coast of Florida, July 30, 1715.)

Van Vorst/Vanvoorst, Simon (Member of Bellamy's *Whydah's* crew who boarded the *Mary Ann* before it wrecked. Van Vorst was captured, tried, and hanged in Boston, November 15, 1717.)

Vane/Veine, Charles (Jacobite and a member of Henry Jennings' crew. Succeeded Jennings as leader when Jennings left for Bermuda. Ultimately, his crew mutinied and abandoned him on a deserted island. He was captured, tried, and hanged at Gallows Point, Port Royal, Jamaica, on March 29, 1721. Vane was one of the more brutal pirates of his day.)

Vickers, John (Deposition, July 3, 1716) ("but whither bound deponent knoweth not." Hornigold may have left to fish the wrecks off the Florida coast) (There is some confusion as to which vessel was the *Marianne* and which was the *St. Marie.* These are French vessels, and the French named the vessel taken by Hornigold in Port Mariel the *Marianne.* Vickers said Jennings "shared the cargo [which was very rich consisting of European goods for the Spanish trade] among his men." Others have stated that while Jennings was ashore, his crew staged a revolt and ferried the cargo to Hog Island where they divided it among themselves.)

Walker, Neal (Son of Thomas Walker Sr.)

Walker, Thomas Jr. (Son of Thomas Walker Sr.)

Walker, Thomas Sr. (Longtime resident of New Providence Island and the Vice Admiralty Judge of the Bahamas until his commission expired with the death of Queen Anne. The biography of Thomas Sr. included the story of Hornigold's encounter with Thomas Jr. in November 1714.)

Walls, Edmond (One member of Hornigold's 148-man crew on the *Ranger.*)

Ward, Richard (Deposition, October 11, 1715.)

West, John (Sailed periaguas in consort with Hornigold and John Cockram, 1713/1714.)

Williams, Paulsgrave/Palsgrave (Sam Bellamy's partner.)

Wills, John (Master of the sloop *Eagle* during the raid on the Spanish storehouses, December 26, 1715.)

Woodale/Woodall, Nicholas (Captain of the *Wolff* and was arrested by Hornigold early in October 1718 while Hornigold was looking for Charles Vane.)

Wragg, Samuel (Wragg and his son, William, were on a ship leaving Charles Town sailing to England when the ship was captured by Thache as he blockaded the harbor.)

Wright, Pearse (Member of Hornigold's crew on the *Bennet* in 1717. Accompanied William Howard and the others of the boarding party that seized the snow and kidnapped Dr. John Howell.)

Yates/Yeats, Charles (Vane took Yates' sloop *Katherine* to escape Governor Rogers' fleet in Nassau. Sought a pardon from the governor of South Carolina. Yates' biography includes the names of the eight sailing with Yates on the *Katherine* who were also granted pardons.)

Brooks, Baylus C. *Quest for Blackbeard.* Lake City, FL: Lulu Press, 2016.

Burbank, Theodore Parker. *Golden Age of Piracy on Cape Cod and in New England.* Mills, MA: Salty Pilgrim Press, 2013.

The *Whydah* was discovered in 1984 by underwater explorer Barry Clifford under fourteen feet of water and five feet of sand. Selected artifacts from the *Whydah* are on display at the *Whydah* Pirate Museum in West Yarmouth, Massachusetts.

Chapin, Howard M. *Privateer Ships and Sailors: The First Century of American Colonial Privateering, 1625–1725*. Eastford, CT: Martino Fine Books, 2017.

Cordingly, David. *Pirate Hunter of the Caribbean*. New York: Random House Trade Paperbacks, 2012.

Cordingly describes Thache's blockade of Charles Town, beginning May 22, 1718.

Cordingly, David. *Under the Black Flag*. New York: Random House Trade Paperbacks, 1995.

Delgado, Sally J. *Ship English: Sailors' Speech in the Early Colonial Caribbean*. Berlin, Germany: Language Science Press, 2019.

Dolin, Eric Jay. *Black Flags, Blue Waters*. New York: Liveright, 2018.

The *Sultana* was a British merchant ship with twenty-six guns. Bellamy became the captain of the *Sultana* and Williams became captain of the *Marianne*.

Captain Lawrence Prince's *Whydah* was a three-hundred-ton British slave ship with eighteen guns.

The *Mary Anne* was thrown up on the shore of Pochet Island just to the south of Eastham.

Dow, George Francis, and Edmonds, John Henry. *Pirates of the New England Coast 1630–1730*. New York: Dover, 1996.

Fox, E.T., editor, *Pirates in Their Own Words*. Fox Historical, 2014.

Goodall, Jamie L.H. *Pirates of the Chesapeake Bay*. Charleston, SC: History Press, 2020.

Jameson, John Franklin. *Privateering and Piracy in the Colonial Period: Illustrative Documents*. New York: Macmillan, 1923.

Knepton, James. *1715*. Tallahassee, FL: Castaway Publishers, 2014.

Konstam, Angus. *Blackbeard, America's Most Notorious Pirate*: Hoboken, NJ: John Wiley & Sons, 2006.

> With the Virginia Capes (Cape Henry and Cape Charles at the mouth of Chesapeake Bay) being over 1,100 nautical miles from Nassau, sailing with the Gulf Stream and at four to six knots or 100 to 150 nautical miles a day, the voyage would have taken seven to eleven days, or substantially more than the four days between September 25 and 29. It's more likely that Thache and Bonnet sailed from Nassau earlier than September 25, maybe between the 18th and the 22nd.

Konstam, Angus. *Pirate Ship: 1660–1730*. Illustrated by Tony Bryan. Oxford, UK: Osprey, 2003.

Johnson, Charles. *A General History of the Pyrates*. Seattle: Loki's Publishing (originally published in 1724).

Lane, Kris, and Bialuschewski, Arne. *Piracy in the Early Modern Era*. Indianapolis: Hackett, 2019.

Little, Denereson. *Sea Rover's Practice*. Dulles, VA: Potomac Books, 2007.

The Log of Christopher Columbus. Translated by Robert H. Fuson. Camden, ME: International Marine, 1987.

Moss, Jeremy R. *The Life and Tryals of the Gentleman Pirate, Major Stede Bonnet*. Virginia Beach: Koehlerbooks, 2020.

> Bonnet's title of major was pursuant to a June 1652 Barbadian law that bestowed military titles upon the landowning aristocracy. The title was not earned for military service.

> Bonnet was a Jacobite sympathizer and "perhaps a supporter."

See Appendix I. A Proclamation for the Suppressing of Pirates, September 5, 1717.

See Appendix V. A List of Those Prizes Taken By Major Stede Bonnet and the *Revenge* or Its Consorts.

Nelson, Laura. *The Whydah Pirates Speak*, vol. 1. Postillion, 2016.

Nelson, Laura. *The Whydah Pirates Speak*, vol. 2. Postillion, 2019.

Oldmixon, John. *British Empire in America*. London: reprinted by Forgotten Books, 2018.

Sandler, Martin W. *The Whydah*. Somerville, MA: Candlewick Press, 2017.

Selinger, Gain. *Pirates of New England*. Guilford, CT: Globe Pequot, 2017.

Szechi, Daniel. *Jacobites: Britain and Europe, 1688–1788*, 2nd ed. Manchester: Manchester University Press, 2019.

Underill, Dave, and Pavlidis, Stephen J. *Captain's Guide to Hurricane Holes: The Bahamas and Caribbean*. Cocoa Beach, FL: Seaworthy Publications, 2018.

Woodard, Colin. *The Republic of Pirates*. New York: Mariner Books, Houghton Mifflin Harcourt, 2007.

Monographs

Brooks, Baylus C. *Blackbeard Reconsidered: Mist's Piracy, Thache's Genealogy*. Raleigh, NC: North Carolina Office of Archives and History, 2015.

Brooks refuted the claim in Johnson's *A General History* that Hornigold and Thache together captured *La Concorde*.

Brooks cited *The Boston News-Letter,* October 28–November 4, 1717, and November 4–11, 1717, as reporting Thache and Bonnet being together at least by early October 1717. (Thache returned to Nassau briefly in August/September 1717 to meet with Stede Bonnet and arrange to become captain of Bonnet's sloop *Revenge,* unless they met at sea as some suggest. The *Revenge,* however, needed to be in Nassau Harbor, a safe haven, so it could be repaired from battle, cannon increased, provisions supplied, and crew added. Nassau, and not a meeting at sea with Thache, would have provided such an opportunity.)

Electronic Sources

British History Online, America and West Indies

Volume 29, 1716–1717

July 14, 1716. Calendar of State Papers Colonial, America and West Indies:

Deposition of Robert Daniell and reference to supporting depositions given. Also note that Col. William Rhett in 1718 led the expedition that captured Stede Bonnet at Cape Fear River.

See July entry for the *Betty* which was then captured from Perrin by Matthew Musson under a commission from the governor of South Carolina and sailed to Charles Town.

Volume 30, 1717–1718

October 24, 1717.

Pirates Library Main—Baylus Brooks> Pirate Reference

Account

Account of the Pirates in the Bahamas by Thomas Walker, March 12, 1714–15.

Board of Trade

Lord Archibald Hamilton's Acquittal, October 2, 1717.

Depositions

Deposition of Robert Daniell, Deputy Governor of South Carolina, July 14, 1716. Daniell stated that Hornigold took the *Betty* from Spaniards "last winter." Hornigold was sailing the *Mary* of Jamaica last winter and then the *Benjamin* so he would have no need to sail the *Betty* last winter. If he had captured the *Betty* last winter, she still would have had the original goods when she was captured by Captain Musson many months later and brought to Charles Town by Joseph Carpenter.

Deposition of Thomas Walker Jr., August 6, 1716. Thomas Walker Jr., said his father and his family left Nassau due to the pirates.

Deposition of Andrew Turbett and Robert Gilmore, April 17, 1717. They discuss April 7, 1717, when the *Whydah* (Bellamy) captured the *Agnes* of Glasgow, the *Anne Galley* of Glasgow, and the *Endeavor* of Brighthelmstone, and April 12, 1717, when the *Whydah* captured a ship belonging to Leith. All captures appeared to be near Cape Charles at the mouth of the Chesapeake Bay on Virginia's Eastern Shore. This was a time after the *Whydah* and the *Marianne* were separated by the storm off the Virginia Coves.

Deposition of Charles Porter, Captain of 140-ton ship *Charles Galley,* September 11, 1717.

Deposition of Fflewelling and Rowe, Surgeon and Mariner on the *Charles Galley,* September 11, 1717.

Deposition of Ellis Brand, Captain of the *Lyme*, to Secretary Josia Burchett, December 4, 1717.

Deposition of *Bostock, Henry,* December 19, 1717. Bostock was the captain of the sloop *Margaret* on December 5, 1717, that Thache captured after he captured *La Concorde* on November 28, 1717. These events were after Thache and Hornigold captured Captain Pritchard's vessel at the Virginia Capes on October 18, 1717. See page 3 of Bostock's deposition for a diagram.

Deposition of David Herriot, October 24, 1718. Herriot does not mention Captain Burgess.

Letters

Letter from the Marquis de Casa-Torres to Lord Archibald Hamilton, January 3, 1716.

Letter by Alexander Spotswood, Lt. Governor of Virginia, to the Council of Trade and Plantations, July 3, 1716.

Letter from Alexander Spotswood, Lt. Governor of Virginia, to the Lord Commissioners of the Admiralty, July 3, 1716.

Letter from Thomas Walker to the Lord Commissioners of the Admiralty, August 5, 1716. (Letter is after Jennings robbed the Florida storehouses. Walker and his family left Nassau and moved to Abaco Island in June 1716 due to the pirates.)

Letter by Admiral Secretary Josiah Burchett to the Governor of Virginia, May 30, 1717. This letter discussed the pirate "infestation" off the Virginia Capes and the lack of naval protection.

Letter by Bartholomew Candler, Captain of the *Winchelsea*, to the Admiralty, July 19, 1717. Captain Candler stated that when he arrived in Jamaica to take command of the *Winchelsea* in March 1717, he found two pirate ships Leeward (west) of Jamaica, each having about one hundred men. One was commanded by Hornigold and the other by Napping. He said he followed them over to the southern coast of Cuba.

Extract from a letter from Richard Perry of Rappahannock, Virginia, to Michjah Perry of London, April 15, 1717. *Marianne* was separated from Sam Bellamy (*Whydah*) as a result of a storm off the Virginia Coves.

Petition

Petition of John Hollidge and Stephen Courtney of Bristol, owners of the 140-ton ship *Charles Galley*.

Reports

Report of Peter Heywood, Acting Governor of Jamaica, to the Council of Trade and Plantations, December 3, 1716.

Report of Captain Matthew Musson to the Council of Trade and Plantations, July 5, 1717. Musson stated that he was cast away in March 1717 in the Bahamas and when he was on Abaco Island, he was told by Thomas Walker and others that Thache in a sloop with six guns and seventy men used Nassau Harbor to "rendezvous" with other pirates. Thache, therefore, would have been in Nassau Harbor prior to Walker's leaving Nassau. Musson's report was hearsay because he did not witness Thache being in Nassau but was reporting what Walker told him.

Musson reported that the pirate leaders appeared to be Hornigold, Jennings, Burgess, White, and Thache. Thache's sloop had six guns and seventy men. Musson's report did not state that the five were there at the same time. Hornigold and Jennings were the leaders. Burgess, White, and Thache were not. Again, Musson's report was hearsay.

Pirates Library Main—Baylus Brooks>Pirate Reference. Lord Archibald Hamilton's Acquittal, October 2, 1717.

Wikipedia (including)

Whydah Gally (last visited February 23, 2022.)

The Great Snow of 1717 (last visited February 19, 2022) (February 27–March 7, Gregorian calendar)

WikiTree, Thomas Walker (ca. 1659–1722) (last visited February 22, 2022) https://www.historyof parliamentonline.org/volume/1715-1754/member/hamilton-lord-archibald-1673-1754.

Index

Acknowledgments

THE IDEA FOR *Captain Hornigold and the Pirate Republic* began about five years ago when Amy Sinclair, one of my former research assistants, and I were discussing her daughter Mya's interest in becoming a writer. Mya showed me some of her writing and we began a fun project of writing alternating chapters. I was impressed with Mya's skill in dialogue and I was able to introduce a narrative character, Abby, a young girl about Mya's age. As Mya's homeschooling demanded more of her time, I continued on by myself. Periodically, Amy would lend encouragement.

Ali Maurer, my sergeant at the Financial Crimes Unit of the Tulsa Police Department, read a few chapters as they were being written and encouraged me to continue.

With COVID-19 on the rise, I left the Financial Crimes Unit in early March 2020 and went into hibernation. That gave me the concentration of time I needed to complete the story.

My son, David, a gifted writer, became my first editor. In addition to his skill as an editor, his suggestions helped craft the story. David has his degrees in art, designed the cover and worked with an illustrator, Tatiana Trikoz, as she implemented his design.

Kay Thurman, my classmate from Washington University School of Law in St. Louis, volunteered to be my second editor. I knew Kay's skills from the time we were on the *Washington University Law Quarterly*. In addition to carefully picking through my draft, Kay called me to task on my use of words and phrases that were not in 1715 vocabulary. "OK" first appeared in an 1839 article in the *Boston Morning Post* and then in Martin Van Buren's 1840 campaign for president. "Ain't" may not have come into common usage until 1749. "Wouldn't be caught dead in . . ." found the light of day in the early movies of the 1900s. Kay made me self-conscious to the point that I learned that the barrel for a "crow's nest" was introduced first in whaling in the early 1800s and the telescope (known as "bring 'em near"), although designed in the 1600s, was not a common navigation instrument until the last half of the 1700s.

Sue Freeman, one of my readers, found a few inconsistencies in the story but her biggest contribution was in the Epilogue. I had written about the tragic death of Captain Hornigold but I had left Abby dangling. A little rewrite united Abby with her family. Sadly, Sue passed away before she could see the book in print.

Shelly Morgan and Melinda Johnson were my additional readers and they too provided helpful comments.

Jane Ryder, Ryder Author Resources, put together a great team that took the story from manuscript to book: Leigh Westerfield, copyediting; Colleen Sheehan, Ampersand Bookery, interior design and layout; and David Argabright, The Editorial Department, proofreading. Jane coordinated those working on the manuscript and took the final steps for publication.

A big thanks to all those mentioned and to all my family and friends who survived my constant chatter about Abby and her friend Captain Benjamin Hornigold. Unfortunately, they will now begin hearing about Hornigold's Jacobite nemeses, Henry Jennings and Charles Vane.

About the Author

MARTIN A. FREY is Professor Emeritus at The University of Tulsa where he taught for many years at The College of Law. He has written a number of paralegal textbooks and has received university and student teaching awards. Upon his retirement, he was awarded a Lifetime Service Award by the alumni of The University of Tulsa College of Law. At his 50th law school reunion at Washington University in St. Louis, he was awarded honorary membership into the Order of the Coif.

Professor Frey was a Senior Adjunct Settlement Judge for the United States District Court for the Northern District of Oklahoma, and for seven years volunteered with the Tulsa Police Department where he was assigned to the Financial Crimes Unit. While he was teaching at The University of Tulsa, Professor Frey served on a number of law school site evaluation teams for the Accreditation Committee of the American Bar Association.

He is a member of the Missouri and Oklahoma state bar associations and has been admitted to practice before the United States District Court for the Northern District of Oklahoma.

After writing about Captain Benjamin Hornigold, Professor Frey dreams of moving to the east coast of Florida, purchasing a metal detector, and scouring the beaches after hurricanes for pieces of eight still unclaimed from the 1715 Spanish plate fleet disaster.

Professor Frey lives in Tulsa, Oklahoma, with his dog, Daisey-Maire.

www.ingramcontent.com/pod-product-compliance
Lightning Source LLC
Chambersburg PA
CBHW071452140726
47997CB00005B/1698